QUEEN OF ROT AND PAIN

THE PALE COURT BOOK TWO

LIV ZANDER

INK HEART PUBLISHING

ISBN-13: 978-1-955871-06-8

www.livzander.com

info@livzander.com

Cover Art: Darling Cover Design

Editing: Silvia's Reading Corner

Warning: This book is intended for mature audiences.

CHAPTER 1
ADA

"Little one." Dark and gutting, a voice broke against my earlobe, its sinister undertone promising a thousand agonies. "Do not believe I will let you escape me." A grinding scoff, followed by an odd wheeze of air. "You are shackled to me forevermore, and death shall be your collar."

Body benumbed, paralyzed, only my mind reeled at the threatening words as I gaped unblinking at whatever came into view. Soft light bathed my surroundings in glimmers of orange. They caught on the golden threads embroidered onto hundreds of pillows in a pile before me, all draped in rich dark red and forest green damask. Tangled limbs and grinning faces poked out from between them, where naked people lounged, chuckling as they stared at me.

All but one.

A bare woman dangled by a noose from a rafter. She twitched and tossed at the end of a rope between the stone frame of a tall, arched window. A line of them overlooked some sort of sprawling garden, where red and yellow birds as big as ravens squawked and whistled in oddly-shaped trees. Heavens, what kind of place was this? A madhouse?

"Quite so," a man whispered into my thoughts, the gentle resonance in his voice like a lure promising salvation. *"Madness shapes the pillars of my court, and insanity its walls. Excuse Leandra and her poor manners... hanging herself in front of my visitors without even greeting you first. So tiresome, this woman's fondness for dramatics, as though she couldn't just quietly slit her wrists. But I ought to be grateful for the hanging. Not as messy, easier on my rugs to be certain."*

Court? What court?

"The Court Between Thoughts."

No, that couldn't be.

The last thing I remembered was... a dark felt hat. Pa standing in the frame of our hut. Light reflecting on something. Metal, perhaps? And then... nothing.

What had happened?

I was shifted, and my eyes landed on lush carpets that covered yellow stone, the rich tan fabric stained red in large puddles here and there, with smaller specks around it. Blood?

How did I get here?

I tried to glance around, but cold apathy froze my entire body into stillness. Why couldn't I move?

"Dreadful, is it not, little one?" A menacing whisper tickled around my temple, its familiarity distorted by a noisy heave, like air sucking into a broken bellow. "This twilight state of half-existence, aware enough for your soul to agonize over it but... Ah! Too detached from your form to escape it."

I didn't so much recognize the voice as I did the smooth cadence it held, and how it sustained its fine composure while slithers of dread burrowed through my unmoving body. It belonged to the kind of man whose roar scared you, but the true terror lay in his unfazed silence.

Enosh.

My God.

My husband.

My... master?

Coldness dug its claws deeper into my flesh. Why did this word resonate in my core like the echo of a persistent prayer? Did it even matter? Shaken and disoriented, I just wanted him to put me in a nest of pelts and feathers, curl himself around me like armor, and stroke the shell of my ear.

I wanted to say his name.

Lips remained stiff.

A strange voice, so unlike my own, resonated from deep within me instead.

Master!

"Yes, I am your master." Enosh clasped my chin, bringing my stiff, dry gaze to meet the cold silver of his stunning eyes set into a ghastly face, one half torn by gaping wounds. "You shall long for me, obey me, and serve me for eternity. And you shall worship me, for I am your god, the keeper of your flesh and bone."

His voice barely registered as nausea clung to the back of my throat. What had happened to him?

Nothing but white bone remained where the wing of his left nostril should be, along with cartilage that clung to a string of flesh. Soot covered much of this half of his face, hiding the pestilent, blistered skin beneath. Something had stripped his jaws to bone and teeth at the far back of one joint, leaving a hole for his breath to wheeze through with each inhalation.

"What to do with my faithless wife, hmm? Ought I to weave you into my throne one joint at a time?" He took my heavy hand and placed it onto the only remaining trace of his humanity, his warm cheek, and the cleaner trails where something must have washed the soot off the unmarred side of his face. Tears? "Shall I shatter your bones into hundreds of pieces as I had to do with mine, so your treacherous beauty will grace it right alongside your terrible betrayal?"

Betrayal?

Cold dread burrowed between my ribs and black fog smothered my thoughts, provoking memories of utter savagery. The *rrk* of cotton ripping, the *shk* of metal sinking into flesh, the rust-stained handle of a knife. Smoky tendrils eclipsed any coherent thought. I understood none of this. What was going on here?

"Shall I tell you, wife, of the many atrocities they have imposed upon me in captivity while you pondered *stew*? Will knowing burden your conscience with guilt the way your disloyalty wears me down with the urge to punish you?" He lowered his monstrous face to mine, nuzzling my cheekbone with the hard, crusty remnants of his nose. "I spent nearly a fortnight in the ceaseless lick of flames, my face burned away by priests in never-ending agony, safe for the three times they decapitated me. Once to note just how my head would return; twice for the mere entertainment of it. And where were you, dear wife? *Where. Were. You?*"

Captivity. Flames. Priests.

Fear trickled across my scalp, pooling inside my head until my thoughts drowned in another blur of memories, only to emerge painfully clear—the attack in the forest, Enosh's capture, how I'd fled to Elderfalls, Pa's sickness, and... and my delay. After weeks of captivity—while the god was undoubtedly contained by fire—he must have escaped the high priest.

Only to find me gone.

Enosh stared down at me, the accusation of treachery edged into his cold, glaring mask of bitterness and disdain. He thought I'd broken my vow, but hadn't I tried to return to him?

Some memories came back to me now, but more remained

a tangled mess. I understood where I was, but I couldn't recall how I'd ended up in Enosh's arms in the first place. Had he come for me? But if so, why had he brought me here of all places?

"Because he just can't let you go," Yarin whispered into my thoughts before he gave his true voice resonance. "Her mind is such a racing mess, I can barely distinguish one thought from another as her soul clings to my voice, shifting into my kingdom."

And what a beautiful voice he had.

It called to me with its soothing intonation and calm undertone. "*Let go,*" it beckoned, lulling my mind into a state of peacefulness. So I did, allowing myself to drift and float away.

Beneath me, the body of a woman came into view, battered and beaten. She rested on trembling arms that lifted her as though offering herself to the heavens. I... I knew this woman.

Yes, it was me.

How strange I looked.

How little I cared.

Mud streaked my face and a wet, brown leaf clung to my black strands. A pink wound cut across my cheek, barely healed. Even against the warm light from the candles flickering in the chandeliers above, deep shadows cast across my otherwise pale features. Red stained the cotton of my blue dress around the belly, the fabric shredded. I didn't move. Not even my chest lifted as though... as though—

"Tsk, tsk, tsk. Where do you think you're going? Unfortunately, I traded your soul away," Yarin whispered before he resonated the room with his airy lilt. "One soul in exchange for ten corpses, as promised. And what a poor deal this suddenly turned out to be, for we both know I could have demanded thousands over the course of eons for this one."

A brutal force gripped my thoughts like a vise, digging,

clawing, scraping. One sharp pull, and I dropped into a freefall toward my body, crashing into it. Something pinned me down, like a death weight on my chest, shackling me beneath unseen chains.

A sudden chill wrapped around me, seeped into my flesh, and planted an ice-cold inkling into the marrow of my bones. The blood I'd seen on my dress, my pale features, how my lungs wouldn't expand. Was I...?

No. I wasn't dead.

"Strange." Yarin's green eyes came into view, and a pout played around his lips. "It seems as though a part of her soul is evading me, sheltering itself in a blind void of nothingness at her very core. Her death came sudden, I presume?"

Pressure expanded behind my ribs until it ached and panic needled my insides. No, I wasn't dead. How could I be if I was right here? My head spun. Delirium crept up on me. Retreated. *I'm not dead,* my mind screamed, *not dead, not dead, not—*

"Shh, you're making my temples throb." Yarin's hush sent a caress of calm across my tortured soul. "Enosh, remember the mortal who kept the fire burning after Lord Tarnem captured you? The one you buried? Seeing your wife's mind crumble, I can't help but wonder about him. It must be dreadful, having your soul chained to your body, only to spend eternity in the ground with no company other than your own mind."

"Mm-hmm, I remember." Bemusement rose into the upturned corners of Enosh's lips, and an inky strand of his hair slowly grew and lengthened where it swept along his forehead. "Ah, my wicked, faithless wife, ought I lower you into a grave and cover you with dirt? Leave you there in your helpless state for as many days as I have suffered for your sake?"

Fear crept into my veins, chilling my blood. Was this truly the man who'd brought rot to the children, rousing a true flicker of affection in me? The gray of his eyes diminished as they narrowed, letting terrifying shadows lower over them as though he imagined me jailed in the wet ground...

...and enjoyed it.

I'm not dead!

"Oh, I heard that one loud and clear." Yarin chuckled. "She thinks she's not dead. Don't they all? Just how did it happen?"

"Mortals stabbed her in the belly," Enosh said, sending my mind into a nauseating spin. "They... might have thought she carried my child. No doubt High Priest Dekalon would have preferred her alive to gain leverage over me."

Mortals stabbed her in the belly.

Thought she carried my child.

Darkness fell over my petrified mind, spinning black shadows into distorted memories. How I'd retched up countless meals. The bowl of sprouted grains. Rose, that wretched bitch. And a blade sinking into my flesh to the echo of a man's voice, *"Who wants to take chances when she might as well have the devil's babe in her belly?"*

Shock overwhelmed me.

My lungs burned.

My vision speckled.

I was dead.

My core filled with anguish, and loss carved itself a home inside my chest, suffocating me with grief. Oh god, I was dead, and so was my unborn baby. They'd killed me. They'd taken my baby from me, the only... the only thing I'd ever—

Oh! I couldn't breathe! I was suffocating, choking on too much pain and not enough air.

Breathe!

My body ignored the command.

Muscles refused to stretch and expand, leaving my chest collapsed around a ball of terror. It burned along my breastbone, searing into my core, burning toward my spine.

Choking me.

Suffocating me.

"Your wife's mind is such a noisy, incoherent place right this moment, it's driving me insane," Yarin ground out. "Keep her like this, brother, and her soul will fall into such despair that not even I can fix it."

Enosh's eyes clenched shut, and three loud heaves wheezed through the hole in his cheek before he growled, "Rise!"

I filled my lungs with a deep inhale, immediately regretting it when the sickening stench of charred flesh and singed hair choked the back of my throat as I wailed, "My ba—"

Enosh gripped my throat as he roughly lowered me onto my swaying legs. "I believed you. I trusted you. I sacrificed myself so you may escape, only for you to abandon me. To break your vow as quickly and easily as any of your abhorrent kind." His hand slipped off my face, the loss of its warmth harrowing as he brought one step of painful distance between us. "My wicked, faithless wife... I *adored* you like no other."

I shivered, the empty space between us like a wall of frigid ice, chilling the still blood in my deathly quiet heart. He'd gone mad with rage. Why else would he talk about betrayal without even a mention of my baby?

Our baby!

Driven toward him by desperation and lured closer by his body heat, I reached my hand for his chest. "I can explain everything, but I need to know—"

"Shh..." He pressed his hand to my mouth, offering a precious glow that tingled along my lips. "I will hear no more of your lies, little one. Your flesh and bone are growing anxious, longing for the Pale Court. It is where you belong, after all, among the remnants of the dead, my cold, cold wife."

"Mm-hmm—"

Horror filled my chest as I swung my hand toward my mouth. I let my fingertips dig beneath his, brushing over the rough patch of skin covering the area, like leathery parchment glued to my lips. I doubled over and sunk to the ground, surrounded by the yaps and snickers of Yarin's corpses.

My soul died a thousand deaths as I reached my arms up to Enosh, begging for comfort as my mind chanted, *Master, master*.

"Yes, I am your master, and death is your true eternal prison." Nothing but the dismissive swat of his hand hauled me onto my shaky legs before he curled his fingers around my chin, lifting my gaze to meet his lopsided smirk. "I shall be your guard, your judge, your punishment, but— Ah... *never* your absolution."

CHAPTER 2
ADA

Weakness curled my spine, and my ribs caved in. Enosh's biting malice shook me to the core, turning me into a trembling, devastated mess. Did he not feel the child? Or did he not care in all his rage? Was it dead? Still in my belly? Had my womb expelled it?

Each time I pried my lips open to give my sorrows voice, the tension of the skin melded to my mouth ached all the way into my nostrils.

I needed to know!

I scratched at the patch of leather, but my fingers quivered too much, my body ransacked by this unholy cold. Why was it so cold?

"Will you not stay a while longer, brother?" Yarin let the stem of a goblet adorned with hundreds of sparkling stones form between his fingers, then sunk his naked body into the ocean of pillows before he brushed his auburn strands back. "Witnessing your marital issues is such a riveting delight, I have half a mind to look for a woman to wed."

Enosh scoffed, "Send us to the Pale Court or my horse, whichever mortal thought is nearest."

"As you wish," Yarin said just as his court faded into a gray fog that wafted over frost-covered bushels of brown grass, his voice a faraway echo. "Watch your boots."

Humid air settled onto my cheeks, woven with traces of wood rot and mildew. Where were we?

My gaze wandered over the misty meadow before they snapped to the trickle of water. A soldier in chain mail stood in front of a tree, stance wide, pressing one hand to the trunk while the other held his prick.

"We found his dead horse wandering toward the Blighted Fields!"

When the soldier turned his attention to the shout, he spotted Enosh standing beside him, albeit too late. "In the name of Helfa—"

Enosh cupped the back of the soldier's helmet. One push, and the man's face slammed against the furrowed trunk with a *clank*. There was a loud *crack*, and the trickle of piss first quickened, then suddenly stopped. The soldier collapsed onto patches of ghost moss with a muffled *thud*, his face a malformed mess of blood and smothered cartilage.

I yelped, but the sound died against my gag.

My husband gripped the torn sleeve of my dress and pulled me behind him toward the open field, my steps as disorganized as my thoughts. He let bone form into dozens of sharp spikes and volleyed them toward the small group of soldiers.

Enosh clasped my waist and bodily swung me into the saddle on a chestnut horse as the soldiers *thud-thud-thudded* to the ground around us. He mounted wordlessly behind me and willed the horse into a canter, leaving the soldiers behind to clasp the holes in their throats as they bled out onto the brittle grass.

I dug my fingers into the hollow between pommel and withers on the moaning leather of the saddle, clasping for balance and the loosest thread of rational thought. There was only so much I could take, and I'd reached my limit even before my death. With Pa likely gone, I was all alone in this crooked world, carrying my grief in harrowing silence.

Denying any and all comfort, Enosh had nothing for me but threats and scorn. The weight of his indifference scrambled my senses, but I needed to reassemble my thoughts. In the back of my mind, I understood where Enosh's sense of betrayal stemmed from. Once I found a way to lose my gag, I had to set my grief aside and explain.

The ride to the Pale Court took a bone-chilling eternity, forcing me to relive my death within my memories, bringing me face to face with my mistakes. How I'd helped Rose with her pain, feeding her suspicion. The damn stone that now likely lay somewhere in the mud, for I didn't sense its weight in my pocket. How I'd wanted to prolong Pa's life only for both of us to end up dead. Probably.

By the time we reached the Æfen Gate, my teeth chattered from the late afternoon chill. Still, it had nothing, *nothing*, on the biting coldness as we descended. It cracked through my bones, permeating me to the shushed organ in my chest until I leaned back into Enosh.

He shifted away.

Another crack to my soul.

Or my heart?

The stench of rot climbed into my nostrils as we entered the Pale Court. Hundreds, if not thousands of animals from varying species—some of which I'd never encountered—lay scattered across the bridges, hung crooked from the banisters, and piled around the dais in different states of decay.

Without a word, Enosh dismounted, not offering me a

single glance as he made his way toward a creature that slumped on his throne like a checkered sack of moldy potatoes. "Hush yourself! The last thing I need now is your constant bewailing to echo inside my head."

I slipped off the horse and carefully tiptoed toward the throne. The faces in it had gone moldy and cracked, crumbling away in chunks and peeling off in blackish layers. With each ascending step to the dais, weaving around the dead animals, the fine hairs on my arms rose straighter. God's bones! No!

Orlaigh lay curled up on Enosh's throne, her face grayish-blue and sunken in, her gray braids thin and brittle. The secretions of her decay had pooled underneath her, staining the white bone of the throne green and black. Maggots oozed from her nostrils, churned on the corners of her milky green eyes, and clung to the teeth of a mouth that gaped wider than it ought to.

My breaths quickened, pulling the poisonous air of decay down my throat and into my hardening stomach. Was this what awaited me? Drying skin and wilting flesh? Maggots eating me from the inside? Had Enosh not threatened a grave?

A scathing gasp lodged in my throat.

All my life, I'd wanted rot for the people. Now that it was upon me, my fear of it was so pressing, I expected my bladder to fail me—if it hadn't already. I noticed no moisture between my legs. Did that mean my baby was still in my belly?

Enosh let Orlaigh's putrefactions fade away, quickly restoring the woman to her former state, and even the dark discolorations vanished from her green-checkered dress. "Quiet now."

"Master, oh me Master. Ye cannae reckon how I worried. All this time, I waited, driven mad with—" She flung two shaky fingers to her lips, sat up, and reached them to Enosh's face. "*Malaichte bas*! What have they done to ye?"

"I am weary and tired. So tired. Do not dare to disturb me while I recover, unless your souls have no flesh left to cling to."

When Enosh straightened and walked away, I chased after him down the dais and toward the corridor. Before he managed to turn into my room, I grabbed his leather-clad arm and gave a tug. Unable to speak, I clawed at the skin covering my mouth, begging him to remove it.

An invisible power forced me to let go of him, and a sob built at the back of my throat as I watched him head for the bed. I couldn't stay like this, driven to the edge of hysteria by a million things that needed said and with the picture of loss stitched into my belly. I needed to explain, but how?

Anxiousness had me shift from one foot to another as I watched Enosh cross the room. I glanced around for a knife, a fang, anything to cut through— There!

I ripped a claw from skeletal remnants I couldn't identify and brought it to my mouth. Even in the looming threat of a wet grave or wiggling maggots, the potential punishments paled compared to giving my sorrows voice along with my sobs. What could Enosh do to me that was worse than dying with my baby in my belly?

Nothing.

One steadying breath, then I punctured the thick patch, giving my whimpers of pain more resonance with each crawling inch of progress. I tore along the gap between my lips, tasting iron whenever I accidentally nicked my lips.

"What have ye done, lass? I haven't seen me Master this— Ah, dia..." Orlaigh watched me from where she stood in the corridor, palms pressed to her mouth as she shook her head, warning me not to do it. "Nay, lass, leave it be."

Not until Enosh had heard me out. He accused me of betrayal. And while I might not be entirely innocent of it, I wasn't nearly as guilty as he claimed.

When the last shred of skin tore, I let the claw *thud* to the ground. "I understand why you're angry with me, but I had reasons for my delay."

Enosh came to an abrupt halt, and after a moment of silence, he slowly shifted his head my way by a single degree, letting a bone crack in his neck. "Reasons..."

I inched toward him on numb feet, letting my palms brush over the cotton on my hips to keep my nerves under control. "After you sent me away on the horse, I fell. The animal just kept going without me. What was I supposed to do, Enosh? I was scared, injured. Look at the wound on my cheek. I didn't know what to do, how to reach the Pale Court. I went to Hemdale, but I knew I wasn't safe there, so Pa and I went higher north."

He sighed as though bored. "Higher north..."

His clipped answers and apathetic demeanor terrified me more than any roar ever could, because I knew that Enosh was his worst self when he hid his feelings behind a bulwark of disdain. And if he turned now to face me, who would I see?

The hurt man?

Or the haughty god?

"Pa was... *is* terribly sick." A thick lump of dread built at the back of my throat. "I had no horse. No coin. When I finally went to get a mule to leave for the Pale Court, priests came to the village, offering a fortune for my capture. People recognized me."

"No horse. No coin. A sick father. Chased by priests. Such dreadful circumstances they almost lend your words an air of truth, but ah... somewhere in your plight, you found pure happiness." He finally turned, his cold mask locked in place, as sleek and rigid as a glacier. "I felt it, little one. I felt the lightness in your chest, the flutter in your stomach, the joy that tingled the nerve endings beneath your skin."

I blinked in confusion. "I… I don't understand."

Two steps, and he tore down the wall of frigid distance between us, filling it with a heat I wanted to melt into. It consumed me, driving out the chill of death as I placed my hand on his leather cuirass. My head tipped back, and I stared up at his mangled face. Oh, his lips remained so perfectly curved. I licked my own at the sight.

He let his fingers sift through my hair, gently detangling the knots as his face lowered to mine, luring me deeper into him. His finger hooked beneath my chin, bringing my lips to hover inches from his, letting the back of my throat purr with anticipation.

I'd once told myself that I didn't care about his love, but I was mistaken. Right now, I needed him to hold me and stroke the hair from my damp cheeks while I cried my heart out over the injustice of this all, the crimes committed to us.

Right this moment, I needed his love.

"Mmm, how twisted this has become, my little one. I sense how much you want my warmth, my touch, my heated skin against yours. And yet it holds no measure to how much I have wanted you. Have I not given you all my attention? My goodwill? My devotion?" His finger hooked deeper underneath my chin, lifting it until vertebras crackled in my neck. "Who… is… Elric?"

My swallow got stuck between a parched throat and the biting angle at which he kept my neck trapped. Everything made so much sense now, from how he must have felt my joy over the pregnancy to how his brother had once more helped himself to my thoughts.

I struggled my voice over the bitter taste of grief in my mouth. "Our baby… if it would have been a boy. My excitement you sensed was over finding that I carried your child in my belly. Still do."

A moment of stillness.

A beat of suspended time.

Stepping back, he once again robbed me of his warmth, even removing the precious pain of his finger on my chin. "Now you have extinguished any doubt in me that you are a liar."

I ignored the sinking feeling in my stomach and how it caused my wounds to itch beneath the blood-damp cotton. "Why would you say such a thing? Can you not sense it?"

"There is... no... child." His voice came forth like the freezing trickle of a wintery creek, treacherously beautiful in its calm cadence. "There never was. There never... will... be."

I placed my palm onto my belly, and a hint of doubt penetrated the anguish in my chest. What did that mean, there never was? I once more shifted my thighs, but sensed no wetness in my braies, nothing that would indicate that I had expelled... but how could this be?

"You're wrong." My tendons stiffened. "I... I had the morning sickness, and—"

"There is... no... child." He stared at me with somber austerity, unshaken conviction chiseled into the hard edges of his jaws. "How dare you serve me this lie to distract from your betrayals."

Anger flared to life at the back of my throat. "They stabbed me three times, but they killed twice!"

A muscle jumped in his jaws. "I might have believed that your mind conjured it up when it was not so, out of your desperate desire for a child. But I told you in the forest that you were not pregnant after your time of fruitfulness. Even told you that our coupling in the forest would not result in one, which renders this a farce." He swallowed. "A most disgusting one."

"Maybe... maybe it's too small that you can't feel it yet."

"I sense everything, from the hair follicles breaking open with new growth to what might become a child settling in its mother's womb."

The room spun around me and my upper body swayed. "You're lying."

"Spare me your theatrics, trying to make yourself look like a fool when we both know you are not." His upper lip twitched, a hairline crack in his detached demeanor. "I have never been anything but honest with you, a fact I now regret deeply. You dare serve me a lie about how you thought yourself pregnant to conceal your betrayal? After I told you how much I grieved the loss of my daughter?"

I flinched. "No. I... The grains, they... there is—"

"There is no child!" The Pale Court shook with the rage of Enosh's shout, bonedust rilling from the walls before the god clenched his eyes shut. When he opened them again, the damage on his mask repaired, he leaned into me, capturing my cheek in the biting trap of his palm. "You never intended to return, for you found this damn happiness I never managed to inspire in you. Or anyone, for that matter. Who is Elric? Ought I hunt him down? Punish him for touching what is mine by setting his corpse into my throne like I have done with... *Joah?* I shall find him, and..."

His voice faded into the rush of my turbulent mind as the last fraying string of my sanity tore with a *pop* at some faraway cranny of my mind. Trembles ransacked me to the core, and I stumbled back into the biting chill of death. What had Enosh told Yarin at the Court Between Thoughts?

Thought that she carried my child.

Thought.

That word echoed.

Had I imagined it all? Had wanted Enosh's promise to prove true so desperately that I'd talked myself into it? Could my mind truly cling to the hope of a child with such desperation that it had wrenched the food from my stomach each morning?

Perhaps I had.

When Enosh shifted in my periphery, once more turning for the bed, I grabbed his arm and let my hand brush over my wounds. "Please make them go away."

Enosh stared at me, his face a still landscape of desolation as his eyes slipped to the wounds. "I find them quite pleasing to look at. You shall keep them, little one, offering us an eternal reminder of your faithlessness."

His leather armor retreated as he stepped away from my touch and toward the bed, where he slumped onto the furs, leaving me behind to stand and stare for a minute or an hour.

For years, I'd wanted nothing more than a child. Within a day, I'd lost it twice. Once to a knife, and the second to Enosh's shout.

They hurt equally.

As the room turned silent around the sleeping god, long after Orlaigh had fled the argument, all that existed was agony. That, and the piercing chill of death, driving me toward the only source of warmth in this cold, cold kingdom.

Enosh.

Dazed and confused, I climbed into bed but, no matter how many furs I draped over myself, my teeth chattered. How strange this was. When I'd first come to the Pale Court, Enosh had been drawn to my warmth. Now here I was, inching closer to where he slept, embracing the heat that emanated from his mutilated body.

My teeth ground together as I brushed my hand over his still face, sensing the thick, sticky soot collecting on my fingertips. I stroked down along his stomach, over the tip of a rib that protruded from mending flesh, and around what looked like a hole in his abdomen.

He must have gone through agonizing pain, and I wasn't sure who to blame for all this. The god for abandoning his duty and enraging the people? Myself for insisting on rotting my late husband, who'd brought me nothing but sorrow? Or my own kind, who'd killed me when I'd only tried to help?

Maybe we all were in dire need of forgiveness.

Something Enosh threatened I would never receive from him, letting me depart a nightmare only to slip straight into hell. I curled up beside him, letting coldness drive me into the arms of the devil who ruled it.

CHAPTER 3
ADA

Only hunger.

Only hunger.

My mind recited the words like a prayer where I soaked in the boiling spring—had for long enough that my skin resembled a dried prune. Salt and sulfur seasoned the stagnant air and the water gently lapped at the stony edges in time to each vibrating gurgle roiling in my stomach.

That strange sensation in my guts—like subtle, yet constant shifts of air—was neither the decay of my innards nor the wiggles of maggots. It was...

"Only hunger."

The familiar *tap-a-tap-taps* of Orlaigh's hurried steps echoed from the corridor, but they stilled at her sigh. "Lass, ye cannae brine in the water for hours like a pork shoulder on a Sunday morn."

I wiped the steam from where it had settled on my cold forehead and frowned at the blackish half-moons along my nail beds. "It's the only place that keeps me from shivering."

Aside from Enosh.

For days, I'd pressed myself against him while he slept and slept. Good thing he did, because I knew he wouldn't have tolerated me near him otherwise.

My ribcage shrank around my organs. "I've ruined this so completely."

"Come now." Orlaigh squeezed the dark water from the ends of my hair, letting the remnants of the walnut dye prattle onto the rock. "Ever seen what happens to cuts of meat when left in a warm place too long?"

"No."

She made a disgruntled sound at the back of her throat. "It'll go gray and slippery as it rots."

When I curled my fingers into my palm, sensing a layer of slick on my skin, my stomach clenched—from hunger. With a sigh, I climbed out of the spring and huddled into the fur she held out.

"How c-can you st-stand the cold-d-d?"

"In time, the cold will mean nothing to ye, or how ye long for… something warm."

That *something* being Enosh.

His omnipotence had turned into a visceral force that pulled me toward him, so strong it sent a wash of longing through me that almost mimicked warmth. It explained how I wanted nothing more but to melt into him.

Not so much how this emotional wreckage between us leeched the remaining blood from my quiet heart…

Orlaigh patted my shoulder as she dried me off, then reached for the broad band of cloth sitting on a rock. "Enough of all this wallowing in yer sorrows. What ye need is sun, lass. Aye, there's not much the fresh air and sun cannae fix on the mind."

I lifted my arms, staring down at how she wrapped the cloth around my abdomen, letting my wounds disappear behind the cotton. "Outside?"

She nodded. "This place reeks of death, and it's not me own breath yet."

"I don't want to leave." I nearly groaned at that statement. A month of trying to escape this place, but now something inside me revolted at the thought alone. "Neither do I want to get stabbed for a fourth time the moment we step outside."

"Reckon ye cannae die of it again, lass." She snorted at what had to be corpse-humor and held one of my dresses out, waiting for me to step into the circle of black feathers. "Certainly not beyond a gate where everyone's dead already, anyway. Those poor souls who survived the wrath of a god dinnae dare come near it. I go there sometimes. Wasn't born there, but the lands are still me home."

Beyond the Soltren Gate.

A new shudder chased along my spine, and my palm circled my belly in some cruel, distorted instinct I somehow couldn't shake. How strangely my fate echoed the one of Njala, calling my thoughts back with its persistent resound.

"I still don't understand any of this." Making it impossible for me to rid myself of this mourning over the loss of something that had never existed in the first place. "How could I've been so wrong? As a midwife...? I retched up every breakfast."

"If I had fish heads for breakfast, I'd retch'em up, too."

"Well..." I couldn't even argue with that. "What of the grains, then?"

"Aye, ye were injured lass, scared and all alone with yer hardships. Of course, yer stomach would've gone sour with worry."

"But—"

"Hush now." She ran the fur along my strands, haphazardly drying them off. "Let it go, lass. All this talk, the false grief... What does it change?"

My chest deflated.

Nothing.

Deep down, I knew I should be relieved at this revelation. I would never be a mother, yet I had to do the motherly thing and find peace in the fact that my child was safe and well.

Also imagined.

When another shift in my stomach vibrated against my knuckles, I quickly dropped my hand. "Maybe I should wait for Enosh to wake so he can take the rot away." The way wrinkles formed between her brows dragged heavily on my confidence. "He'll... make it go away, right?"

"Lass, have ye ever met a man who woke from a nap in a mood other than sullen and irritable? Removing rot takes me Master—"

"Great effort." I swallowed nothing but air faintly tainted with the rancid onset of my own decay. "Yes, I remember. I just can't imagine he would be quite so cruel."

A humorless chuckle vibrated her chest as she gestured for me to step into my slippers, then ushered me into the corridor. "Nay? Then ye have lost yer wits right along with the beat of yer heart."

Maybe I had.

Personally, I blamed the wedding.

After I'd given my vows, Enosh had lifted his mask of the bitter god one vulnerable inch at a time, letting me glimpse the loving man beneath. He'd spoiled me with the sweetest words and the most tender of touches. He'd torn down the last of my hate-forged defenses, leaving my cold, silenced heart helpless and exposed.

With his mask back in place and seemingly poured from iron, what fate would await me once he woke?

My fingers went to my belly once more, pushing the feathers where the cotton beneath caught on my wounds and burned. "I want these gone. Can't stand how they still cause me agony. Do you think he'll truly let me keep them forever?"

"Ach, lass, everything will be awright." Her words smoothed over the pressure of dread in my chest, but only until she stopped, held her arms out, and pushed the sleeves of her checkered dress past her wrists. "So long as ye brave yerself for the worst."

Sour gall burned at the back of my throat as I stared down at the deep red wounds on Orlaigh's arms, like rings of raw flesh past her wrists. "You've never showed me these before..."

"Because ye never asked how I died," she said as she tugged the fabric neatly back over the wounds, continuing toward the bridge. "Ach, how angry me Master was for letting the little lady get taken away, her belly round with his babe. Aye, I've warned her, but who listens to old Orlaigh? Chaperoning her was like herding a bunch of flea-ridden cats."

"What did Enosh do?"

Shrugging, she crossed the throne room. "Dragged me behind his horse until Eilam came for me breath."

My muscles tensed at the sound of that name, until my feet faltered to a halt at the first gaping hole in the bridge toward the Soltren Gate. "If I go outside and Enosh wakes, he'll think I'm trying to escape."

Orlaigh's voluptuous body shook with a chortle. "No matter which direction ye run, lass, ye will always end up straight in his arms. If me Master had any fear of you escaping, I reckon he would not be sleeping the time away."

Shoulders slumping, I nodded and weaved behind her,

around the holes of the decrepit bridge. Death was my collar. The Pale Court was my cage. And my chain...? A pressure inside my chest, like an invisible force that urged me to turn around.

It strengthened as I navigated along the sharp rock walls that snaked toward the chirping birds. Whereas the Æfen Gate had an incline, this tunnel opened straight into a cutting breeze that pulled on the bright green bushels of grass spread before us.

My mouth gaped open as I turned back toward the gate, blinking quickly to adjust to the sudden brightness out here. The wind tousled through my hair, letting smudged blonde strands flutter across my face before the gusts broke against the rock, scattering into a dozen whistles.

I assessed the archway set into the stone of a mountain, which extended in ledges of rock to both sides. From there, they spread across the landscape as far as the eye reached, coming together in gray chains that rose and fell through meadows of lush green.

I reached my hand toward the cloudless sky, ignoring how the sun intensified the contrast of dark veins webbing across my arm. "It looks as though I can almost touch it."

Orlaigh smiled, climbed onto a boulder, and patted the sunny spot beside her. "The living used to call this mountain Brockenberg."

Gravel crunched beneath as I walked over and sat beside her, moaning at the sudden warmth of the rock against my palms. "They spoke a different language here?"

"A great many." Her gaze went adrift on a landscape seemingly abandoned, aside from a small group of horned sheep that munched on the vegetation sprouting between the rock not far from us. "Aye, the little lady could recite poems in four different ones."

"How did you come to these lands?"

"Me mam and da came to these lands by ship, serving a fine household."

When she squinted, I let mine follow her line of sight but could make out nothing but specks of gray and green. "So high up, and I don't see a single village. No towns. No roads."

"Ah, they're there if ye ken where to look." Her lips pressed into a fine line before she swatted a fly. "Hergenheim Castle, the town of Steinau, the Duke's Road going between them... it's there, sleeping beneath a blanket of vines and thorns."

Would Enosh decide a similar fate for the lands beyond the Æfen Gate? Or would he just kill every poor man with the name Elric, thinking that... Just what exactly was the thinking? No matter how often I mulled over his words, they remained a convoluted mess.

"Looks like its nearly summer in these lands." Yet another strangeness, along with the purple flower I plucked from a gap in the rock, where more of it grew without any soil. "Who was Joah?"

Orlaigh tilted her head ever so slightly toward me, side-eyeing me for a moment. "Ye dinnae remember, lass? I told ye on the dais once. Commander Mertok."

I flinched.

Commander *Joah* Mertok.

"Right." An unnerving pinch ached my ribs. "You only mentioned it once, and Enosh rarely bestows the honor of calling someone by their given name, so I forgot."

Enosh had mentioned his name when he didn't believe how I'd thought myself pregnant. Not only that, but he'd threatened to hunt *Elric* down and weave him into his throne.

Like he'd done to the commander...

... who'd touched what was his.

My temples ached at the onslaught of questions whirring through my head. What did that mean? Had Joah and Njala become lovers after he took her away? And wouldn't that make sense of his threats? The depth of his gaping disappointment? His acute distrust?

Shaken by Enosh's shout and the devastating truth about my pregnancy, my mind hadn't comprehended his words as anything but rage-sparked nonsense. But it hadn't only been rage, had it?

The god was *jealous.*

One fact, however, challenged that conclusion. If Njala and Joah had indeed developed feelings for each other, why had he slit her throat when Enosh had closed in on them? Had his sense of duty to Lord Tarnem outweighed his love for her?

"Commander Mertok slit her throat as... as an act of revenge," Enosh's voice resonated in my mind, as well as the hesitation it had held when he'd told me on our way to Airensty. *"Her soul departed quicker than I could act."*

My breathing flattened.

Quicker than he could act.

Enosh had once explained to me how souls departed slower when death came suddenly. Did that mean Njala had seen hers coming? Because her death had been... what? Anticipated?

Even planned perhaps?

Had she fallen so hopelessly for the commander that she'd chosen death over returning to Enosh? The idea alone gave me chills, and my hand lifted toward my stomach as agony infiltrated my core once more. I could never condemn my baby to death over forbidden love, or—

There is no child.

I dropped my hand back to my lap. What reason did I have to grieve a child? What right did I have to assume that I understood a wink of dying with one in my belly?

None.

I shifted on the rock until I faced Orlaigh. "When Lord Tarnem sent his daughter away with the commander, did the two fall in love?"

Everything in the old woman stilled, safe for how the wind lured wisps of white hair from her braid, her pale skin speckled with the first signs of rot around her ears. I took that as a *yes.* So I was right.

"If ye ken what's good, lass, ye best dinnae bring up such talk inside the Pale Court."

Good for whom?

Enosh knew of her emotional betrayal and how she'd never grown to love him, only to do it with another. Why else would he mention Elric and Joah in the same sentence, threatening to do with one as he had with the other?

Devil be damned, I'd shoveled myself into a hole inside a muckheap. Enosh accused me of betrayal—perhaps the one thing he judged harsher than any other offense—and on top of it, he accused me of infidelity.

Could I blame him?

Once bitten twice shy might be a mortal saying, but likely no less true for my god husband. With no child in my belly, I had no explanation for the joy he'd sensed within me during a time of such terrible hardship for us both. All I was left with were explanations for my delay, and even those had started to take on the echo of excuses.

Because I *did* have doubts.

They'd cost me everything.

My goal.

My life.

My husband's trust.

As it so often went with distrustful minds, Enosh had conjured up his own explanation for all this. The same he'd experienced once before, making it a reasonable choice in the head of a man… another man.

Internally, I laughed.

Heavens, as if I didn't have anything better to do but find myself another of those. God or mortal, either way, they were nothing but trouble and could slowly but surely kiss me where no sun ever reached.

I sighed. "Why did Joah slit her throat?"

Orlaigh shook her head ever so slightly as she flung her hand at what had now become a small swarm of flies. "Lass, let old tales rest."

I pulled my knees against my chest, giving the wind less surface to rob me of the sun's warmth. "She didn't want to return to Enosh, so she asked Joah to kill her instead, right?"

Perhaps Njala had never wanted the baby in the first place? Once again, the woman's story left me confounded, tossing me puzzle pieces that refused to fit, no matter which way I turned them.

No matter how long I stared at her, Orlaigh provided no answer. Neither was I foolish enough to ask Enosh. He might just snap at the mere mention of it, turning this into a mind-boggling mystery I might never uncover.

Unless I asked Joah…

For a moment, my veins seemed to have a pulse as they buzzed beneath my skin. Only the warmth of the rock. If I ever grew bored of my eternal state of decay, I might get to the truth of all this, but not before I'd somehow placated my enraged husband. But how? How to convince him of my flawed but sincere reasoning?

Orlaigh eventually rose under huffs and puffs. "We best get back before the flies start eating away at us. Pesky beasts."

I hurried behind her into the Pale Court, fanning my hand

before my face to keep the flies from settling on my lips. "They'll leave us for the dead animals soon enough, or so—"

I stumbled to a halt by the edge of the bridge, all former holes meticulously filled with the whitest bone. Not a single dead beast remained anywhere, a sight that let another shift of air roil through my guts.

My husband was awake.

CHAPTER 4
ADA

Paralyzed, I stood on the bridge, eyes hesitantly drifting from the white patches of bone to the dais, and up from there. Enosh oversaw the chamber from his throne, chilling the Pale Court with the aura of his cold presence.

The phantom beat of my heart pounded in my ears, triggering the impulse to run. More powerful was the instinct to go to him—an innate compulsion rooted in my core, which pushed me toward him, no matter how my mind screamed its warning.

Come to your master.

His command echoed within me, quickening my steps as I crossed the bridge, even as my fingertips curled into my palm. Would he ask me to my knees and plunder my mouth? Turn me around and fuck my arse until I tore, then pull out and spread his seed on my face? On the wounds beneath my navel? I dreaded that he would do all those things and worse...

Dreaded more that he would do none.

Ascending the dais was nothing but a blur of gutting trepidation and unbearable longing, of knowingly walking into trouble and embracing it for the sake of his body heat.

"That is close enough, little one." He regarded the way I came to a painful halt from the apathy of his silver eyes, set into a cruel scowl I recognized all too well. Dreaded it! "Kneel before your god."

I sunk to my knees willingly before he would make me, finding a shred of dignity even in this semblance of a choice. "You're still furious with me."

A grin hushed across his mouth, only to die at the cutting twitch of his upper lip. His black strands hung damp from his head, telling me he'd bathed. His white shirt was tied across his brawny chest, but it didn't hide the flaming red cuts which still wept from behind the bindings. Heavens, he hadn't only scrubbed the stench from his skin, had he?

He'd peeled it off.

"No, little one." His calm voice didn't detract from its dark undertone, gravelly and unsettling. "Such a fickle emotion, fury. It rushes into existence, only to drift away a moment later. Disappointment, however, echoes caution for eternity. Orlaigh, leave me with my wife."

I watched her disappear into a corridor, then looked back at my harsh husband, his face restored to all its irresistible beauty. Oh, he could deny his anger all he wanted, but I saw it… the seething rage that drew fine lines across his stoic mask, the simmering fury that thawed its sharp edges.

If only I could rip it off as he had his skin.

Bypass the cruel, arrogant god and go straight for the man beneath. The one who'd come to trust me, willing to put his caution aside, along with this toxic bitterness between us.

I needed him. Desperately.

And I knew he needed me, too!

I let my eyes plead for leniency, for the faith he'd once placed in me. "I would have returned to you."

"And so you have, delivered by death." Leaning over, he placed his elbows onto his thighs, letting his hands steeple between his knees. "Crawl to me."

Every proud fiber of my being bristled. "You're punishing me for something I didn't—"

"Crawl!"

My hand reached forward on its own accord, a sight that let humiliation flood my insides. Inch by squirming inch, black feathers caught on the porous bone as I climbed the dais like his pet, and the humiliation ebbed away. Reshaped into an excited tingle beneath my skin as I crawled toward the only source of warmth in this place, no matter its icy core that was my husband's stony heart.

When my face came into reach, he clasped my chin hard enough it pulled my bottom lip from my teeth, but the remaining distance between us ached me the most. He smelled... different. Wrong. Dark. As bitter and biting as his mood.

His gray stare sunk to my lips, but it never quite reached there as he quickly called it back to meet mine. "Mmm, look how your hair has lost its luster, your skin its softness as it succumbs to decay."

Ba-boom-boom.

A sudden beat startled me where it drummed in my ears, amplified by a rush of blood that burned beneath my skin.

My heart?

Another followed, letting the veins on the back of my hand fade along with the churning in my stomach. Had he removed the rot from me?

I took a needless breath, only to release it into a whimpered, "Thank you."

“Thank me?” A scoff. “I have done it for my sake, not yours. Whyever would I subjugate myself to your stench?”

Anger needled itself between my ribs, and my brain urged me to ignore it. Nothing good ever came of rebelling against his godly whims when he was like this.

“You don’t exactly smell like freshly-plucked flowers, either,” I snarled, which put the hint of a tremble on his chin.

“Courtesy of my faithless wife.”

“You’re full of contempt and insult.”

His eyes dropped to my mouth again, staring at it for a minute or ten before he rasped, “Says the woman full of deceit, with lips that whisper the filthiest of lies.”

I lifted my face to his, letting the warmth emanating from his mouth seep into mine. “For something that appalls you so, your eyes give it a great deal of attention.”

He blinked and shifted back.

Just as quickly, his features hardened further—if such a thing were even possible. Curse this mess, he was colder than ever before. With a push against my chin, he shoved me back by a freezing inch that sent a carpet of goosebumps across my skin.

“Mmm, my wife is so cold, suffering the never-ending embrace of death,” he crooned as he regarded the bumps on my arms with a positively mean smirk. “Ought I to warm her?”

Worn down by days of biting coldness, my dignity collapsed into a mewl without consent. “Please! Oh, please… I’m begging you, make the cold go away.”

“At long last, my wife has learned how to beg, and it only took a knife to teach her. Tell me, little one, do you deserve my touch? The warmth of my embrace?” When I said nothing for long moments, knowing there was no answer that wouldn’t paint me either needy or pathetic—possibly both—he chuckled. “Now, now… how could I abandon my cherished wife the way she has done with me?" One hand went to the ties on his black breeches, opening them as he shoved the leather down. The other stroked along the contoured outline of his shaft, reached inside, and took out his jutting cock. "You may warm your hands on this."

Heat funneled into my belly in equal measures of rage and rapture. I should have told the hateful bastard to go fuck himself. Instead, I eagerly wrapped my hand around his thick length, moaning at the feel of his glorious heat against my knuckles.

He hissed, and the muscles in his powerful thighs flexed and contracted before his mouth pulled into a lopsided grin. "Mmm, you weren't usually *this* enthusiastic."

"I wasn't usually this dead, either."

A muscle jumped in his jaws. "It appears as though not even death could cure you of your insolence."

I lifted my chin, offering at least a smidge of defiance while my hand worked his length. "It tried. It failed."

"Indeed—mmm..." Strings of groans tumbled from his lips as I jerked the tight clasp of my palm down his swollen length. "Yes, stroke me. Harder, little one. Much harder. Your hand is oh-so cold."

Scooting closer where I kneeled between his legs at the foot of his throne, I lubricated my palm on the dark pink weeping slit on his crown. Tightening my hold, I let my fingers run up and down the flare with quick pulsations, soaking up the warmth it left around my tips.

Curses, this shouldn't have excited me so. Warmth pooled right between my legs at the familiar shape of his cock, the weight of his flesh as the heavy thing fought gravity. Oh, how deliciously warm he was!

When Enosh bucked into my fist, I ran my hand down along his shaft. His cock stiffened fully in my hold, and I sensed the rapid rush of his heated blood in a large vein that disappeared into his root. Once at the base, I fondled his sac, tracing the tawny seam at its center, which caused his breath to hitch.

Mine, too.

I brought my other hand up and enclosed his cockhead with it, gathering more of the translucent seed he wept in copious amounts. Once lubricated, I pumped his length with both hands, working the engorged flesh with hard jerks until it smacked and squelched.

"Ah, little one, how I have pondered your punishment." Enosh sunk deeper into his throne. "What to do with my faithless wife? Put your sharp tongue on my balls."

When he spread his legs as wide as the gathered breeches below his knees allowed, I sunk my face to his heavy sac. I set my tongue against the underside of one testicle and lifted it, sensing the weight and the velvety skin which encased it. His masculine groans vibrated in the air when I sucked it into my mouth, only to release it and do the same to the other.

He ground into my face, snickering how I moaned at the swath of warmth from his sac pressed against my nose. "If memory serves, then your mouth can do better than that..."

"You're terrible."

I gripped his smooth, glistening crown, squeezing its flare until it wanted to pop out of the tight grip of my palm. But I didn't let it, milking his cockhead until Enosh's buttocks tightened. His hips lifted toward me, and I placed the hard tip of my tongue at the base of his cock. In one, slow, languid motion, I ran it up along his length the way he liked, letting my hums join his ragged breaths.

When I wrapped my lips around the head, he fisted my hair, the touch rough and demanding. It sent a wonderful tingle into my scalp. His hand followed my rhythm for one bob of my head, two, three. At the fourth, he pushed down until his cock hit the back of my throat.

"Deeper!" His command fought for dominance against my pitiful gagging sounds as his other hand came to my face, only for his fingers to squeeze my nostrils shut. "Open for me, little — Ah, ah, ah, I said nothing about pulling back! Did you not claim that you would have returned to me? To this? You will open for me. You will show me just how glad you are to have this cock in your mouth once again." Panic seeped into my stomach until I gasped for air, widening my throat far enough for his length to force itself past the urge to retch. Only then did he release his clasp on my nostrils. "Such an interesting observation among your kind. Corpses, that is. You need no air, but I have yet to meet one with his soul bound who can suppress the innate reflex."

I wanted to tell him to go to hell, but it sounded more like, "Gh-mmh-cr-uh..."

"Ah, little one, I ought to drape you over my lap and spank the rot off your ass for what I am certain was an insult, but ah... how nice your voice vibrated around my cock." A guttural groan, followed by a shivering thrust of his hips. "Mmm, yes, take me deep. Swallow all of me, and I might feed you my hot seed. Would you like that? For my spent to scorch along your throat and land warm in your belly?"

A tingle ignited around my clit as I nodded, working his length deep into my throat until my chin sunk into his tightening sac. My hands rested on his hips, soaking up his warmth. His breathing came faster, harder—as did his thrusts as he bucked into my mouth, his grip on my hair so ungiving it burned.

Burned so good!

Another tight grunt, then he gave a final thrust as he pushed my head down, keeping me locked between the aching pressure in my throat and the quick pulsations of his hips. A first shot of seed splashed hot against my throat, blistering around my esophagus before it seared down my trachea. Then another, and then a third.

A shiver wracked my entire body as his spent warmed my insides, but large parts of my body remained cold and frigid. It wasn't nearly enough, and I grabbled at Enosh's upper body as I pulled my mouth from his still-jerking cock, lips parting to beg him to fuck me. Devil be damned, I would take a spanking if only he put his hands on me.

"Enosh, I'm so cold," I whimpered. "Please, touch me."

"Mmm, begging so nicely." Tugging on his breeches, he put himself away and leaned forward once more, bringing his mouth teasingly close to mine. "No."

He rose and stepped away toward the dais.

My insides convulsed when the warmth of his seed faded away, right along with his body heat as he descended, leaving me behind without even a pat on my head.

I pushed myself up to stand and hurried to the edge of the dais. "Where are you... Why are you leaving?"

He didn't bother turning around. "Because I am done with you."

He was done with me...

My throat bobbed with a scream and my knees shook underneath me. This was not the man I'd married. This wasn't even the god who'd first held me captive.

This was worse.

So much worse.

A crueler version intent on punishing me for something I didn't do.

Red-hot rage pounded along every single one of my ribs, giving me the semblance of a heartbeat. "You're a fucking bastard!"

He halted. "Careful now, little one. While I may be a bastard, I am also a god… and I advise you *not* to push me."

I shifted my balance onto the balls of my feet. One more word of insult, and he would retaliate—his arrogance seldomly left him another choice.

Yet it was his arrogance I was after, and how it sometimes crumbled when his anger was too great. How much of it did it take to blow off his mask? To get to the man beneath?

Taking a steadying breath, I lifted my chin. "I have yet to meet a man who doesn't think himself a god. Just because you happen to be one doesn't make you any less of a bastard, and a poor husband along with it."

"A poor husband?" He swung around, stomped up the dais with a promising twitch on his upper lip, and promptly gripped my throat before he let his snarl cut along my temple. "Even as they threw bladders filled with oil at me, then shot burning arrows to set me aflame, I fought them to ensure your escape to the Pale Court."

"And you failed, because that brainless horse of yours didn't get me anywhere near the Pale Court before I fell off," I snapped as I leaned into his bruising hold on my throat, pressing against his chest until my nipples hardened at his closeness. "You're not the only one who suffered, Enosh. *I died*!"

"And I did not!"

A flinch wrecked through me at his roar, and how bone *crack-crack-crackled* beneath our feet. Should that reassure me? Scare me? Which one?

"I'm sorry for how much they hurt you." Regretted even more how it had turned him bitter, as though resolved to make me hurt the way they'd done with him. "I thought of you every day."

"Had you?" His heavy breath broke against my earlobe, but

it quickly changed into the caress of his lips. They hovered along my cheekbone toward my mouth, merely stroking the tips on the fine peachy hair covering my skin. "That amasses to many days indeed, my annoyingly beautiful wife with poisoned lips that tempt me for a taste."

My core fluttered at the premise of his kiss. He wanted it as much as I did; I sensed it in how he shifted toward me, back, then toward me again—torn between his desire for affection and the fear of betrayal.

When his lips parted at the corner of my mouth, letting his heated breath fan my need for this kiss into a scorching flame, I arched my neck. I clenched my eyes shut and rose onto my toes. Higher. Higher yet.

Coldness.

I opened my eyes.

A frigid veil settled onto my heart as I stared at his polished chin. He held it high, his lips so entirely out of reach, yet it didn't hide the smirk on his mouth. Neither his air of self-satisfaction over how he'd played with me like a cat with a bird after breaking one of its wings.

"Just how much did my dead wife want that kiss, hmm?" Staring down at me, he thumbed my bottom lip. "A pity... I have no appetite for your lies."

CHAPTER 5
ENOSH

My little one stared up at me with a flicker of rage, but it quickly drowned in the blue depth of her glistening eyes. "Sometimes you make it so damn difficult not to hate you."

A vise of pain wrapped around my ribs, but I would not let my posture betray it, giving her surface to stab where I ought to be numb... but was not.

How unexpected.

Irritating.

Utterly absurd.

What was her hate but a fitful remnant of her mortality? Was she not dead? Terribly cold, yes, but oh-so wonderfully chained to me, her god and master? Never again would she want to escape us.

At least in this, I had succeeded.

"Quite so." My thumb itched to trace the shell of her ear, to comb the knots from her hair, but I banned the urge to the memories of how this woman had cost me insurmountable suffering. "After all, it was not love that brought you back to me, was it?"

My words turned to ash on my tongue. Bitter, bitter ash. It clogged my sinus cavities, choking me along with the stench of my own skin, driving me mad with the urge to peel it off in layers.

No, whatever affection I'd thought she had for me had been a farce, likely inspired by nothing else but my wife's ambition to see me return to my duty. So enthralled had I been by this woman and her painful honesty, I'd vowed to open the Pale Court the day she loved me.

A foolish act borne out of this annoying need to make her wholly mine—flesh and bone, soul and heart. Something that seemed to come so easily to mortal men like *Joah*, perhaps even this... *Elric*, where my divinity somehow left me lacking.

A tremble hushed across Ada's pale bottom lip. "How could it be when you treat me like this? You viciously fucked my mouth!"

"Ah, but that is not nearly the heart of why this... encounter angered you so, is it? Little one, you would have let me fuck your mouth until your neck snapped in half in exchange for a single touch of my hand upon your head."

And I'd wanted to touch her.

Wanted it still.

Succumbing to this damnable need, I pinned a strand of her blotchy hair behind her ear. Bloat in her stomach, atrophy gnawing on her muscles, corrosion curdling her blood... My cold wife was rotting away this very moment and, somehow, I wanted her still.

Had not been able to let her go.

How could something this false continue to rouse tender feelings within me? I needed to rid myself of them. Strangle whatever affection I'd foolishly allowed to blossom in my—

Pain stabbed my temples.

My court faded away.

Time stalled and stumbled.

Searing heat flared across by body, sending a nauseating whiff of ash into my nostrils. Through the fog of looming delirium, I clenched my eyes shut, but it only amplified the echo coming from the black cleft that was my sanity. *Elric... Oh, where is my beloved Elric?*

I blinked the fogginess from my mind, only to stare straight at my wife, the source of my agony. She could not love me...?

Then hate it shall be.

"My poor wife, left even without a word of praise over how deep she took me." I let my fingertips stroke over the black feathers of her dress, reminding myself of the wounds she carried beneath and why. "Not a single caress of my finger around the shell of her ear. Not even a mumbled, *mmm, my love, your skilled mouth feels so good.*"

All things I had offered her freely and generously, doting on her for hours, giving her my undivided attention, and never leaving her unsatisfied. Gentle touches. Words of praise. Fine gifts. Not once had she found any appreciation for it.

And I would never offer it again.

Would never elevate her above the others of her wicked kind ever again. What was she other than flesh and bone for me to rule, to use as I wished, no matter how depraved?

"I don't even recognize you anymore." Her eyes glistened with what had to be the last of her tears. "Everything I told you was what I thought true."

My muscles tensed.

And I'd wanted to believe it.

Here she stood, my wedded wife, her ribs too pronounced from too little food and with a new scar slashed across her cheek. Not to mention the fact that she was quite dead...

Hardship was written across her battered body and could not be ignored. The fall off the horse was plausible, along with the story of her dying father—for she had mentioned it before—or the lack of coin.

Not so much her joy.

The one I could never inspire.

"For centuries, I've ridden the mortals' lands, sensing their many hardships and their heavy limbs, even without such dire circumstances as yours," I said. "Oh, little one, I've been rather tempted to rein in my rage, my disbelief, and this biting jealousy over the mortal whose name echoed in your thoughts."

Until she'd mentioned the child.

Remnants of fury flared in my veins, heating my blood to such a degree that her corpse body mindlessly shifted its balance toward me. It only angered me more, this longing for my warmth she couldn't suppress, making it no more sincere than anything that had come before.

However...

It was my due, nonetheless.

And I would make use of it until the coldness would be nothing more to her but a thing to accept. Yes, my little one would learn what it felt like to want something so desperately... only to be denied.

She clenched her eyes shut for a moment, not letting her tears escape, precious as they were. "There was no other man."

Liar.

Liar!

My muscles tensed beneath my skin and my mind fogged once more. I'd been chewed up by the lying teeth of a woman before, for I had understood so little of the power they could wield over any man, be it mortal or god.

And still it was not the bodily betrayal that angered me so. Flesh and bone held no memory, no devotion. The mind, however, did—breeding a disconnect in a place where my power had no say to make it otherwise. Why had she resisted me so? Had I not tried to please her?

"Hear me, Adelaide, you could have whored yourself toward the Pale Court in your difficulty, and I would not have judged. Never that." I shoved my fingers beneath the weight of her hair, gripping it tightly to justify touching it in the first place. "Make no mistake, I would have killed every man who touched what is mine. I would have forgiven you, if only it meant you'd stood by your vow and this candor of yours I'd come to appreciate so greatly. It is the *dishonesty* I cannot forgive, the fact that another inspired what I cannot, and how you tried to hide it behind the most *hideous* lie."

"If you think I had nothing else to do but smile at other men with that slashed cheek of mine," she pushed through clenched teeth, "then you're mad."

My eyes slipped to her lips.

Perhaps I was.

Why else would I want to kiss her? To take her into my arms, this woman I had come to care for so deeply—perhaps more than I wanted to admit to myself.

"Who would not go mad during a fortnight in the lick of never-ending flames?" I yanked her closer to me—torturing her, torturing me, agonizing us both. "I bleed like you. I hurt like you. The only difference being that I cannot die. Truly, little one, it has done the state of my mind no favors."

Her chest expanded with another futile inhale, the dark veins of her oxygen-deprived blood still prominent above her collarbone. "Clearly, because you sound insane."

"Yes, little one, utterly deranged." So much so, I pulled on her hair until her head tipped back, bringing my mouth near hers. Oh, how I wanted to lose myself in her kiss and the false comfort it promised. "For nearly a fortnight, all that kept my mind from shattering anew was the thought of how you waited for me. A fortnight, little one. A fortnight, and not even a fucking furlong closer to the Pale Court, but overly joyous over something *you are not telling me!*"

Defiant little thing she was, Ada ripped away from my touch, punishing us both. "I was happy about the baby!"

Righteous fury flooded my veins until my skin bristled. "Oh, yes, the *baby*. The baby!"

My shout resonated in the chamber, right along with the sudden groans of a corpse in my throne as though I had asked his opinion. Lord Tarnem's muffled grunts pounded behind my temples right along with the echo of my wife's cruel lie, and delirium loomed over my thoughts once again.

I was unwell.

Not enough recovered.

"Quiet!" I shouted.

Ada's eyes flicked between the silenced throne and me, but ultimately settled on me with a blaze of new anger. "Just because it turns out that I wasn't pregnant after all, doesn't mean that I hadn't thought myself—"

My hand rose alongside the violent beat of my heart, tempting me to seal her deceit behind yet another patch of leather. One she would certainly cut open again, for my wife was dead but no more obedient for it. My motion alone stopped her words. Unfortunately, it didn't call back the pain they'd already unleashed in my chest.

"Two centuries of mourning the death of my unborn daughter..." The agony of her loss aching fresh and fierce like a stab to the heart. "Of all the lies to veil your betrayal, perhaps even your faithlessness, you chose this one? *This one?* When you knew how much I'd wanted to die—"

I stopped myself.

No, I would not allow her to drive another knife into my ribcage. Would certainly not let her see how she just had.

I stifled my ragged breathing.

Smoothed the tension off my face.

"You shall answer this question." Leaning into her, I let my exhale tingle along the side of her neck, tormenting her with longing, punishing her with the premise of my warmth. "You say you would have returned... So tell me, little one, have you been this convinced the entire time?" Another exhale, and she turned her head, slowly shifting toward me. "Did you ever wonder what it might be like if you escaped? Did you ever... doubt your vow to return?"

A flinch. A slow blink. And then...

...silence.

Cold. Dead. Silence.

Aside from how she gulped—likely swallowing whatever tale she'd considered serving me for the fraction of a moment. A courtesy I could certainly appreciate, but it made her no less a liar.

Liar!

Prickling heat seared beneath my skin until her bones brittled at my command and the dais crackled beneath us. I wanted to grab her neck and drag her into a deep grave—bury her beneath dirt and let her rot—as that was how much I hated her for making me... hurt, ache, long.

Feel.

Hated myself even more because I could not do it. And I could not do it. And I could not fucking do it.

My chest constricted.

What was wrong with me? What had this woman done to me? Why could I not bring myself to be nearly as cruel to her as she deserved? As I ought to! Was I not above the fickle emotions of mankind? Was I not a god, and she a mere dead mortal?

All strength left me.

Her internal deterioration stopped.

No, I could not do it.

Didn't dare ponder on the name for the reason.

"Look at you, your lips so pale." So bloodless, not even my thumb left an imprint behind as I pressed down on her bottom lip. "Who did this to you, hmm? Who dared to hurt my wife? You saw them? Know the names of those who caused this, yes?"

She nodded. "Three of them."

"Good. Now, make another mention of a child, and I *will* shovel you a grave." I turned away toward the bridge to the Nocten Gate. "Orlaigh!"

"Enosh..." Ada called behind me and when I looked back at her, she asked, "Do you know anything of my father? I... My memories of the attack are blurry at best, but I know he was there. Got injured trying to protect me. Is he alive? Will you at least tell me this?"

"The moment I found you, I hurried to the Court Between Thoughts to have your soul bound." I shrugged and continued down the dais. "I cannot say what became of your father."

"Did you kill people there?"

Not yet. "Everything in due time."

I once more delivered her flesh from a new onset of decay, safe for a small speck that resisted my power—paid for with a wave of weakness that clawed at my mind. Oh yes, what a poor husband I was...

"Always chasing me old bones," Orlaigh muttered as she hurried toward the Nocten Bridge where I stood and waited.

I removed the rot from her body down to the expanding brittleness in her bones at the cost of a sway in my torso and a blur in my vision that expanded rapidly. Rest. I needed more rest.

"Prepare yourself to head to the nearest town in the Nocten lands within the next days," I said. "You shall find out which god these people pray to while I will ride beyond the Œten Gate. I need to assess the lands, for I have allowed the world to fall away from my rule for far too long."

"Yes, Master." She dipped her head. "Just dinnae send me out through the Æfen Gate, or they'll string me up by a tree. Ach, I bet me howlin' arse the Pale Court is surrounded by priests and soldiers."

"So I shall hope."

After all, I required an army.

A large one.

CHAPTER 6
ADA

S*even tens and two.*

Seven tens and three.

I stared up at the ceiling above the spring, how the dim glimmers of light melted with shadows in constant ripples and distortions. All my life, I'd considered being burned at the stake as one of the hardest deaths.

Until I'd drowned myself.

Nine tens and three.

Nine tens and four.

My back rested against the rocky bottom of the spring. When another rush of gloriously hot water lifted me ever so slightly, I inhaled, weighting down my lungs with more water. Who needed air when the second warmest place at the Pale Court turned out to be at the bottom of this spring?

One hundred.

One.

Two.

Three...

I closed my eyes against the sting of salt and listened to the deep hum of the water as suspicion flooded my mind. Thrice Lord Tarnem had grunted and groaned in my presence, each time with an urgency as though his life depended on it—an odd thing indeed, for a corpse.

What would he tell me?

My fist hardened around the smooth fang in my palm—the one I'd once torn off my dress in an attempt to cut open Lord Tarnem's mouth. I'd dropped it when Orlaigh had walked in on me, and it had gone ignored since, having sat so close to the throne where no beasts dared to roam for rest.

Whatever the man knew had the old woman fear that she might end up right next to him. But what did it have to do with me?

Perhaps nothing.

Most likely nothing, but I was at a loss with my husband and death turned out to be a rather dull affair. No sleeping. No eating. Enosh kept his distance, which was as much a blessing as it was a curse. All day, I did nothing but rot... and drown.

Nine tens.

Nine tens and one.

Tiny bubbles of air tingled where they latched to my skin as I sat up. Orlaigh had left for the lands beyond the Nocten Gate seven counts ago, and Enosh had ridden out the Œten Gate long before that.

Time to have a chat with a lord.

I climbed out of the spring, and the first swells of water drooled from my mouth. The salt bit the back of my throat, but only until I rose and folded my upper body over, letting more of it pour from my nostrils.

My brain caught fire and my eyes welled. When I gasped for air, a gurgling flutter teased my lungs until a barrage of violent coughs squeezed out most of the remaining water.

I haphazardly dried myself with a fur, then shucked on my chemise and turned toward the throne chamber. No need to bother with a shoulder pelt. Coldness was my constant companion—the faster I got used to it, the better I could resist Enosh's divine gravity.

The chatter of my teeth echoed from the brittle bone as I crossed the bridge. Tremors ransacked my body and my chest convulsed, letting lone droplets of salty water run from my nostrils only to collect on my chin. Drowning was not elegant.

I hurried up the dais...

...and hit a wall of warmth.

"Who walks about my court?"

My muscles strung tight at the haughty lilt in Enosh's tone. Ugh, my husband was home.

He slouched on his throne in battle armor, his black leather cuirass intricately tooled with flames roaring around bodies on spikes. Could he be any more dramatic? With his leg draped over one armrest, he looked positively bored.

Never a good omen.

"Mmm, my dead wife, here you stand, drowned, once again challenging everything that had been true to me for so long. For eons, not a single corpse ever ignored the innate reflex to breathe... until you." He lowered his leg and let his heavy boot come down with a *thud*, then straightened his spine. "Oh, look how you shiver, your hair still wet, your skin damp."

"Concerned that I might catch a cold?" I clasped the fang tighter, hoping he would not sense it and ask questions. "Why are you here? I thought you rode out."

"Your husband has returned early... joy, oh joy." Sarcasm dripped from his voice as he spread his arms out wide, as though presenting himself as a gift he knew I wanted to return. "So grateful were the mortals beyond the gate when I emerged, they fell to their feet, prayed, and brought me a virgin. A young... *warm*... virgin." Whatever he saw in my eyes—a spark of green rage, most likely—put another smirk on his mouth. "But alas, I have a cold wife at home to return to."

I didn't like how my hackles rose or what this might say about the feelings I'd developed for him before my death—not to mention my mental state. "I'm humbled."

"Not nearly enough. We shall rectify that." A pat on his thigh. "Come, little one. Sit on your husband's warm, warm lap so he may cure you of the cold."

A shudder raked me over. "I'd rather drown myself some more."

His lips twitched. "On my word, I shall be on my best behavior."

My toes curled because his promise smelled decisively like shit. "If I wanted to listen to such dung, I'd head to the nearest tavern and drown myself in its latrine instead."

"Sometimes it seems as though death has emboldened you even further."

"Because I have nothing left to lose."

"You would be surprised..." His jaws clenched and the depressions beneath his cheekbones filled with shadows. "Whatever have I done to earn your suspicion? Do you not trust my word?"

The fact that I trusted it was half the problem. "You coaxed me into the empty hope for your kiss, allowed me to press myself against you, and deliberately teased my mouth to search for yours... only to reject me."

And he would do it again.

I was dead, not stupid.

He would hit me right where it hurt the most, dangling the bait of his warmth in front of me, snaring me with those lips which had once whispered the sweetest compliments. The perfect trap, innocently perched on the throne, carrying the disguise of patience with each slow *pat-pat-pat* against leather-clad thighs.

"Come now." His command let my balance shift toward him. "Enough with your impressive display of obstinance while your bones ache to obey their master."

Obey, they did.

Curse those bones, my legs carried me straight to him, but he would never command such obedience from my soul, and in extension, my mouth and whatever came out of it. At least for as long as he would allow me to keep it...

Enosh clasped my waist and pulled me onto his lap, chuckling at the way I moaned at the sudden heat beneath my buttocks. "Ah, my love, pout all you want, but the fact remains that not even the spring warms you better than I do."

"True." I let myself go limp against his chest, letting the fang disappear in a cranny between bone. "But the company is much better down there."

"My wife is irritable again." He pushed the cotton of my chemise down, exposing one breast to the chill. "Such insolence ought to be punished."

Lowering his head to my nipple, he let his warm breath blow around the bud in a circle. His tongue followed, lapping it into a hard pebble before he suckled it between his hot lips.

I moaned in delight and arched my back, feeding him more. "Why are you so cruel?"

"I promised punishment." Which he quickly initiated by letting his hand slip beneath my chemise, rearranging me on his lap until his finger gained access to circle my darkest hole. "Am I not a man of my word? Have my threats ever been idle?"

I gasped as the pad of his finger drummed against the puckered skin. "No."

"No." He dipped inside, only for his finger to retreat and

continue to vibrate against the softening ring of muscle, making me seek it out with shifts of my hips. "Mmm, little one, I told you that you would learn to love this. And so, you have. What a pity that your enjoyment renders this quite useless as a punishment. Unless…"

Leaning deeper into his throne, he let his other hand reach around and grip my chin. He shifted me until the back of my head rested on his left shoulder. He hooked my legs over his, spreading me wide.

His exhale broke against the side of my temple, where the corner of his lips rested. "Who is Elric?"

Remembering his threat of what he would do if I ever mentioned the truth again, I only said, "Nobody."

"That's right, little one. *Nobody.* Because no mortal man could possibly touch you the way I do, knowing every fiber of your form by heart." His other hand rearranged itself, a finger in each fold that framed my cunt, and a third that drummed my arse. "Your heart no longer beats, yet I can hear it in my memory, its crooked cadence. Listen…" A startling rhythm pounded to life inside my chest, sending a skin-prickling rush of blood through my veins. "Ba-boom-boom. Ba-boom-boom. Oh, how I loved listening to it while you slept."

He brought his fingers closer together, pinning my clit between them. Then he rubbed them up and down, pulling the throbbing nub and its little hood along with it. At each downward motion, his finger dipped into my arse, sending little sparks into my heating flesh.

"You cannot imagine how much effort it takes me to give you this much sensation," he crooned into my ear as he quickened his motions, rubbing me toward completion. "See, my love, your body no longer lubricates on its own. You can feel, yes, but your nerves are corroding more with each of your useless breaths, dulling your sensitivity. Yet here I am, pulling you against the warmth of my chest, rubbing your cunt toward your acme of pleasure. And what do you say to me for this, hmm?" When I only moaned and bucked against his touch, he pinched my clit harder, drummed his finger faster against my needy hole. "The correct answer would be, *thank you, Master.*"

The roots of my teeth ached with how I pressed them together as I pushed the words through their gaps. "Thank you, Master."

"We shall practice this some more." His hot breath clung to the fine wisps along my temple as his other hand kneaded my breast. "So close, I can sense how your muscles tremor. Does your master make you feel good?"

I hissed a dozen curses, called him twice as many things, but it all ended in a guttural, "*Yes...*"

His finger pushed deeper inside me, filling the tight channel with warm pressure as his knuckles shifted around my clit. "And because I make you feel so good, you say...?"

I rocked my pelvis to follow the rhythm of his touch, chasing my release. Oh, so close! "Thank you, Master."

"Better, but not good enough to deserve any pleasure." His hands disappeared, leaving nothing on my cunt or my breast but a frigid pain that ripped a small cry from me. "Yes, this shall make the perfect punishment. Dare touch yourself, and I shall relieve you of your hands."

Frustration mixed with fury.

Curse this devil and his games!

I kept my face as straight as possible, not letting a single mewl or sigh voice my dismay. "Perfect, yes, but rather predictable. Or do you think I expected, for even a second, that you would bring me to completion? You're toying with me. Don't think for a moment that I don't know it."

"Once again, I seem to find myself in a predicament where my wife and her punishment is concerned. How dreadfully complicated this mortal custom proves itself to be... marriage." In one quick move, Enosh swooped me off his lap, only to lay me over it like a girl who'd ruined her new ribbons. His hand shoved the cotton of my chemise up to gather around my middle before his fingers dug into the flesh of my buttocks. "How about this? One strike of my hand for each day I spent being cut up, burned, and spread wide in places we ought not to mention. Yes?"

A shiver of uncertainty trickled across my body, leaving pebbled skin in its wake for my husband to snicker at. I'd been whipped, beaten, and paddled many times in my life, yet his suggestion caught me off guard.

As did the reaction of my body.

Draped over the god's lap, I found myself rocking against his thigh in search of friction, more fervently whenever he circled his warm hand over my buttocks. He didn't seem inclined to interfere with how I rubbed myself on him, and I had no interest in stopping, chasing any sensation to replace the dullness of death.

The humiliation would burn something fierce if he spanked me, but not nearly as hot as the impact of his palm on my chilled skin. My nipples hardened at the thought of his hand slapping my arse, setting the skin ablaze for days to come. If he did it right.

I dug my fingers into the leather of his breeches, braving myself for his first strike. "Do it."

"Do not command me, little one. You might be my wife, but you are not my equal. Try again."

I swallowed past a knot of pride the size of my fist, nearly choking on it. "Please spank me, Master."

"If you so wish."

Tendrils of nervous anticipation weaved through me. My muscles tightened, turning me stiff as I braced for his first strike and the uncertainty of how much strength it would hold. How many times was I due? Would he allow me a few moments between each to let me gather my composure? What if he—

I gasped.

Not at the first strike, but how his fingers glided from my buttocks to between my legs. Enosh circled my entrance with one finger, spreading my wet lust around the needy flesh before he dipped inside with two. Each sensual thrust pushed me against his thigh, teasing a new throb into my clit and sparks of pleasure into my womb. Oh, I wanted more!

"I take no pleasure in hurting you..." a beat of considering silence, "...too much."

His fingers pulled out of me at lightning speed, only for his palm to come down on my buttocks like thunder. Pain crackled through my skin, through my muscles, and into my bones. It wrenched a squeal from my throat, which came out as nothing but a puff of air that parted my trembling lips. By the time its remnants tumbled from my tongue, they shaped into a long moan as the pain faded into wicked, blissful heat.

"Perhaps I have never acquired the taste of it... until now." Enosh's breathing altered as he slipped his hand between my legs once more, letting his fingers fuck my drenched cunt. "And even this arouses you."

I wiggled, not in an attempt to escape my punishment, but to dole out one of my own with how my ribs shifted over his swelling length. "No more than you."

"As impudent in death as she was in life."

Slap.

His next strike disabled my lungs, turning my splutter of curses into a tangled mess of dying whimpers and groans.

Even without air, the scorching pain, the intense pleasure of it, made me feel warm and brutally alive.

A caress along my cunt followed, if to tease my clit or simply to wet his fingers and worsen the impact of his punishment, I couldn't say. Didn't care, either. I only moaned at how his fingers hooked and curled with each thrust, letting me clench around them. I was so close again.

So damn close.

Slap.

"Did you think I would let you come?" he tsked. "No, little one. I might tease you for years, torture you like this for decades."

He continued his pattern of brutal, shuddering swats interwoven with teasing, pleasure-inducing fondling on my cunt until my mind surrendered to the sensation of all-engulfing heat. Heat of pain. Heat of anger. Heat of pleasure.

Just... heat.

Enosh lured me toward release more times than I could count through the haze of rapture, only to abandon me on its biting ledge. Between my sore bottom, my aching muscles, and my flayed pride, my convulsing womb enraged me the most—how it tethered at the edge of harrowing bliss without bursting into release.

At Enosh's next swing, the heat seared straight through my muscles, crumbling all tension, making me hang slack from his lap. Tears blurred my vision, not from pain but from the distressing need and disappointed want.

His next swing never landed.

"I counted seven. Not nearly enough, though I daresay you are sufficiently warm now."

Hands on my waist, he lifted me and sat me on the infuriated flesh of my bottom. With one hand, he stroked my tousled hair back, while the other trailed a finger along the underside of my eye, from the outer corner to the inner one, collecting a tear which he presented to me on the pad of his finger.

"This, little one, is your very last tear. There are no more left in you." His ungiving stare held mine as he licked it off, then swallowed it with a moan. "Mmm, what a gift you gave me."

CHAPTER 7
ADA

Hot anger spiked between my ribs.

Stripped of my pride and my last tear, I blinked Enosh's face into focus, from the smug arch of his left brow to the non-smile framing his lips. Devil be damned, did his facial muscles ever tire of faking cruel detachment?

I was sick of seeing it and my palm itched with the urge to slap it right off. Where I had understood the source of Enosh's anger before, now I could no longer bring myself to care. My own anger was growing thicker with every nasty encounter, every attempt at prying that damn mask off, which left me with only emotional cuts and bruises.

I'd tried to explain, to apologize, to reason... had even tried to unleash his carefully camouflaged rage. Nothing worked. Just what did it take to lure the King of Flesh and Bone out of his skin?

Might as well try that slap.

The moment my arm lifted by a mere inch, Enosh's eyes

flicked to the limb in question before they pinned my gaze down like nails. "I advise you to reconsider."

My spine snapped straight at the sharp undertone that roughened his voice. "You spanked me!"

"How could I deny my wife? *Please spank me, Master...* Oh, how she pleaded. And so, I gave in, cherishing my wife as I ought to." His arm came around my middle, shifting me on his lap until I hissed. "Ah, how nicely your bottom throbs in lieu of a pulse. I daresay the imprint of my hand on your ass makes for a lovely mark. Now, if you wish for another spanking, you only need to say so." For the fraction of a second, his smugness contorted around the edges, letting his pretense slip beneath the snarl on his upper lip. "Strike me, and you can be certain I will retaliate, for I have *never* raised my hand at you in anger, nor whipped you or beaten you for any of your many transgressions."

My arm sunk right along with my shoulders, because half of it was true. Enosh had never caused me physical pain—at least, not the kind that came without pleasure. Except for when he'd twisted my legs, and even then, he'd quickly dulled the pain away.

Still, I couldn't ignore how his eyes returned to ungiving coldness, positively unfazed and remarkably severe to any unknowing stranger... but not to me. I saw how his thick inky shadows of lashes betrayed a potential crack for me to squeeze through and reach the gentle core of his heart.

It was there, I knew.

It had to be.

I straightened on his lap and let a strand of his raven hair run through the clasp of my fingers. "Aside from your excursion beyond the Œten Gate, I haven't witnessed you leave to spread rot."

His face turned impossibly stiffer as his gaze followed the

motion of my finger, watching how I trailed my nail over the tooled motifs on his cuirass. "What?"

"For the children," I clarified. "Wasn't that our agreement? I return to you no matter what, and you rot the children?"

A scoff, then he harshly gripped my wrist and removed my touch as I figured he would. "Our agreement is null and void, for you did *not* return."

Now I dared a scoff, along with how I once again ran my nail along the furrows in the black leather that spun across his chest. "I'm here, am I not?"

"Delivered by death."

"If that's not the ultimate definition of returning no matter what, then I wouldn't know what is." Continuing upward along his high-cut collar, I let my fingertips trail over his hardening jawline. "Besides, you never clarified the specifics. All I know is that I'm here, and you're not out there."

His brow arched higher as though to say, *your obstinance knows no bounds.*

In truth, I couldn't bring myself to care about my old goal of getting Enosh to resume his duty. What did I care about the likes of Rose, who'd gotten me killed? The priests who'd chased me? What had anyone at Hemdale ever done for me, aside from casting their harsh judgment?

Enosh dug his fingers into my cheeks, turning my face away for his teeth to lay siege on the still artery on the side of my neck, where he nipped me. "The gall you have, my little wife, expecting that I would spread rot to the sons and daughters of those who have wronged me."

"They have wronged me, too." I leaned into his rough touch and tilted my head, inviting his teeth to torture me while I cupped his face. "Yet here I am."

"Here you are."

Another harsh nibble here, a sensuous lap of his tongue

there. I'd once called Enosh unpredictable in his godly whims, but that was before I'd spotted his pattern of divine punishment.

My suggestion angered him, and his arrogance left him no choice but to hide it behind the excruciating ecstasy of his hot lips against my skin. He would work me into another frenzy, soaking his bruised ego in my unanswered puddle of want.

And I would let him.

Rejection burned twice as much when the blood was heated—one of the three things I knew could make the god's rage grow too large to be contained by a mask. And if one wouldn't do... well, then I had to try for all three at once.

And pray I wouldn't end up woven into the throne.

Faking a moan was easy enough as he let his slow, deliberate exhale fan along the length of my jaw. Dear god, only the devil himself could make me writhe on his lap and ignore the pain of bruised seatbones in search of the rock-hard bulge hidden beneath his breeches.

I let my thumb trail over the arch of his brow. "Stand by your promise and spread rot."

As haughty as ever, he slapped my hand off his face with a *tsk*, all while gently playing with the curls between my legs, letting tingles spread around my labia. "I have half a mind to rot that tongue of yours instead."

I stopped my writhing, willed my throat to suppress all sounds of pleasure. "Am I free to go, then?"

His fingers stilled around my cunt for as long as it took him to push a boisterous laugh from his lungs. "What makes you think that I will let you leave?"

"Since our agreement is null and void, I'm under no obligation to remain with you for eternity."

He clung to the smile the laugh had left on his lips and

stroked two fingers inside me, his palm rubbing against my clit at each thrust. “You are still my wife.”

“A poor one by your standards, just as you’re a terrible husband by mine.” Curses, the way he shoved me around until his hard length pressed against my arse wasn’t helping my focus, but I wouldn’t give in so easily. “Might as well divorce.”

That earned me the crushing clasp of his hands on my waist as he turned me to straddle him. He yanked me by my hair until my face nearly collided with his, bringing my mouth just close enough to his, as though luck was on my side for once. Yes, this would play out as planned. Maybe.

Enosh’s breathing quickened against the shell of my ear where his lips circled in non-kisses. “Oh, naive little mortal. Wherever would your brittle legs carry you if not back to the Pale Court? Back to your husband, your god, your master?”

My gaze wandered to Lord Tarnem, whose eyes rested on me, but he would have to wait. “Is Yarin not also my master?”

For a moment, I could have sworn I heard Yarin’s chuckle somewhere in the back of my mind... until Enosh’s hiss pulled my attention back to him.

“Scheming to escape me again so soon?” He clasped my chin and brought my lips to his, leaving no more but a hot sliver of quaking breath between them. “A fortnight in freedom and my little one believes herself something other than mine? I would have chased you to the edges of the world.”

“No need to chase me,” I whispered against his lips, following them, shifting my head in pursuit of them whenever Enosh evaded the impact. “I would have returned.”

“Liar.” His breath teased my mouth to chase his seducing lips. “You told me you considered freedom. That you had... doubts.”

“Yes, I had doubts.” I rocked my hips, rubbing myself against the length of his cock as I moved on to the second thing that never failed to impact him—honesty. "Who was the man in the forest? Was he real or only in my imagination so I could justify the things he made me... *feel?*" At that last word, the tremble of his lips shuddered the air, and his fingers loosened their clasp on my cheeks. "I doubted you would ever return to your duty after the attack, cursing my dying father to wander for eternity. So what was the point in coming home and leaving him behind to suffer alone?"

I shifted back and let his hand fall off my face, fighting the invisible pull toward him so I may inspect the chinks on his face. A small wrinkle between his brows. A slight gap between his parted lips. A gaze that slipped to my lips, strained to meet my eyes, then slipped again.

"I doubted all those things." With another rock of my hips, I leaned over once more, and brushed my lips against the corner of his mouth, delivering the final blow—affection. "But then they found the corpse of a rotting boy, and I realized that I *wanted* to return to you. Not for a deal, or a vow, or some ceremony, but of my own choosing. Because the man I was returning to was worth it."

Aching for this kiss, I pressed my chest against the groaning leather of his armor, shivering at the mercy of desire. My lips hunted for his, encouraged by how his stuttered breaths gave me guidance. Heavens, Enosh's entire body quivered against mine.

Kiss me!

Our mouths connected.

My lips scalded, not from the heat of his kiss but how they dragged over the sharp emerging stubble along Enosh's jawline as he turned his head away, sanding my anticipation back down to anger.

"So ambitious," he growled and shifted his head back, staring at me with a positively smackable grin. "Did you believe me foolish enough to fall for your deceit so easily? To allow those lying lips anywhere near mine?"

"No." I flexed the fingers on my right hand. "I figured it might take a push, ill-tempered and arrogant as you are."

I lifted my palm.

I thrust it at his face.

With a hiss, Enosh gripped my wrist, bringing my futile assault to a predictable halt nowhere near his cheek. "You dare try to strike—"

I slammed my mouth to his.

Pure, violent heat melted my lips, letting them shape so perfectly around Enosh's. It was all-consuming, the feverish passion that softened our bodies against each other, burning me to the coldest, innermost part of my core.

Enosh's lips first stiffened, then trembled. Then they parted on a groan, inviting me deeper into this kiss. Releasing my wrist, he brought his arms around me, holding me in place against the upward thrust of his hips. But instead of letting his breeches vanish, he busied his hands on me, letting them stroke, caress, and palm wherever they reached while holding me tightly. So tightly.

I let my fingers map the familiar arch of his brows, the sharpness of his cheekbones, the way his jaws shifted with our breathless kiss, only to trail down his cuirass. And what if I took his heavy cock out and mounted him? Would he let me?

Agonized by his skillful fingers and deprived of any release, I made quick work of untying his breeches. My plan hadn't included to fuck him, but what would it hurt to show him my want?

I shoved his breeches down, released his fully erect length, gathered my chemise, and sent my cunt searching. When his crown nudged at my entrance, I slid down, impaling myself on him.

I moaned.

"Ada..." Enosh groaned.

My skin pebbled at the guttural sound around my name, and a second time when his hard flesh filled me with pressure and warmth. Heavens, I'd forgotten how thick and how impossibly long he was.

I rubbed against him, spreading my legs as wide as the throne would allow to take him deeper. God, he felt so good, pushing me down on him, shifting his hips so perfectly in rhythm with mine.

"Ada," he groaned once more, with his hands tightly pressed against my body. "I ought not to—"

I pressed my mouth to his, clawing at his cuirass in search of the strong chest on which I'd slept many times. Oh, I'd missed this so much. I had missed *him* so much, and I didn't want to consider why.

Little moans and whimpers tumbled from my mouth as I fucked him harder, faster. Tingles swarmed my clit each time the needy nub pressed against the base of his cock.

"I'm so close," I whispered against his lips before they melded against his in another fiery kiss. "Mmm, Master, please make me feel good."

Enosh stilled so fully, so absolutely, it rendered my blood into chilled slush. "Stop."

"What?" My hips only slowed their rhythm, and my lips suckled his unmoving bottom lip, trying to rekindle what little warmth remained. "I didn't mean to say that."

"Exactly. Now get off me before I make you."

My stomach convulsed.

My hips stilled.

I slowly shifted back and lifted my eyes to his, expecting a grin, a smirk, an arched brow... anything that would indicate he'd once more toyed with me.

But what I found instead was worse.

So much worse...

Enosh stared into the nothingness of the Pale Court, the focus of his eyes as detached as his mind seemed to be. And then it happened. Something I'd thought impossible with this virile, lusty god.

He softened inside me.

"So ambitious indeed." His voice was as void of anger as it was of arrogance, and I didn't know what to do with that at all. "Even in death, my wife won't stop pestering me, feeding me the sweetest kisses and words to achieve her goal. If only death had not betrayed deception."

My core hollowed. "No. Enosh, I—"

"Nobody ought to accuse me of breaking my vows." Rising, he slipped me off him and tucked himself away. "However, I shall choose the manner in which I fulfill my oath to you, for when I ride beyond the Æfen Gate, it will not be to spread rot... but death."

I clasped my arms around myself at the sudden draft whistling from beyond the Æfen bridge. Groans and shuffling resonated in the tunnel and the nipping stench of rot filled the throne room. What was happening?

When my eyes caught on a figure emerging from the shadows across the bridge, I stopped breathing, filtering out the reek of death, but not its grizzly sight.

Oh, my god...

Dozens, no, hundreds of children entered the Pale Court, from boys near fighting-age who dragged their smashed limbs toward us to pox-speckled toddlers who scooted across the bridge. A young girl, half her head amiss, carried an infant in the cradle of her arms, stripped down to bone and sinew.

I shivered. "This is awful."

"Awful? No. This is what you wanted, is it not? I am

opening the Pale Court to those children you love so dearly. Their skulls shall stack into columns, their skins span a canopy above them, and their ribs shall encase the beauty of my court."

One after another, the children dissolved into the white powder of bone. It swirled into all directions at once, shaping pillars carved with motifs of forests, walls that rose toward the arched ceiling, and wide staircases of bone, polished to a shine. A palace formed around me, furnished with alabaster tables, life-sized statues of beasts, and elaborately carved chairs, padded with what had to be woven hair.

It was beautiful.

It was terrifying.

More horrid was how five children limped toward me, their eyes veiled in white, their bodies torn to shreds for they must have laid in the piles for years. Decades. Their groans echoed from the wall of bone that rounded the dais, battering straight into my heart with its odd resonance.

"Kneel."

My knees hit the ground. "What are you doing?"

"Your coronation, my love." Enosh hooked his pointer beneath my chin and lifted my gaze to his. "Are you not the wife of the King of Flesh and Bone? You have the kingdom you wanted... and now, its queen shall have her crown."

My thighs gave out as the children reached toward me, and my arse sunk onto the heels of my feet. I clenched my eyes shut, but I felt it—their tiny hands squeezing my head, their spindly fingers digging into my hair.

"Rise," Enosh commanded.

So I did, opening my eyes only to watch the children dissolve. The pressure around my head, however, remained.

I reached my shaky hands upward, sensing the smooth bone spreading out and thinning like a circular nest of branches. My fingertips glided over bumps here and there. *Knuckles.*

"Your crown, my queen," Enosh whispered into my ear. "The Queen of Rot and Lies? No... not quite regal enough. Ah! Now I know. The Queen of Rot and *Pain*. Your rot, my pain."

No matter how I yanked on it, the crown of little hands and fingers wouldn't lift an inch. "You melded it to my head!"

He twirled a strand of my hair around his finger, then seemingly weaved it around my crown of bone. "There, you have achieved your goal. Take your victory, Ada. Take your victory, but spare me your deceptions."

He turned and climbed a staircase that spiraled above his throne, leaving me behind shaken, devastated, and defeated. Yes, I'd gotten the god to stand by his vow and open the Pale Court to some of the children, but it didn't feel like a victory at all.

It felt like loss.

Bitter. Aching. Loss.

CHAPTER 8
ADA

The Pale Court had turned into a maze of corridors, bridges, and staircases—a tangled labyrinth that knew no bounds and seemed to swell with each child who shuffled through the gate.

Its inhabitants?

The god, who sequestered himself away in the highest room above his throne; old Orlaigh, who cursed all the stairs she had to climb; and me, its rotting queen.

Oh, and my entourage of corpses.

They followed me everywhere—two boys who reached no higher than my hip, and a girl with one arm—serving no other purpose than to punish me. *Clack-clack-clack* made their flesh-bare heels as they tottered behind me down the southern staircase, making sneaking about the court impossible.

Not that it mattered.

Once again, Enosh had seen to my appropriate attire. Thin braids of white and gray hair lined my bodice. From my waist down, it fanned out into small, translucent circlets which shaped the train of my dress—quite possibly made of nails, though I couldn't be certain. A fringe of bony fingers ran along the train's seam, joining in the clattering, brain-grinding, macabre symphony of decay as I rushed about court.

I turned toward the throne room with purpose in my steps. With Enosh once more asleep, as though my failed ruse had exhausted him about as much as a fortnight of fire, Orlaigh remained the only potential obstacle between me and the truth. Something I'd prepared for, and...

And this was not the throne room.

"Curse these corridors!" I came to an abrupt halt inside the archway of what I called the great hall, appointed with a large table—where nobody ever ate—and chairs with backrests of carved antlers. The dome-shaped ceiling was decorated with thousands of white feathers, which hung from strings of skin. "Whatever did he do to the stairs toward— Ah!"

The children followed me up one short set of stairs and down another. At the next turn, we followed a narrow corridor toward the throne room, its walls shaped from the brightest bone and tooled with vines of roses and birds' nests.

As expected, I found Orlaigh sitting on the painted dais with a book in her lap and promptly handed her two of Enosh's shirts. "Before he fell asleep, he requested you wash these."

"Ach lass, me bones start squeaking halfway to the spring with how vast the Pale Court has grown." She struggled herself up, sighing as she took the shirts and frowned at the small spots of blood. "That deamhan, making such a mess of it. Where did these even come from?"

From my toe, where the bit of blood I had left pooled each day, until Enosh sent it rushing through my veins with a startling beat of my heart. "As if he'd tell me."

"Curse the man, this will take forever to wash out."

Good. "Best get to it. I don't think he'll sleep much longer."

She stared at the children and furrowed her brows before her gaze met mine. "Ach, lass... ye were good for me Master's head up to the point where ye got yerself killed. Now he's stuck in such a rage and as mad as ever. Ach, he'll keep me in his service for another eternity, never setting me soul free."

"Is that why you ratted me out? Not letting me escape so I may replace you? So you might find rest?"

Fine wrinkles formed around her pursed lips. "Can ye blame me?"

"No." Not anymore. "Death is rather boring state whenever Enosh isn't busy punishing me."

"It could be worse."

"Yes, I presume he could have weighted down the train of my dress with little skulls." My husband knew exactly how the sight of these children ached me, no matter their lack of awareness over this morbid display. "Whatever affection he might have held for me, if any, has all turned into endless hate."

"*Hate?* Ha! Those he hates become a crown upon his head." Book clasped beneath her arm and shirts bunched against her chest, she walked down the dais. "Those he loves get to wear one."

"That's not love, Orlaigh." My sarcastic laugh echoed from the walls. "He melded children's hands to my skull. Enosh is worse than ever before."

"Aye, he is." She lifted a scolding finger in the air as she turned toward a corridor. "Worse than a god in rage..."

... is a god in love.

My throat constricted, and my mind wandered back to the day I'd died. How Enosh had placed my hand upon his cheek, right where tears had washed off the soot from his marred skin.

Had he wept for me? Cried over my death?

Maybe a god's love wasn't gentle or kind... Maybe it was all-consuming, devastatingly painful, and destructive in its lack of moral restraints. Maybe he had given me his heart after all—the one he'd claimed he didn't possess—immediately broken by my doubts, delay, and death.

When Orlaigh's unhurried steps finally faded away, I turned toward the throne.

As always, Lord Tarnem watched me through the dull veil clouding his eyes where his face protruded from between intertwined roots of bone. The rest of him wove around the backrest of the throne in a tangle of limbs, making it impossible to say which arm or leg belonged to which corpse.

The claw I'd stashed away between the bone was gone, likely consumed in the construction of the palace. It was of no consequence, thanks to Enosh's generous disdain.

Leaning over, I reached for one of the digits that strung along the seam of my train. With a sharp pull, I ripped the finger off, then broke the brittle thing in two. A tap against the splintered edge confirmed its pointed sharpness.

Yes, this would do quite nicely.

I lowered myself onto the throne and, with a determined thrust, punctured the patch of skin that covered Joah's mouth. "You first."

A cloud of rancid breath hit me in the face, making me nauseous. It intensified with each tearing inch of progress as I cut the leather, making me gag as though my stomach had anything left to relieve itself of.

Joah's green-speckled eyes squelched as they focused on me, as though the liquids of decay had collected in their sockets. Still, he was handsome as far as two-centuries-old corpses went, with tattered long brown hair and full lips, now cracked and dry. Enosh had restored the corpses some before he'd bedded down, but if they had retained their ability of speech remained to be seen.

When I'd assured myself of the presence of an actual mouth, I leaned back so he wouldn't have to strain his eyes so much. "Were you and Njala lovers?"

There was a crackle at the back of his throat—like brittle leather stretching much too thin—before the black tip of his tongue pushed against the back of his gray incisors. "N-nj..."

"Yes, Njala. Were you lovers?"

"Uh-waysh."

I sensed my facial muscles pull into a frown. Uh-waysh? "Always?"

Whatever did that mean?

His mouth gaped open, letting the remnants of leather at the corners of it tear like old parchment. "Fre-hever... love Nj—"

When a *pop* resonated from the black cavity of his mouth as though a sinew or muscle had torn, I quickly pressed my hand against his sinking jaws before the entire thing would come loose and rip off. "If you loved her, then why did you slit her throat? Because she wanted you to?"

"Yesh."

Goosebumps sprouted along my arms. "And condemn her baby to death?"

His face vibrated in my clasp as he tried to shake his head where it sat embedded into bone, letting stiff vertebrae *crack-crack-crackle* at the base of his neck. "No. To save—"

Pop.

The weight of his lower jaws dropped into my palm and I frantically shoved at his limp face. "No, no, no..."

"Hrk-hmm... nhh..."

"Save how?"

"Gkrrr..."

A heavy swallow bobbed down my throat as his skin tore beneath his ear. Heavens, there was no use. His lower jaws would separate soon enough, and no holding it in place would give me any intelligible answer.

At least not from him.

I gingerly removed my hand from Joah's face, then turned my attention to Lord Tarnem. As always, he grunted and heaved, pressing the tip of his tongue against the leather covering his mouth, which I made quick work of.

The gray-haired man opened and closed his mouth several times, wafts of decay souring the air between us. "Ada."

I shuddered.

He knew my name.

Should that surprise me? Because it shouldn't. After all, he also knew the size of my breasts and the lewd sounds of my pleasure, considering I'd groaned into his face on several occasions.

I pulled my knees against my chest as I draped the heavy train of my dress over the armrest of the throne. "I have questions."

Another stretch of his mouth revealed a tongue still moist enough to slither and curl as though it relished the rare taste of freedom. "And y-you shall... shall have your answers."

"Why did Joah—"

"After you pledged me... your he... help."

Internally, I groaned. "Or I might just peel your face off in layers until you talk."

"Child, I have been at your husband's mercy for... oh, for two centuries. Such threats mean nothing to me."

Neither did I have the patience to wait this out with how

Orlaigh often guarded the throne room like a dog its bone. Literally. "What do you want?"

"You will convince the god of my... my innocence, so he may grant me rest."

A sad little laugh vibrated in my chest. "I can't even convince him of my own innocence. Besides, why would I bother to help an old man rotting in this throne over something that is little more but a mystery to me and something to relieve me of eternal boredom?"

"Old, rotting man..." I sat at his eye level, yet he managed to stare down at me with all the arrogance of nobility, even in his state of decay. "I am a lord."

"And I am a queen." A tap against my crown vibrated all the way into my skull. "As it so happens, I've recently grown sick of helping others only for myself to end up worse than before. Like dead, for example. Now that I gave you your mouth back, you can convince him yourself when he wakes."

"She will make certain he won't believe me, as she always has."

"Who?" When he tilted his head as much as the throne let him, giving me the weight of his stiff, milky stare, I sighed. "Orlaigh."

"Yes, Orlaigh," he said. "Dear child, my success stands and falls with yours. If you convince our Master of your innocence, my own might follow. In part..."

That piqued my interest. "What's all this got to do with me?"

"Your pledge."

"Fine, I give you my promise, for whatever it's worth these days."

"A great many things if I am correct in my suspicion. Now listen, and listen well." He cleared his throat, sending me back half a foot with another puff of sour air. "It is true, the god and

I had a disagreement over the amount of corpses he promised me for an army."

"Enosh told me Njala came to talk sense into you."

He laughed hard enough that the expanse of his chest let ribs crack against the ungiving cage of bone that trapped his body. "Yes, she came. And then she vanished, spirited away by the commander of my own forces."

My guts constricted, and for once, I was certain it was neither hunger nor maggots churning my stomach. "So, Joah took her away of his own account?"

"Hmm, yes."

I choked on a spike of shock as imaginary puzzle pieces reshaped before my mind. One after another, the echo of many accounts from different people distorted, only to rearrange into a grotesque picture that left me reeling for its meaning.

Yes, Joah and Njala had been lovers.

Always.

Forever.

Even before Enosh?

The shocking intensity of this possibility left me stunned and feeling rather stupid because the hints had all been there. Had Orlaigh not once mentioned how Njala had been found in the stables with a man? Had it been Joah? Why else would he have stolen her away?

I blinked myself out of my daze. "They had an affair, and you broke them apart when you gave her to Enosh."

"As a lord with no son, no heir, a daughter's reputation can carry the weight of alliances for generations to come," Lord Tarnem said. "Stained as it was, no other man of nobility from neighboring parts would have her, but the god does not care about such things. Before Joah could put a bastard in her belly and render her worthless, I promised her to Enosh, silencing the damaging gossip while securing a powerful ally."

"Worthless." That word stung deep enough it poked a sense of solidarity toward Njala and how she'd shared in a woman's plight same as I had. "Why keep Joah on as the commander?"

"Dismissing him would only have given credibility to rumors."

"So Enosh didn't believe that you had no part in her disappearance, which prompted him to accuse you of keeping Njala away from him so he would bend to your demand."

"When he marched his corpses to my castle, I had no other choice but to capture him. To keep him my prisoner and my lands safe until I retrieved my daughter, contained the proof of her disloyalty, blamed Mertok, and returned her to the god as a sign of my goodwill. As you can see, child, gods make poor prisoners. He freed himself, and his corpses flooded my lands with the fury of their master without one more word spoken between us."

"But when Enosh closed in on Njala, she refused to return to him and instead, chose death." My palm glided to my bodice, pressing against the braids of hair to soothe the sudden itch beneath. "And because she'd never wanted Enosh's child to begin with, she chose death for the both of them?"

"Did she?"

A moment of brittle silence stretched between us, filled with the phantom beat of my heart and a dull ringing at the back of my mind that begged for my attention. Joah had shaken his head as vehemently as one might expect of a corpse this old, telling me they'd meant to save the child? From what?

I gulped.

Or from *whom*?

I pressed my hand against my parched throat. It started as a tremble in my chin, that moment when a startling question ripped the world out from underneath me, sending me stumbling off the throne.

Had Enosh even been the father of this child, or had Joah—

"No, this can't be..." My mumbling faded into silence as I lifted my gaze to Lord Tarnem. "Njala was already pregnant when she left the Pale Court and ran off with Joah, is it not true?"

"Yes, she was."

Njala came and left as she pleased, Enosh's voice resonated in my mind before it shaped into Orlaigh's odd lilt as it whispered, *Chaperoning her was like herding a bunch of flea-ridden cats. Foolish, foolish girl.*

The question pounded louder inside my skull, making me choke on a wave of dread. "Who was the father of this baby?"

The corners of Lord Tarnem's lips twitched. "Child, you might very well be the only one capable of answering this question."

"She saw him. All this time, she secretly met with Joah." I wrapped my arms around myself. "If she continued her affair with Joah, he might have been the father of the child."

A self-satisfied smile came over the lord's face. "The *mortal* child."

The one Enosh had sensed.

My mind wobbled somewhere between wary suspicion and wicked sanguinity as all strength left my corroding muscles. Pain stabbed me in the belly, sharp and cold. I looked down at myself, halfway expecting my bodice to stain red from wounds bleeding anew.

I sunk to the ground, trembling. Fought the heart-wrenching hope spreading through my core and how it might set me up for harrowing disappointment. No, I could not go through this again. But how could I avoid the impact and potential meaning of this revelation?

Enosh sensed all the dead.

All the living.

But not his brothers.

I pressed a hand to the wounds on my belly and circled them as overwhelming sorrow dulled my senses. Again. If Enosh could not feel his divine brothers, then what were the chances that he could feel our divine baby?

CHAPTER 9
ADA

Orlaigh squatted over a wooden tub beside the spring, running one of Enosh's white cotton shirts down the washboard. She hadn't noticed my approach since I'd outran the children while lifting the weight of my bony train. Her cheery caroling resonated in the cave, a song about a dragon who guarded a secret.

My breath shook.

How fitting...

I'd known she was hiding something, but never had I expected that it might affect me to a degree that my entire body vibrated with fury and fear alike.

Fury that I'd died pregnant.

Fear that I had not.

Or the other way around?

My stomach plunged to my knees. No, I was doomed either way, for the truth—either truth, really—would shatter my soul. If my theory proved true and I had died with a child in my belly—

I pressed a hand to my mouth, muffling a sob as agony,

sharp and digging, spread around my heart. No, I could not possibly survive it. Might die a second time.

Same if my theory proved wrong.

My hand circled my belly again, every go round like a caress to a hope I could *not* afford, either. What if Lord Tarnem's goal to get himself out of the throne had taken advantage of my situation? My desperation? What if I fell for a lie?

What if there was still no child?

My stomach clenched, shifting around the gases of decay once more. Mercy god, I would descend into a hysteria that would make Enosh look reasonable.

What was true? What was not?

Only one woman knew.

Taking a steadying breath, I opened the clasps of my hands and let the fringe of fingers *clank* to the ground where I stood beside the dark rock. "Foolish, foolish, Ada."

Orlaigh spun around so fast, her soles squeaked on the stone floor, hands hovering wet and dripping over the ground. "What?"

My lungs hardened against the pressure of unease that expanded within my chest. "Who fathered Njala's child?"

Face going still, shaky fingers disappearing into the checkered fabric of her dress, mouth a hard line, she glared at me in shock. "Whatever do ye mean?"

I took a step toward her. "Who was the father? Enosh or Joah?"

"Ach, lass." Sliding one leg forward, she struggled up to stand. "Yer mind's muddled."

The roots of my teeth ached with how I clenched them. Of course, she would deny it all. Might even try to twist things around, unleashing doubt and confusion.

I would not let her.

"Oh, quite the opposite," I said. "I feel as if I'm seeing things clearly for the first time."

"It's the grief talking." A grandmotherly smile crossed her face—one I didn't trust a bit. "Let me help ye out of this dress so ye can soak in the water and forget."

"No doubt it would serve you well if I did." And hadn't she eagerly tried to convince me to let go of my grief? "I spoke to Lord Tarnem. He told me everything."

"Dinnae go listening to lies, lass." Her smile wavered around the edges. "Ach, the man will say whatever he can to get me Master to release his bones from the throne."

"Just like you will say whatever you can to keep yours out of it." Even if it came at the cost of my heart, not to mention my sanity. "*Oh, if me Master ever finds out the truth. Foolish, foolish, girl.* Do you think I forgot how I found you arguing with Lord Tarnem that day? You accompanied Njala when she left the Pale Court. Will you deny that she met with Joah?"

Her hands balled into fists. "Ye dinnae ken what the little lady was like—"

"I know that she chose death for herself and the child, likely because she feared what Enosh would do if he ever found out the truth." My words triggered a spread of gooseflesh along my skin. "Do you deny it?"

"Lass—"

"Who fathered her child?"

"Ada—"

"Who?"

"I dinnae ken!" Her shout echoed off the stone, and deep furrows carved along her forehead as she fumbled with the cotton of her dress. "What was I but the old wet nurse to be shushed about as though I've never lived a day in me life? So many times, I warned the little lady...Oh, how I scolded her."

"Yes, nobody listens to old Orlaigh," I said. "Njala loved the commander, didn't she? Never stopped loving him."

"Ach, we women cannae afford to love. I told her so. *Many times*. But she would not listen! What could I do? Tattle to the god? See the little lady punished?" She pressed a hand against her sternum and swallowed. "I've nursed the lass from me own breast since she was a wee thing, as though she was me own. Only days after I lost me own child."

My guts knotted up at the familiarity of her pain, but I couldn't let that soften me in my determination to uncover the truth. Would not continue to care more about everyone else's sorrows than my own.

And mine were dire, indeed.

"It's true then." My legs turned brittle underneath me, and I pressed a palm against the rock for support. "All this time, she secretly met with Joah. Was he the father?"

Orlaigh tsked, "Lass—"

"Was he?"

"Who can ken such a thing? Ach, the world is full of bastards, raised by their unknowing fathers, be it a king or a kitchen drudge."

"But you knew it was possible, plausible, even. Especially since the baby was mortal." And that fact brought precious remnants of tears to my eyes, not enough to pearl down my cheek, though they blurred my vision. "What if Enosh cannot sense a godly child? What if I died pregnant, after all?"

"What of it?" Orlaigh shifted from one leg to the other, lifting her arms and letting them flap against her sides. "What does it matter now?"

"It matters a great deal to me!" I shouted, hating how this ordeal leeched away the self-worth I'd finally found for myself. "All my life, I've been called barren, an unwoman. One husband called me worthless; the other calls me a liar. I'm sick of being at the mercy of everyone's false judgment!" Against the tremble in my hand, I dared another heart-shattering caress of my palm around my belly. "I might be carrying a divine child in my belly."

"Or ye might not." The bite in her tone clawed at my narrowing throat. "Even if the babe was the commander's..."

Sharp and harrowing, the potential truth of her words punctured straight into a heart that still hadn't fully mended from the agony of losing a child twice. Oh, I was so stupid, it hurt.

There was a third option I hadn't even considered.

What if all my assumptions about Joah and the baby were true, but not how it related to me? None of it made me any more likely of carrying a child in my belly, divine or otherwise.

My hand slipped off the rock.

The ground shook.

Or maybe not, but my legs snapped like twigs underneath me anyway, letting me sink to the damp, harsh ground. No, there would be no comfort in this mess, no liberating discovery.

Only agony.

Only suffering.

"Lass, it hurts me to see ye so." Drying off her hands some more, Orlaigh walked over, squatted down, and stroked my arms. "Who says that gods can even sire children?"

"Who says they can't?"

"Lass, three gods as old as time." She arched a bushy brow. "Not one has a child, and the world is better for it."

My stomach knotted into a hard ball beneath the pressure of my hand. I thought back to Eilam's kiss, stiff and unskilled, as though his lips had never touched a woman's before. Perhaps they hadn't, but Yarin was a scoundrel who likely spent most of eternity beneath the skirts of women, dead and alive.

What if Orlaigh was right?

My stomach hardened.

But what if she was wrong?

"I had all the symptoms..." I whispered, clinging to the thinnest thread of faith. "I might be a poor fisher, but I'm a decent midwife."

"Even if ye're right, lass, it doesn't make ye any less dead." The slow shake of her head carried all the weight of a thousand bitter truths. "Even if its father is a god, does that make the child undying? Able to grow between bloat and maggots?"

My teeth ground together until a molar shifted under the strain, threatening to pop from my gums.

Dead or alive.

Divine or imagined.

How would I even prove any of this? Was I to cut myself open and rummage through my innards? That sounded crazy even to me, once again making me wonder if I'd simply lost my wits along with my life. What if I was a liar, even to myself?

My pride reared in my chest.

No, I was no liar.

Morning sickness. Achy breasts. The grains. I died pregnant. Call it instinct, but I sensed it deep inside me with each caressing circle of palm around belly.

But if I went to Enosh with talk of a child, he might very well make good on his threats, for he could not feel it. Neither could his brothers—

Realization smacked me in the face, painting me as foolish as everyone else involved in this mess. Hadn't Yarin mentioned something about some of my soul resisting when he'd bound it? What if not mine had resisted, but that of my child?

My lips parted on a gasp, only for an unexpected name to tumble from my lips. "Eilam."

Orlaigh frowned at me. "What's with him now?"

"He said something when I died about, um..." Devil be damned, what had he said? Something about life? Too much life? "I don't remember, but I feel like it's important. Maybe they can't feel the baby, but they can feel that *something* is amiss. At least two of them. I need to talk to Enosh. He has to notice it, too."

"Ye are dead, Ada." Orlaigh's voice was soft, yet my hackles rose at the nape of my neck as though not even my skin trusted her anymore. "Ach, the little lady was too young. The foolish thing never thought of consequences. For two hundred years, I've paid for me mistake of giving in to her plea to see her lord father. Aye, she betrayed me as much as anyone, running off with that... bastard."

My muscles stiffened. "What are you saying?"

"If ye tell me Master now... if what ye think is true... Ah diah, he'll weave me into his throne, all over a child in yer rotting belly." A pleading look. "Have ye no mercy?"

"Mercy?" I shook my head and shifted back. "And who has mercy on *me*, huh? Not you, that's for certain, for you have known this all along. I've dragged guilt with me for years, and I won't drag misery with me for eternity because of the mistakes others made some two hundred damn years ago."

The moment I scrambled to my feet, she grabbed my arm, her grip too strong to suggest grandmotherly care anymore. "Two centuries, lass. I cannae let ye send me into his throne now."

My ears pricked at the nip in her undertone. A warning?

She will make certain that he won't believe me, Lord Tarnem's words floated through my head, *as she always has.*

As she would now?

I looked back at her. "Will you throw me to the wolf once more?"

"Before it bites me in me howlin' arse, aye, I will. Does that make me the villain? Did Njala not betray me the same as everyone else, leaving me behind for the god's wrath to chew me up when I'd only shown her leniency?"

"Perhaps you were too kind, same as me." I rose, shaking off her hold. "Something I'm trying to rectify."

Her lips pressed into a thin line for a moment before she smacked her tongue. "Not at the cost of me bones."

A chill shot up my spine, cooling my raveled mind enough for my brain to recognize the threat. Enosh might think me a liar, but I was nowhere as skilled as Orlaigh—a woman who held enough of his trust to keep the truth from him for two centuries where I held none.

"Not at the cost of mine, either," I said. "You said it yourself; he loves me."

"Aye, loves ye to death."

I shuddered.

Stepping away from her, I turned, then fled toward the *clack-clack-clacking* that resonated the passage back into the Pale Court. My mind spun and my heart ached, but I couldn't allow myself to succumb to either. How could I approach this without sending myself straight into the throne?

If I hadn't gone to Orlaigh in anger, I could have avoided pitting her against me. Could have conjured up a way to tell Enosh the truth. Preferably one that didn't contain me blurting, *I am maybe carrying your child, after all. Njala ran away with Joah of her own choosing.* Or, the worst option yet, *The baby was probably never yours.*

Well, it was too late now.

Devil be damned, my skull ached under the pressure of my crown and how my brain frantically tried to compose a plan.

More so when the corpse children huddled up to me with their grinding *clanks* and *clonks*. What to do?

I pondered that question for what felt like an eternity as I combed through their tousled strands until an idea struck. What if I avoided Enosh's suspicion and Orlaigh's deceitfulness altogether and went straight to one of the other gods?

I frowned.

Not Eilam.

Aside from the fact that I trusted him the least—not that Yarin could be called trustworthy by any means—his court was the world. That was a pretty big place to go looking for a god.

But what about the Court Between Thoughts? I'd been there before. Could I somehow go there again? Would Yarin notice the potential of a divine child and convince his brother of it?

It was an option.

My only one.

I just needed to find out how I could get there, given that it was no physical place. At least, I didn't think it was. If I remembered correctly, then it was between my thoughts... wherever that was.

In her wariness, Orlaigh would be of no help with this, leaving me no other choice but to pry hints from Enosh. And while I was at it, I could contemplate how to explain to a god that he'd been made a cuckold...

CHAPTER 10
ENOSH

I observed my wife from the concealing shadows of a horse statue, my mind well-rested from days of sleep, yet no less confounded. Perhaps even more so.

Ada sat on a daybed I'd created at the center of a pavilion... eight pillars carved from bone, with triangular sheets of skin stretched between them for a roof. A gentle breeze from the Æfen Gate weaved through braids of hair where they created sheer curtains around the structure, each strand decorated with white feathers.

What was I to make of this?

In my anger, I'd given her a crown shaped from the little fingers of children—a punishment for her ruse of feigned affection, her talk of how she'd chosen to come to me, and a stolen kiss that had wrecked my defenses. And what did she do?

She made it look *stunning*.

My ribs shrank around my organs as though I had only punished myself. There she sat on a pile of gray furs, plaiting the mousy brown strands of a girl—one of three child corpses I had commanded to follow her, offering her yet another reminder of how she'd tormented me with the most hideous lie.

Ah, what a mistake.

These children had neither soul nor awareness, yet Ada must have washed the filth off their emaciated bodies. They sat on the ground by her feet, their tatters replaced with clean tunics and the two boys' lackluster hair neatly combed.

If anything, my punishment served as a reminder of why I had come to admire this woman. Had come to love her?

My breath stuttered at the premise of having allowed myself to love once more. Such a terrible emotion, love; perhaps the only emotion capable of soothing a heart one moment, only the rip it in half the next. What else explained this... this shift in me?

My mind wandered back to how I'd held her draped over my lap, resonating through the Pale Court with the loud smacks of my palm meeting her reddened backside. It had aroused me, yes, but the pain I'd instilled on her body had ached me more. So much so, I had stopped at seven.

What was wrong with me?

I was a man of my word, never false in my threats and promises, be it suffering or death. Yet where my wife was concerned, I could not seem to uphold a single one. No matter how she angered me—as though intent on unleashing my wrath—something always stopped me.

Something that soothed.

Something that hurt.

Ah, now she placed a kiss atop the girl's head, sending a sense of nervous reluctance to burn along my veins. Ada's care for children knew no bounds, extending beyond death where she offered their bodies dignity and love.

It did nothing to cure me of how uncertainty crept in, and the relentless confusion about this entire ordeal.

Orlaigh walked up beside me, frowning at the way Ada placed a makeshift shoe onto the girl's foot. "What's the lass doing now?"

"Caring for the children entrusted into her keep." This... *something* shifted beneath my ribs, a sensation as unwelcome as it was persistent, no matter how hard I had tried to deny its existence. "Would such a woman truly use a child as a lie to hide her deceit?"

My age-old servant cocked a brow, giving me the whole weight of her concerned stare. "Are ye growing doubts about her betrayal, Master?"

I bit down on the tip of my tongue.

Was I?

My mind had been... unwell after I'd escaped the priests, exhausted from a fortnight of the most horrendous torture. Shaped after mankind, I suffered its shortcomings, its flaws. I made mistakes. Might have reacted rashly, overwhelmed by thousands of memories of past betrayals and shocked by my wife's disappearance.

"Has she not proven her upright character more times than she has strayed from it?" I countered. "Did she not look convinced of her own lie?"

Ada was no fool, but she was a woman scorned, having wanted nothing more than a child. A mortal's form was capable of doing wondrous things in conjunction with a soul's desires—even wrench food from a stomach. What if she had truly thought of herself with child?

Orlaigh's gaze lowered to the ground as she fingered a faded ribbon on her dress. "The looks of mankind are deceiving. Yer own words."

My breathing altered. "Indeed."

Was I a fool for a liar once more?

I observed my wife's rounded spine, and how she let her palm glide from sternum to belly where she circled once, twice. Why would she display such mannerisms if not for grief? False, yes, but no less painful.

Had I wronged her?

My chest tightened. How utterly strange that she could suppress the reflex to breathe, yet not the urge to caress something that was not there. Oh, she'd wanted it so dearly.

As had I.

Had wanted nothing more than a woman and a child... many children. To make a family. A desire that had grown over centuries of watching them in their glorious innocence, pure and untouched by mortal's depravity.

Now, it would never be.

This, the mortals beyond the Æfen Gate, had ensured in their stupidity. Oh, look what they'd done to my Ada, her body so cold, her heart so terribly quiet, robbed of its odd cadence.

Look what they'd done to *us*.

Wicked, wayward mortals.

"I shall ride beyond the Æfen Gate and assemble my army." And bring justice to those who'd dared to touch my wife, then to those who'd dared to touch me. "Ah, death will walk the lands once more until the soil trembles in fear."

Orlaigh shifted beside me, stroking over the faded ribbon with more fervor. "Will ye fix the corpses in the throne before ye leave? Aye, their constant bewailing is grating on me poor nerves."

That took me aback. "How so? They have been blessedly quiet for decades."

She swatted her hand at the air. "Ach, reckon ye haven't seen them yet since ye woke, and how the lass cut their mouths open."

Cut their mouths open.

Their lying mouths.

An itch started beneath the skin along my arms, bringing my attention to the stench of ash and how I wanted to scratch myself bloody for it. My wife had dared yet another transgression. Why?

"She spoke to them?"

"Aye, I saw her sitting on the throne, whispering as quietly as a wood mouse in a bucket of corn." Orlaigh shrugged. "Maybe hushing secrets, maybe hushing lies. Who can say?"

Lies.

On instinct, every single muscle on my face stiffened with wariness, a reaction forged in the endless lick of flames and hardened in the chill of heartbreak. Was there no end to women's fickleness? My wife's scheming?

"Aye, the lass said ye're worse than ever before," Orlaigh went on. "Ach... the disgust in her eyes when she speaks of me Master. The hate."

Hate.

The blood heated my veins with a new ripple of suspicion. "Nothing good ever comes when traitors put their heads together, whispering between them under the cover of their master's sleep."

"I told ye..." Orlaigh said. "From the beginning, I told ye that this one has her wits about her."

And that she would run from me.

Was she trying to?

My fingers curled into my palms. Mmm, the dead had little interest in escaping me for I was their master, yet even in death, my wife proved obstinate.

She conspired with those who'd wronged me, had inquired about my brother, and even drowned herself to throttle her desire for my warmth—the latter being particularly impressive.

A muscle twitched near my temple. What if she tried to find refuge with my brother? Was she that desperate? Or was she trying to find a way to rid herself of Yarin's shackles on her soul? Escape me into eternal death?

It was possible.

Such a frail thing, a soul, requiring a form to cling to. No soul-bound corpse had ever achieved breaking the shackles, for it required a great deal of self-mutilation. An act utterly against a mortal's sense of self-preservation.

But then again, no corpse had ever managed to drown itself at the bottom of my spring, suppressing the innate reflex to breathe.

Only my wife.

My wicked wife.

Dread tensed my muscles at the premise of losing her. Losing her for eternity. Ought I to make her a new collar? A new chain? Five chains?

A brutal surge of anger scalded my veins, burning me from the inside. More painful was the rise of an entirely different compulsion—a possessive urge to put my little one into a cage of bone.

Better yet, my throne.

An unforgivable act.

Ada would forever hate me.

No, she *already* hated me.

Did it matter then?

Had the feelings between us not wilted away past the point of forgiveness? Of saving? Was she not mine to do with as I pleased, unconcerned of her judgment? Or was I once more too harsh? Too quick to judge?

I took a deep breath, trying to calm a heart that was

fraught with pain and distrust. "I ought to think on this."

"Think on this?" Orlaigh's fingers gathered more checkered fabric from her dress, kneading it. "Well... while ye do, I best keep an eye on her."

It wasn't so much her words that gave me halt, but the way a toe curled in her shoe. "Why so restless over something that does not concern you?"

"Ach, Master, it's been two hundred years, but not a day goes by where I dinnae regret the part I played in the little lady's disappearance." Orlaigh's pale lips thinned into a fine line. "The least I can do is watch out for yer heart and warn ye. Aye, it would break me own to see ye betrayed yet again."

The creases on her forehead supported her words, so why this hardness in my stomach, why the heightened senses where my ears pricked at each of her inhales? Aside from her... misstep, had she not served me for two centuries? Had kept me company in all those decades of isolation?

Yes, she had.

"Watch her," I commanded, then turned toward the spring. "Inform me if she speaks to the corpses again, or if she steps even a toe outside this court."

"Yes, Master."

I crossed the Pale Court and its many bridges, finding no joy in my creation for how my veins throbbed with anger. Oh, my resourceful wife, likely searching for a way to escape me among the memories of those who had failed to do so.

When I reached the spring, I undressed and slipped into the water. Its heat ripped a moan from me as I waded along the outline of rock. Until steam climbed into the back of my throat, rancid and biting, ripping a gag from me.

Ash.

Bitter, bitter ash.

It drove me mad, the disgusting stench that refused to

abate, no matter how often I bathed, scrubbed, oiled myself. Why would it not lessen?

Because it was trapped.

Under. My. Skin.

Calling upon the generous amounts of bone stored across the Pale Court, I let a knife form in my palm, its tooled handle rough against the pad of my fingers. One steadying breath, then I brought it to my arm.

Sharp and burning, the bone blade carved itself beneath my skin, letting rivers of blood vein down along my arm. They collected around my elbow, *drip-drip-dripping* onto the water where they formed circlets of crimson, seasoning the thick air with iron.

I pressed down on the flap of skin, trapping it between thumb and blade. With one swift motion, I peeled off my flesh, laying my embedded veins bare.

Shred after shred, I relieved myself of the bitter reek for a long while, peeling it off me wherever my hands reached. Whenever a new tatter of pink-tainted membrane flapped onto the damp rock, I submerged the body part, letting the salt burn away the foul putrefactions.

"Not again." No other but my wife emerged from the dark corridor and walked up to the edge of the spring, one of her arms pressed against a boy's chest to keep him from falling into the water. "How many times will you shed yourself like a snake?"

I was a god shaped to perfection, yet I turned my face away, hiding my temporary disfigurement with how I'd peeled myself down to meat. "As many times as it takes."

My little one remained utterly still where she stood and stared down at me, her golden tresses woven through the spindly nest of fingers that crowned her head. How beautiful she was. The prettiest, most dangerous corpse. Why had she come?

A heavy gulp went down her throat. "Need help with your back?"

Her unexpected offer instilled as much surprise as suspicion. "Are you jesting?"

"You fused children's fingers to my skull and gave me an entourage of corpses. *Clack. Clack. Clack.* All day long, they clatter behind me with their bony heels," she said, which explained the meticulously tied shoes on their little feet. "It's driving me to the edge of madness. No, Enosh, I'm not jesting... I just feel like skinning you alive."

"Ah, a wife peeling the skin off her husband, what can this be if not true love?" Either that, or yet another ploy. Likely the latter, but I was curious to see what she had planned now, so I reached her the knife. "Indulge yourself."

CHAPTER 11
ADA

Enosh stared up at me from a face flayed to weeping flesh, turning my stomach upside down and my guts inside out. If this compulsive urge to skin himself had anything to do with my remark on his smell, I couldn't say, but I regretted mentioning it.

I took the bone knife from him, then jutted over my shoulder back at the children. "Can you tell them to sit down? Or at least stand back? I'm in no mood to fish them out of the water again."

Their bony little bottoms *thudded* as they hit the stone, where they folded their legs and stared up at me. Beside me, bone dust shaped into a deep bowl.

"Taking the skin off alone will do little," Enosh said, the ends of his dark brows tainted red where they regrew above his unmarred lids. "You ought to pour water over the exposed flesh before my skin mends, which will happen quickly."

I squatted by the edge of the spring, taking in a whiff of rusty metal as I watched tiny strings of fresh skin web across his face. "I can tell."

He observed me from his silver eyes, the bridge between them already fully restored to flawless skin, not a single scar in sight. "Does it appall you? The blood? The inflamed flesh? The throbbing veins? My ruined face?"

"I've seen worse on you." Heavens, his handsome face was the source of at least half my problems. "Turn around."

To my surprise, he did so without fuss or reprimand. "Why go through the trouble of washing the corpses, little one? Surely, you have noticed the progression of their decay?"

I sat down, gathered the train of my dress, and let my legs dive calf-deep into the spring on either side of his body. "The way the skin on their bellies lifts and shifts makes it pretty clear that you're not... maintaining them."

"Answer my question."

The severe undertone in his voice put a tremble into my stiff fingers as I set the blade down to the left of his spine. "You know full well why I'm doing it. Otherwise, you wouldn't have given them to me in the first place."

"Yet more evidence for how much love you hold for children," he said with a sigh. "Never will my wife cease to confound me, even in the expected."

"Take a deep breath."

Sharp as it was, the blade sunk into his skin easily against the expanse of his inhale, then cut downward. Angling it almost parallel to the sway of his muscles, I ensured I took mostly skin off.

Mostly.

Blood welled from the spots where I used too much pressure, carving into his flesh as nausea bubbled at the back of my throat. I'd skinned plenty of rabbits in my life, but none had ever grunted as Enosh did, the god quivering against the bite of the blade. Devil be damned, why had I offered this?

Because I needed answers, even if I had to cut them out of him.

When the blade severed the skin at the height of his waist, I quickly reached for the bowl and dunked it into the spring.

Splash.

Water hit wound.

Enosh groaned, pulling his shoulder blades together and arching his back. "Continue."

I set the blade down beside where tiny droplets of blood wept from the exposed flesh, only for new growth of thin skin to encapsulate it. "It only takes seconds to mend. Is it like this for all of them?"

The shifting of muscles on Enosh's back came to an abrupt halt. "All of them?"

"Your brothers."

There was a pause that lasted a second too long for comfort before he said, "Yes."

One word.

It carried an edge of caution.

A whole-body shiver wracked through me, and the silence of the cave echoed. I'd searched for him the moment I'd noticed how the black veins on my hands had disappeared, but what if Orlaigh had gotten to Enosh before me? What had she told him?

I ran the blade down with one hand and used the other to press on the loose skin so it wouldn't fold over and get in the way. "You once told me that the Pale Court shaped around you when you... came into existence. How did you learn of your duty? Who taught you what to do?"

"Who taught you how to breathe?"

I flinched when I severed the second strip and let it slip off the blade, where it hit the ground with an awful *slap*. "So you're saying that you just knew? All three of you?"

Splash.

He once again pulled his shoulder blades together against the impact of the steaming water, letting a pink river form along his spine. "Such curiosity about my brothers."

Only how to get to them. "I remember the Court Between Thoughts. Rich fabrics. Pillows. Warm light. So different from the Pale Court."

Silence roared between us, vibrating against my heart with such ferocity it nearly mimicked a heartbeat. Every memory of every encounter I'd ever had with Enosh urged me to shut my mouth.

I circled my hand around my belly.

No, I need to do this.

Taking a useless but comforting breath, I pressed the blade to the right of his spine. "I don't remember how I got there."

More silence.

"Neither how I ended up in your arms, as though pieces of my memory are missing." A slice. A grunt. A splash. "You found me dead in the village, didn't you?"

Enosh rolled his shoulders, letting the joints crackle under the release of tension. "You called to me from among the dead, your voice panicked. I came as quickly as I could..."

"I was scared. The moment they chased after me, I knew." My head shook all on its own. "Knew it wouldn't end well. Felt it in my guts, really. I internally screamed, asking you to come save me."

He turned his head slightly, just enough for me to glimpse his perfectly angled cheekbone draped in smooth skin. "In this, I have failed you. I will not deny it."

Oh, he'd failed me in so many things, but mentioning any of that now would neither change the past nor help me set right the future. "Did you cry for me? You had tear tracks on your face."

"Does it surprise you, little one?" He slowly turned, his face fully mended, yet something broken seemed to sit at the depth of his mercury eyes. "Do you believe gods do not weep? That we do not suffer and ache? Hope and wish?" Pouting, he reached for the scar on my cheek, tracing the puckered skin. "Mmm, I wept over your dead body, Ada. I grieved your death. I celebrated it. Then I grieved it some more."

"Celebrated," I repeated. "Because you knew I would never want to escape you again. Not after you had Yarin bind my soul."

"Mmm, the living warm but the dead obey." A twitch of his upper lip. "Except for the Queen of Rot and Pain... who does neither."

"Do you regret binding my soul? Taking me to the Court Between Thoughts?" A swallow ran down my throat, thick and painfully dry. "To Yarin."

"Yarin. *Yarin.*" Enosh shifted his lower jaws around. "You seem to have taken a rather strange interest in my brother. Your... *master.*"

I dropped my gaze to the ground, as though fearing he could read the truth from my eyes. "It's just... so curious."

"Curious?"

I was treading on thin ice, I knew. "How he shapes out of thin air. How his court appears and fades. Just how does one get there?"

My breath stilled.

Wrong question.

Enosh's features turned to stone, so stiff and ungiving, not even his upper lip twitched anymore. "Do you wish to seek him out?"

Yes. "No."

His hand shot out of the water and gripped my crown,

pulling my head until his lips brushed against my earlobe where he whispered, "Liar."

My rotten heart dropped into the pit of my sour stomach. What now? Tell him the truth? Lie myself out of this mess?

No, I might have been a poor fisher, but I was an even more miserable liar. I was no liar at all! But that didn't mean I was stupid enough to blurt the truth. Yet.

"You have nerves calling me that," I snarled as I gave into his hold, easing the tension on my skull. "As though you've never spoken a lie."

He scoffed, "I have never told you anything but the truth."

Against his grip on my crown, I angled my head until my lips pressed against the shell of his ear. "Liar. You told me Joah killed Njala in an act of revenge, where we both know that she asked him to kill her. That she refused to return to you because she did not love you. She loved him."

He flinched as though I'd stabbed him.

Ice-cold fear shivered down my spine. Not over how the tremble in his hand vibrated into my skull or even how he stuttered out a never-ending breath. No, it was the endless silence that followed that made me fear for a life I'd already relinquished.

His chuckle shattered it, a terrifying sound like claws scraping over my skull. "No, little one, she never found love for me."

I swallowed, but it lodged in my throat, producing an ugly gagging sound. "Enosh, I—"

"And how could she have, hmm?" He yanked on my crown, nearly ripping me into the water wasn't it for how he climbed out of the spring with one quick, fluent movement and gave a shove at it. "Am I not a monster? The devil?"

I scrambled back, legs kicking and arse scooting, only to crash into a wall of little corpses. "Enosh, what are you—"

"Who could love such a cruel bastard?" He yanked me up by my crown and dug his fingers into my waist until it burned. "Not you. Never you. Oh no, all you have for me is hate and deceit."

My feet left the ground.

The cave shifted, spun.

Enosh swung me over his shoulder, letting the world turn upside down as my face slammed against his shifting back muscles. "Mmm, my faithless wife, once again scheming her escape. A collar cannot keep her. Chains cannot hold her. But I know a place that can."

His throne.

Now I've done it.

Numbness spread from my terrified core into every brittle bone, every quiet vein, every dull fiber of flesh, sending me into paralysis. *Clack-clack-clack* made the children as they ran behind us, the sound so grinding it sent me straight into hysteria. No! No no no!

"Please, not the throne!" I grappled at his back, clawed at the barely mended wound along his spine until skin and flesh collected beneath my nails. "Oh my god, please! Not your throne!"

"Whyever not? Have you not made friends there?" He hurried along the dark corridor, leaving wet footprints on the ground that changed from rock to bone as my palms shifted over his wet skin. "I shall weave your body into my throne between them, so you may hush and whisper, hate and scheme. But one thing you shall never do, my beloved wife, is escape me."

"No!" I drummed my balled hands against his back, pounded into the ungiving wall of damp, naked muscle. "I didn't plan to escape!"

"No? You weren't trying to find a way to reach the Court Between Thoughts?"

"Yes, but—"

"Maybe to break the shackles on your soul. More likely to find refuge with the god who placed them. I should have known the moment you called him your master..." His voice dripped with venom, poisoning my thoughts with panic. "Do you long for another master, little one? For the sweet things he whispers into your mind? Oh, Ada, I ought to warn you, my brother is not quite right in the head."

"None of you are!" I screamed my lungs bloody through the black fog distorting my vision, and the blur of lines beneath me. The dais? Oh my god, oh my god, oh my god. "I carry your baby!"

He stopped so abruptly his next footfall never landed, the force of it slamming my face against his back.

Thud.

Pain spread across my face.

A morbid nocturne resonated the throne room as Lord Tarnem and Joah moaned, grunted, and wailed. But the truth once more crumbled under rot and decay.

Enosh didn't move for one ragged breath, two, three, letting the bit of blood I still possessed pool around my spinning thoughts. Should I tell him everything? Nothing? A little bit at a time? What if I told him—

"A change of heart." He swung around. "A grave it shall be."

CHAPTER 12
ADA

Cold, freezing panic surged, locking my joints into place and numbing my fingertips. "What?"

"Are we not agreed that I am a man of my word?" Enosh let black breeches shape around his legs as he descended the dais. "I have threatened a grave, have I not? This time, little one, I shall not waver. I shall *not*."

Shifting on his slippery shoulder from the sudden turn, I clasped at air. "No! You can't do this! Enosh, please! Not a grave! No! Orlaigh is the liar! Njala's baby was nev-ghh... mmh—"

My lips refused to part.

Mumbles died against leather.

He'd gagged me.

Sharp and piercing, dread stabbed into my belly and deeper, as though my bladder wanted to give. Panic pounded inside my chest like a heart shaped of fear, jumping with each step Enosh walked toward... Where was he taking me? Outside?

I blinked against the white and black floaters in my vision

as I bounced, shook with each of his quickening steps, and shifted around until the stab wounds on my belly burned beneath the motion. My focus melted with my never-ending surroundings.

Bone. Stairs. Bone. Bridge. Bone.

Corpses.

Behind me, children funneled in from the hallways. They ran after us, their little bodies in different states of decay, but they all had one thing in common.

Shovels.

The children dragged the white bone spades over the ground, the *crrr-sh-crrr* louder as they passed us. No, this could not be happening. Not a grave!

"Have I not been a lenient husband, keeping the rot from you? Containing my anger, regardless of your many transgressions?" Enosh carried me through a corridor of darkness and out into the chilling lick of the night. "Oh, little one, I have warned you. So many times, I have warned you, but my wife does not listen."

My body stiffened into stone as my senses sharpened. The sweetness of spring flowers wafted around my nose in all its mockery. Moisture settled on my exposed calves, right beneath the tight clasp of Enosh's arm. Where was I? Oh my god, what was that noise?

My ears pricked at the *hrk* of shovels digging into dirt. Close. Closer. When Enosh suddenly stopped and turned slightly, I saw it.

Numb panic soaked into my muscles, disabling my lungs, drowning me in a sea of righteous fear. Beside me loomed a deep black grave, empty aside from the few children who still climbed out to line beside the others along the gaping hole.

"Ghmmm!" I hammered my fists against Enosh's back and

waist, tossing and thrashing until the wounds on my belly screamed. “Mhmm... mmm...”

Enosh jumped into the grave, making me toss on his shoulder with such force, I barely registered how he lowered me onto the damp, cold ground. Somewhere, an insect buzzed. Something slithered around my ankle, wet and cold.

No, I had to get out of here. Had to—

“Shh...” Hand pressed to my sternum, Enosh pinned me into the dirt, letting a root poke against my neck as he brought his lips to my ear. “Seventeen days and nights is what you still owe me. The grave shall be your fire, all-consuming. Rot shall be the lick of its flames, biting into your flesh.”

“Rkhh!” I squirmed beneath his hold and, when he loosened it, I wrapped my arms around his neck and clamped my legs around his waist. “Hkmmh... mmh...”

“Let go of me.”

I held him tighter, clinging to him until my joints burned and the pop of knuckles resonated in the night. No, I would not let go. Would not let go. Would not—

“Even now...” An exhale sputtered from his lips with the same violence as his fingers trembled on my chest. “Even now, I want to take you into my arms... the cold, lying corpse that you are.”

Nothing happened for long moments. Neither of us moved as dirt rilled from the walls of my grave or came down in clumps where the children lined its edges. Was he... hesitating?

A spark of hope.

Please hold me!

I ran my hand from his neck into the weight of black hair still damp from the spring, pulling until his temple pressed against mine while he continued to kneel over my body.

No, he would not do this.

Not to me.

Right?

Enosh slid his arm under my back, not lifting me, though I sensed in the tension of his hand that he considered it. "How blessed you are to hate me so."

Stricken with fear, I shook my head ever so slightly. Oh, I wished I could hate him the way any normal, rational woman would if she found herself in a grave beneath her undertaker. But I was not normal, for I was dead. And I was not rational, for my unborn child was likely alive.

"If only I could bring myself to hate you," he whispered, his voice chillingly absent of any emotion, "perhaps then this age-old heart in my chest would not ache so at what I must do."

His arms retreated.

My limbs slipped off him.

Panic pounded my head.

No. No. No!

He effortlessly climbed out of the grave, leaving me behind with my mind stunned. I trembled so violently, my limbs flopped about uncontrollably. Would he truly bury me alive? No, Enosh would not be this—

Something hit my eye.

I clenched both shut, swinging my hands to my face to rub the burn from them. But the assault continued with each *shk* of a shovel, followed by a *patter* of dirt raining down on me.

Nausea swept from my stomach, biting along my esophagus, only to trap itself inside my mouth. Oh, my god. He was burying me alive! No. No. No no no!

When another chunk of loam landed heavily on my chest, I turned around. I struggled myself onto swaying legs. Out. I needed out!

The dirt came faster from all directions, creating piles around me that seeped into my shoes, caught between my toes where it rubbed and itched. Each time I looked up, more of it hit my eyes, blurring the outlines of the children lining my grave.

In my panic, I clawed, dug, and scratched at the wall of compacted earth. I had to climb out. Had to—

A nail broke off, the flesh beneath too dark, and turning darker with each second. I stared at it as my stomach shifted, writhed, and swelled. Rot. I was rotting.

He was rotting me!

I screamed, but only grunts made it through the leather.

I waded toward a corner to try it there, but I kept on slipping, ripping off chunks of loam, helping with my burial.

Master, my mind wailed and screeched. *Master, please!*

My stomach heaved and my chest convulsed, amplified by the biting stench of decay that blew from my nostrils at each panicked exhale. Gravity abandoned me and I fell on my arse, my legs halfway buried in damp, cold dirt.

More came from above, pelting down on the roof of rotting arms as I buried my head underneath them. Back and forth, I swayed in a self-consoling manner, humming an old lullaby as my mind stiffened in the clasp of madness.

The *shk* of shovels and the *thud* of dirt faded against the comforting sound as my lips stumbled over the words. "...a-and the b-b-babe with the ro-hoasy cheeks... mmh... da da mmh... and fell to s-sleep. And if the babe's still w-warm come morn..."

My voice faded away.

A gulp hiccupped from my lips.

My *parted* lips.

What was happening?

Detangling my arms from around my head, I brought a hand to my mouth, letting a dirt-caked finger stutter along my bottom teeth. My gag was gone. But how?

I glanced down at my finger, letting the moonlight glint off a nail already regrown with only a faint smear of blood remaining around its bed. Where was he? Should I look?

Carefully, so carefully, I allowed my gaze to drift upward. The shoveling had come to a stop, leaving the children to stare down at where I cowered in a grave half-filled.

The fine hairs along my arms rose at the eerie silence. It couldn't be trusted. Shouldn't be trusted. Seconds passed. Minutes. Maybe hours.

Where was he?

Did I want to know?

My diaphragm convulsed, trapped between the dread of sitting in this grave and the fear of what would await me outside of it. Had he left? Had this just been a lesson? Or was the true lesson waiting up there if I dared to climb out?

My eyes wandered to the pile of dirt at the edge. I could if I wanted to. Did I want to?

Shaken and scared, I pulled my buried legs from the dirt, rose, and staggered toward the edge. Once I stood on the pile, I let my foot find purchase right above a root. Another was in easy reach just above me, which I gripped to struggle myself out of the grave.

The children parted as I dangled at the edge, kicking my legs and pulling on bushels of grass. Once I had enough solid surface beneath my chest, I swung one leg up, then the other.

I stood and stepped away from the hole, shivering, clutching my arms to ward off the biting cold of night. Where was I?

Glancing around, I recognized the line of hills that cut through the landscape and the many boulders scattered here and there along the windy pastures beyond the Soltren Gate.

A heavy breath.

Not mine.

I shuddered. He hadn't left.

Enosh sat only a few feet away from me on a boulder, his silhouette shrouded in darkness. Knees pulled against his bare chest, he held his head with a clutching grip to his tousled hair. Why had he stopped? Why was he... like this?

On instinct, my throat tied up and my foot lifted toward the grave, trembling at the coldness it promised. Maybe I should get back in there?

Enosh turned his head and looked straight at me, his cold, cruel mask gone, revealing a face contorted in pain. "Why can I not do it?"

CHAPTER 13
ADA

My bones chilled.

I hugged myself and took a step away from this man… this stranger who looked nothing like Enosh.

The branches of a nearby willow warped his features as they shifted in the biting breeze, casting shadows across the valleys of his sunken cheeks. From this angle, the moonlight reflected off his glistening eyes, leeching all color from his face to pale anguish.

My throat narrowed. *A trick?*

He rose and turned toward me.

My right heel lifted from the ground.

He stopped himself. "You are scared of me."

"S-scared of y-you?" Equal parts of fury and fear shifted in my core, volatile and erratic, putting me on edge. "You to-ossed me into a hole, let me rot, and commanded child corpses to b-bury me alive. I'm *terrified* of you!"

His lips parted as though to justify his actions, only to press into a thin line as he lowered his head and raked a hand through his raven hair. He gripped the roots and yanked, mumbling beneath his ragged breath. He shifted from one leg to the other, not like him at all.

Who was this man?

He lifted his gaze to me once more, his expression so unguarded it showed every distressed crease between his brows, every agonized distortion along his twitching jawline. What was I supposed to do with that?

The next time his lips parted, an audible gulp resonated the night before he stepped toward me. "Forgive me... please."

Hackles rising, I stumbled back until the skeletal remains of a child's foot crunched beneath my heel. Enosh never asked for forgiveness, and certainly not with a *please*, making this stranger terrify me more than the god ever had.

Because I didn't know him.

Didn't know what to do, what to expect, or why he kept shifting his balance without pouncing.

I dug my dirt-caked fingers into my bodice, quivering under the stranger's pleading stare. He paled with each passing second, as though Enosh's mask of cruel indifference bled right off a face that looked ages old, wrinkled by the hardships of a hundred lifetimes.

He took another step toward me. "Little one—"

"Do not come near me!" I shifted my torso against the wall of little skulls and bony chests. "Leave me alone."

His brows drew together, closely framing the pained look in his eyes. "I cannot."

He took another step.

Slow. Deliberate.

And another.

Panic clogged my throat anew, and every instinct in my body told me to run. *Run!* Where? Anywhere that wasn't here; anywhere that wasn't with him.

"Come to me. Not to your master, but... to me." Stalling his advance, he opened his arms, beckoning me into his embrace. "I only wish to hold and warm you."

I fought the ghostly tug beneath my breastbone—how it pulled me toward the arms of a monster, with the warmth emanating from his fingers as a lure.

A trap.

No, I would not fall for it. Would rather drown than succumb to his promise of comfort. Comfort I'd wanted. *Needed.* Had begged for, only to be denied over and over again!

I didn't want it anymore.

Not from him.

Refused to need it still.

I raised my hand as though it might ward off the devil. "I would find more warmth in the embrace of a corpse!"

He flinched. "Ada—"

"Don't call me that!"

A dozen hairline cracks veined across my quiet heart, bleeding liquid anguish into my rib cage. *Little one. Mortal. Wife.* I could handle all those things, but not my name.

Not from his lips.

Not after... this.

Sidestepping along the line of children, I advanced toward the gate. "Do not come closer."

He didn't.

Nor did he allow more distance to grow between us, mirroring my steps up the slight incline.

I understood I couldn't escape him, for each of my steps existed only at his permission. All I wanted was to run from this traitorous tug in my chest, this ache to throw myself into his arms—if only for long enough to prove that I could.

Another sidestep.

My foot caught on a rock.

I stumbled forward, paddling the air. By the time I regained my balance, Enosh had crept up on me, keeping less than a foot's distance between us that quickly filled with warmth.

My eyes flicked to the gate.

I bolted.

Even before my foot left the ground, Enosh slung his arm around my middle and pulled me against the all-engulfing heat of his body. "Calm yourself."

"No!" Anger flared to life at my core, and I shoved at his chest. "Let me go!"

"Never." His other arm came around my waist, anchoring my hips against his body, submerging me in the scent of ash sprinkled over snow. "Call it obsession or call cruelty. I am close to calling it something else entirely."

A scream dislodged from the back of my throat as I shifted and wiggled, fighting against his tight grip and its glorious heat with everything I had. But no matter how I squirmed, he only held me tighter.

"Shh..." he whispered against my ear. "Please forgive me."

The way he hushed me and dared to ask for forgiveness fueled my anger into rampant rage. I squirmed, elbowed, kicked. My hands balled into fists, hammering his chest like a woman possessed while my mind tumbled into a frenzy.

It was too much.

Too fucking much.

The shock of my death, the child in by belly, the bitter loneliness of my miserable existence fraught with everyone's scorn... I deserved none of this. Was tired of everyone pushing me around like chattel!

"I reacted in anger, for little terrifies me more than the thought of losing you." Enosh's voice turned rough and shaky. "But I ought not to have done this. Forgive me."

"You buried me!"

Slap.

Enosh's face jerked back, the imprint of four fingers rapidly shading the bottom of his right cheek where I'd struck him.

I froze for only a second before I lifted my chin. "Go ahead. Throw me right back in. Make it twenty days... make it a month!"

He swallowed.

He cupped the back of my head and pulled my face against his pounding heart, letting his lips brush over the shell of my ear. "I love you."

His words fractured something inside me, pulling my legs out from underneath me. I didn't want his love—it was too painful, too unpredictable, too damn destructive.

Enosh held on to me, trying to steady me on wobbly legs. Eventually, he gave up and let me gently sink to the ground, lowering himself with me as he kept hugging me, hushing me.

"I hate you." For holding me the way I'd needed him to—instead of being his cold, indifferent self—turning me into a needy, trembling mess.

"I would rather have you hate me for eternity than not have you at all." His lips brushed the corner of my mouth, kissing me as he brought one of my legs over his, positioning me astride him. "But at least allow me to love you."

The way he pushed me down onto his growing erection sent a jolt through me. "No!"

"Shh..." he hushed me once more. "Is this not what you want? Not what you long for? My kiss? My attention? The heat of my cock between your legs?"

Squirming in his hold, I lashed out at whatever came into reach as my mind descended into violence. Red lines streaked his neck and chin where I scratched him while shrieking like a banshee.

Maybe I'd made it out of the grave, but my sanity had not.

Or maybe I needed him to retaliate—to strike me, spank me, bury me. Anything to contain how I longed for him, ached for him to hold me tighter as I rocked my hips toward his.

But Enosh neither dodged my assaults nor made me stop. No, what he did was much worse. *So much worse.*

He let me.

Enosh tolerated it all, shoving a finger beneath my dress, pushing my braies aside before he ran a knuckle over my clit. "Keep going, little one. Scratch me. Strike me."

I did.

My core heated with every scraping attack, each slap of my palm, burning away the sorrows that had worn me down for too long. Too long. Everything, from the gossip I'd endured and the judgment, to the unfairness, I released into my balled hands.

And it felt good.

Freeing.

A sudden swath of warmth against my cunt told me Enosh's breeches had vanished. Leaning slightly back—his palms braced against the grass on either side—he lifted me up with his hips, increasing the delicious pressure against my sex.

That felt good, too.

Losing precision and vigor, I kept dropping my little fists against his chest with hollow *thuds*. All the while I shifted my hips faster, rubbing myself on his rock-hard shaft until my nipples grew to aching points, but... oh, it wasn't enough.

"No, my wife would not want to escape me, would she?" He stared at me, the red lines on his face already vanishing. "For I am the beat in her heart, the blood in her veins, and the heat she desperately clings to."

My insides clenched at the smugness hiding in his undertone, nothing but the trace of his arrogance simmering beneath the surface of his baritone. I observed the faintest twitch on his upper lip, as though his mask tried to return.

But I wouldn't let it.

Refused to continue this madness.

I would shatter that mask tonight.

Instead of wasting time on another attack, I shifted my hips until his crown nudged my entrance. When I pushed back onto his cock, he clenched his eyes shut, letting his groan mingle with my whimper.

I quivered at the mercy of feverish heat and how I rocked him deeper into me. Mmm, how his cock pulsed inside me, hot and hard, warming me in ways he'd denied far too many times.

Enosh stuttered out a breath and let his forehead drift against mine. "Mmm, how nicely your needy cunt grips me."

I thrust against him, joining in our shared rhythm as I succumbed to the warmth it provided—a shred of wicked comfort in a hell of eternal cold and heart-rending solitude. I chased every spark that tingled around my clit, every convulsion in my lower belly.

I shoved his chest until his back hit the grass, loving how it made him lengthen inside me. His hands wandered to my waist, pushing me down with each of his upward thrusts, letting my clit press against his hard body.

When Enosh's breathing quickened, he expelled a guttural groan. "Say my name!"

I bore down on him, grinding and rubbing, until an all-consuming burn erupted between my legs. "Enosh—"

Scorching, sweltering, red-hot heat rippled across my core, spreading into every limb, into the tips of my fingers, my toes, and even into the roots of my hair. Everything tingled, sending a whole-body shiver across me, leaving my skin a landscape of pebbles and raised hairs.

Enosh sucked in a breath, stiffening beneath me. His hips

stalled—they always did before he reached his peak. Gods were unpredictable; men were not.

I slipped off him and scooted up to his chest.

Behind me, his unfinished cock slapped against his stomach, but it was his agonized groan that brought a smile to my lips. Enosh stared up at me with widened eyes. He bucked underneath me uncontrollably, dug his hands into my waist, frantically shifted me toward his cock once more.

But it was too late.

He grunted and jerked underneath me as he spilled his seed over his stomach. Or onto the train of my dress? Who could say?

"Friction." I leaned over, letting the tip of my tongue lap at his earlobe. "It is in your nature to move, buck, and rub in search of it. But remove it while you succumb to pleasure, and it *hurts*. You might be a god, my master, yet that won't keep your cock from making you look rather mortal in this moment."

His hand shot to my crown but a second later. "It seems as though you are begging for punishment."

"It seems as though you stopped begging for my forgiveness."

A beat of hesitation.

For the first time, my husband seemed positively stunned, choking on this damn arrogance of his. His face blanked, leaving every parting and closing of his lips utterly exposed with nothing left to hide behind.

With a sigh, he eventually released my crown, and a hint of pain moved in the depths of his irises. "Will you forgive me?"

That would depend on what forgiveness bought me. "You nearly buried me alive."

"Only nearly, and not quite alive." When I said nothing, letting the silence stretch thin between us, he finally nodded in defeat and raked a nervous hand through his hair once more. "I was… convinced you were scheming to escape and find refuge with my brother."

"And you weren't entirely wrong."

He stilled, and even his chest stopped mid-inhale. "Explain."

"You want my forgiveness for tossing me into a grave?" I sat straight, reacquainting myself with the man beneath the mask and how out of sorts he looked. "I will explain, but you will listen until I am finish—"

"Little—"

"No interruptions!" I ignored the snarl coming to his lips, the flash of teeth as though he were close to biting my mouth off. "Then you will take me to Yarin so he can confirm what I've told you is true."

His lower jaws shifted and his eyes narrowed. "You have a great many requests."

"And you have a great many things in need of forgiveness." And it was time that he learned exactly why. "Do you want it, yes or no?"

"I shall be so quiet while I listen," he ground out. "For your forgiveness, I shall do this."

And I blurted it right out.

"Njala has been in love with Joah even before she came with you to the Pale Court. The affair brought Lord Tarnem no political benefit, so he broke it up and gave her to a god in exchange for an army." I watched first confusion, then old misery crack through Enosh's face in the shape of wrinkles webbing from the outer corners of his turbulent eyes. "She continued to see Joah whenever she left the Pale Court—something Orlaigh tried to talk her out of but could not. And so, she helped keep it a secret."

His features hardened. "You sound rather certain."

"Because I can prove it."

Maybe. Hopefully.

I told him about the day I found Orlaigh scolding Lord Tarnem, how I couldn't keep any food down in Elderfalls, and how the grains had sprouted. The more I told him, the more his body stiffened against mine. When I told him of my chat with Lord Tarnem, Enosh tilted his head back until his throat bobbed as he stared at the black sky.

"Enosh, the daughter you thought you lost was mortal for a reason... You were able to sense her because she was never yours." I took his hand, flattening his palm atop my wounds. "This one, you cannot sense, not as what it is. But I know Yarin and Eilam sensed *something*. Tell me, have you ever felt anything amiss on me since I died?"

He didn't move, didn't speak.

Only gulped.

His eyes glistened with the wreckage of age-old beliefs and the destruction of a lie that had turned a loving man into an enraged god. His face showed every wrinkle of anguish forming between his brows, every twitch of shock jumping along his jaws, every tremble of doubt hushing across his bottom lip.

"I..." Shaking, his fingers brushed over my belly, "I have."

Another spark of hope.

Another stab of pain.

As expected.

Enosh's gaze trailed toward the child corpses as though he couldn't bring himself to look at me, and something else shaped on his features—something I'd never seen on him before.

Guilt.

When he brought his eyes back to meet mine, he cupped the back of my head and tugged, only to let a whisper break against my ear. "Guilt and sorrow, hope and sin. The madness of their whispers lies within."

Light blinded me.

I clenched my eyes shut and my ears pricked at the cacophony of moans and laughter, interrupted only by the *clinks* of metal against metal. The smell of moist air faded, along with the songs of crickets, quickly replaced with the sweetness of wine.

That, and Yarin's voice.

"Oh, how I love surprise visitors. You have arrived just in time for the fun."

CHAPTER 14

ENOSH

I pulled Ada against me where we stood at the center of my brother's domain, her legs as unreliable as the staggering beat of my heart. "Do you know where you are?"

She nodded, eyes frantically going from the pile of red and green pillows in the center of the room to the man whose lips were currently wrapped around my brother's length. "The Court Between Thoughts."

"Quite right, Ada." Yarin lounged naked on a daybed of red velvet, one hand pushing the corpse's copper thatch of hair closer, the other balancing a metal cup in its palm from which he sipped. "And how delighted I am that you have chosen to— Oh my, sweet thing, would you look at yourself? Whatever happened to your hair and... is that a crown of *bones* upon your head?"

I let a jacket shape around me, having arrived nearly as bare as I had left the spring in my... unforgivable burst of fury. "Make yourself decent."

"Afraid your wife will find too much appreciation for my form? We both know I'm the handsomest among the three."

With a chuckle, he tossed his cup across the room until it *clanked* against the sandstone wall, then thrust into the man's gagging mouth. "Pathetic, how you claimed you've never had relations with a man, yet you suck with such vigor. Go on, finish me off."

I turned my wife away from the debauched scene, and myself with her. "This is a serious matter."

"When is anything pertaining to you ever not serious, hmm? You've always... always been— Ah, yes! Swallow everything. Mmm, look how you suckle my cock. I don't believe for a second you have never bedded a man." A pop resonated behind me. "Anyway, you've always been the broody one, Enosh... always so serious. My favorite, to be certain, but oh, such a bore. Ada, has my brother ever suspended you from a harness of skin, fucking you while corpses pinch your nipples and another pushes a femur up your tight—"

I let out a warning hiss. "Dare speak to her like that again, and I shall—"

"What? Stab a bone spike through my throat, as is my favorite brother's preferred way of killing? I don't think so." Because he knew full well I held little power here, where everything shaped at the whim of thoughts. "Well, I didn't think you have. For a god, you *are* rather prude. Have you come to ask my advice on matters of your marriage? As it so happens, I am an expert in all things pertaining to the mortal heart."

"You are an expert of sin and insanity." When the unhurried *hrk* of buttons pressing through fabric resonated behind me, I turned to face my brother, and how he closed the golden clasps on his richly embroidered green felt jacket. "When you bound her soul, you spoke of something that... resisted."

"Out!" he shouted over his shoulder, chasing soul-bound corpses from the pillows like rabbits from their burrows, sending them to scurry in all directions. "I don't recall—"

"Sheltering itself away in a blind void of nothingness." Ada stepped away from the embrace of my arm and toward my brother, her hair nothing but a tangled mess of bones, grass, and loam. "That's what you said."

"Had I? Interesting... not." Yarin strolled over to a round table, plucked a grape from the diamond-studded platter, and popped it into his mouth. "Anything else? There are souls to collect and thoughts to shape. Unless you wish to put aside your dull character for a moment, brother, and partake in my corpses together with—" His eyes shot to my wife, and he tilted his head as a grin shaped his lips. "Did you just tell me to shut up? Nobody has ever told me to— Actually, many have told me to shut up, but never through their thoughts. Oh, Enosh, she is so very special, this one."

Yes, she was, yet I had allowed century-old doubt to come between us. "Does she carry my child? My *divine* child we cannot sense?"

All mirth fell away from him, lending his posture a straightness I'd seldomly witnessed on the God of Whispers as he stepped in front of Ada. "A divine child, you say?"

My knees shook.

No, not mine.

Ada's legs trembled, threatening to snap, no matter how well she hid it behind the dirt-smudged fabric, feigning strength where I knew she had none left. I did not need to sense her soul to know it was agonized, my brother's potential answers equal in their torture.

"I sense..." Yarin clenched his eyes shut, a mere inch of distance between the tips of his fingers as he hovered them from her forehead to her chest and lower. "Sadness. Anger. So much. A hope you fear, a fear you hope. And... nothing." His fingers stopped, clenching and unclenching below her navel. "A void that will not answer me. Right here."

In her belly.

Something I had sensed whenever I'd delivered Ada's flesh and bone from decay, shrugging it off as nothing more but yet another part of her embodied resistance to me. To us.

Time stuttered to a halt.

How blind I'd been.

"You feel it, too?" Yarin set his grass-green eyes straight on mine and, when I nodded, he sighed. "I hold no control over it. Never have I encountered something like this before."

"Eilam said something ab-bout—" A sob cut through Ada's voice, her bones heavy with pain. "That there was a lot of life in me... more than in others."

"So he sensed something amiss as well." Yarin tortured his upper lip. "Are we agreed on what this is, then, Enosh?"

"It is Elric." The sound of the name sparked old anger in my core, only to flare into bright joy before it died into paralyzing sadness. "My divine child, trapped alive but unable to grow in the belly of my dead—"

I grabbed Ada's arm where she swayed beside me, pulling her against my chest before she collapsed to the ground. My ears pricked at her wail, and my muscles tensed at her violent tremble as her entire weight pulled on my arms.

"My ba-ha-aby." Her high-pitched scream shattered from the yellow stone before it penetrated my chest, needling straight into my heart. "Oh my god... Oh my god— Ah!"

Unable to steady her on legs that continued to sway no matter how I willed them, I picked her up and cradled her tightly against me. "Shh..."

Her little fists pounded against my chest once more, but quickly died down, only to hang limp from her quivering body. Face contorted into a hundred wrinkles of pain, she cried without tears, each sniffle and sob like a bone blade digging between my ribs.

My blurred gaze shot to Yarin. "Do something!"

"Hush, hush, shh..." He placed his palms on her temples and brought his whispering lips to her ear. "Listen to my voice..."

It faded into nothing but hums and murmurs, unintelligible to my ear, though I sensed how Ada softened in my arms. Her stare lost itself in the nothingness of the arched ceiling and her muscles slackened. No more than a breath later, she stilled.

I commanded her lungs to expand and retract, focusing on an even rhythm so she may find comfort in it, then allowed her eyes to flutter shut. Together, Yarin and I placed her soul-bound body into a twilight state of subdued consciousness that closely resembled sleep.

"Her soul is in such anguish, it is fighting my bonds." A rare glint of something other than amusement came over Yarin's eyes, his voice void of his usual aloofness, stripped down to a growl. "What have you done?"

My stomach convulsed.

Where to begin?

I swallowed past a knot at the back of my throat, coiled in a tangle of emotions I had little experience with. "Most recently, I prepared a grave for her, lowered her into it, and had corpse children fill it with dirt."

"Brother, when you try for the affections of a woman, *you give her flowers,*" he turned away on a scoff and slumped back on the daybed, letting another appear across from it, "not bury her beneath them."

Excruciating sorrow strangled my guts.

Every inhale burned within my lungs, searing, scalding, charring its way straight into a heart I'd claimed I did not possess, only for it to bleed out all over again. A punishment I received gladly, for I had never deserved it more.

I stood there, a god shamed into silence, consumed by guilt

and utter self-contempt. Oh, how I'd wronged my wife. My little one had not lied. No, she'd truly tried to return to me, and what had I done...?

What had I done?

I had driven her away. Punished her for a betrayal she'd never committed, causing her nothing but excruciating pain. Three times, she'd lost the child she always wanted. First to a blade, then to my blindness, and now to the truth.

And I had lost it, too.

For the second time in my cursed existence, I'd lost a child. Njala's daughter might not have been mine, but I had grieved her just the same. Now I grieved again, yet my pain would likely never compare to the agony Ada must have carried all this time.

All by herself.

Because I was not there.

Had left her alone with her sorrows.

Instead of defeating the loneliness of my existence with her by my side, I had abandoned Ada to it. How could I ever undo the damage I'd caused between us in all my glorious ignorance?

"Pray tell, Enosh, how can this be?" Yarin pushed himself up to sit, formed a golden goblet in his hand, and took a sip. "My mind is utterly confused. Dazed, truly. How come we felt Njala's baby, clearly mortal, but this one evades us in all its godly arrogance?"

Ada could likely not perceive it, but I sat on the daybed across with her and stroked the shell of her ear the way she enjoyed. "Njala—"

"Oh, I think I figured it out." He chuckled, but even my brother failed to give it its usual air of cockiness. "My, my, my... Enosh. And here I thought you do not share your women. Not such a prude after all, I see."

On any other day, I would have slit his throat and bled him out on his pillows, but I could barely bring myself to lift my head. "Orlaigh kept her reckless infidelity a secret, in all of mortals' never-ending depravity."

Trapping me in false grief for two centuries over the loss of a daughter that had not been mine. Oh, she'd concealed her betrayal well. Had riled me up against my wife the moment I woke, poisoning my mind with wariness and suspicion.

Where I expected fury and the urge to return to the Pale Court to weave her into my throne, I only found forlorn sadness.

Apathy.

Fatigue.

Two centuries of rage and distrust, and what had it given me? A dead wife full of justified anger, a child lost at the expense of my own, and a broken heart that beat ardently for both of them.

I loved Ada.

Loved her like I had never before, with no precaution over the pain it had already caused me, nor the pain that was certainly yet to come. I loved her with a ferocity that was not save for me or her. Certainly not for this world.

How to fix this?

I'd been so full of old hate and wariness, letting it snare me, corrupt me to such a degree that I'd hurt the most honest woman to walk this earth. The woman who had chosen to come to me. Might have held affection for me. Inklings of love?

But that was before...

Before I'd condemned to carry mortal's viciousness carved into her belly. Before I'd refused her my warmth, even though I knew the harrowing coldness of death. Before I'd given her a crown of children's fingers. Before I'd lowered her into a damn grave.

"An immortal child..." Yarin mused as he ran his thumb across his bottom lip, staring at the tip of his boot where he'd crossed his legs at the end of the daybed. "It just occurred to me that I might have sired thousands of those, unknowingly leaving them behind in the rotting bellies of countless whores. Not even I can find anything to laugh about that. You know full well how much I love children... such pleasant thoughts in their heads."

I pulled Ada's limp body tighter against me, taking another searing inhale until the lick of shame scalded my core. "It cannot die, or its decay would have noticeably affected her womb, but it cannot grow, either. This... void in her belly has not altered since her death, remaining the size of a pea at best."

"Unless..." His nail tapped against the bottom row of his teeth a few times. "Unless you can convince our beloved brother to restore her. With her soul bound to her intact form, your woman is but a breath away from life."

Eilam's breath, for he was the god of life and its absence. Where most mortals spent their existence without ever crossing my or Yarin's path, each one had met my brother at least once.

"Rebirth." A capricious flutter came to my chest, rousing a hope that collapsed into despair but a moment later. "He will never agree."

"Hmm... Yes... the drowning."

And likely that one beheading six centuries back... "Among other things."

"No, you are quite right, Enosh. He will refuse." Yarin raked his fingers through his auburn strands, then propped his arm beneath his head. "Unless you leave him no choice but to agree. Nothing vexes him more than a good old sweep of annihilation."

My shoulders stiffened.

If memory served, my last act of rage had devastated the lands beyond the Soltren Gate to a degree it had still not recovered after two centuries. Oh, what a mess that had been. Should that cause me hesitation?

Drowned lands, devastated towns, the decimation of entire bloodlines mortals valued so dearly… What was it to me? The Pale Court would forever endure, sheltering my wife and child within.

Yet one problem remained.

"My wife has a kind heart, carrying so little of mortal's corruption." What had gained her my admiration now proved an issue. "I shall have the high priest's head, this much I vow, and I will destroy this false god they pray to. She will understand. But the rest of the retched lot…"

… needed to die, too.

How many?

Only my brother knew.

Ah, I'd told Ada that her hate did not bother me, so as long as I had her. Perhaps I was a liar after all, for I wanted little more than for her to love me back. Yet the moments where I showed mercy to the wicked had softened her toward me.

Mercy would not return her breath.

Only devastation.

Yarin sighed. "They stabbed her in the belly. Surely your wife must now see their offense and carry a hint of hatred?"

"A hint will not do."

"A hint is all I require for my whispers to go unnoticed. As always, my powers are at your disposal. Interest free."

"Now I know you're up to no good." Eager to twist my wife's head where I wanted our love to be true, and not tainted by illusions of any kind. "I do not want you anywhere near her thoughts. Unless she leaves me no choice."

"Such jealousy is unbecoming of a god," he *tsked*. "I presume you could try to... make her see sense."

Make her see sense.

My heart burned, and for once, not at the feverish mercy of shame and guilt. No, it was the searing edge I would have to balance, whetted with the choices of saving our child or gain my wife's love.

Could I achieve both?

Perhaps one with the other?

But something else burned inside me, too—a sudden realization that made me curl around Ada's still body. Death was her eternal prison, tethering her to me if I ensured she remained in my presence. In life, she'd slipped me once, and she might slip again.

Yes, Eilam could give her life.

And life meant freedom.

CHAPTER 15
ADA

I awoke to the sensation of my head being lifted, only to sink seconds later. Up again. Down. Something brushed over my back in caressing swirls, with deviations of serpentines up along my spine. A finger?

Blinking my eyes open, I caught familiar glimpses of the few black hairs scattered across Enosh's bare chest. I rested against him, naked, blissfully absorbing the all-engulfing heat of his body. How long had I been like this?

"I feel you rousing." Enosh pressed a kiss to the top of my head. "Are you well?"

Was I?

I assessed the ease of my inhales, the laxness in my muscles, the gentle hum beneath my skin at this wash of warmth. In truth, I felt better than I had in a long time—my sorrows not gone but somehow, not as suffocating.

Which could only mean one thing...

"Yarin did something to my head, didn't he?"

"Your soul was suffering, shattering right before my eyes." Enosh's fingers trailed along the side of my head, scraping over my scalp until it tingled, making me lean into it. "My brother merely calmed your thoughts, allowing you to... come to terms with things in a dream-like state."

Come to terms.

My teeth wanted to clench, but I forced my jaws to shift. From the moment I'd learned the truth, I knew that convincing Enosh of my innocence would not give me back my child, only his trust and goodwill. A sense of normalcy between us—whatever that meant.

It was enough.

It had to be.

I took a deep breath, pulling a lungful of ash sprinkled over snow down into my chest. Enosh smelled like a thousand sins and salvations, like my lover and my husband. My captor, whose scent swaddled me in the comfort of familiarity.

Comfort I'd told myself I no longer wanted from him, the man who had twisted my bones but mended my dignity, who had put me in the collar of a prisoner and the cruel crown of a queen. What a lie.

I needed it.

I needed *him.*

Had wanted nothing more for the past month but to curl into his broad chest, to hide away from the world and what it had done to me. Wanted to escape the coldness of death, and instead, soak my bruised flesh in his heat.

As though he felt it in my bones, Enosh wrapped his leg around mine, continuing to draw symbols along my back. "You are safe. Nothing and nobody will ever harm you again." Shoulders curling, legs angling, I made myself so very small, rolling myself up like a cat.

Beyond us stretched a circular room, its walls engraved with motifs of oak trees surrounded by long bushels of grass that swayed in the breeze.

His room.

Enosh had shaped it the day he opened the Pale Court, appointed with elaborately tooled furniture made of tusk and bone. Thin braids of hair hung from the high ceiling, each decorated with teeth, fangs, and nails. They reflected the magical glimmer coming from the bone and *clanked* together in a monotone symphony.

Realization seeped into me when his nails parted my hair with ease, letting a mumble roll from my lips. "My crown's gone."

He cupped my cheek and gingerly brought my gaze to meet the calm gray of his eyes, set into a face dusted with several days' worth of black stubble. "And the two boys and the girl are at rest."

I ran my thumbnail over his thick, stubborn whiskers, loving the way they scraped at my skin with quiet *hrk-hrk-hrks.* "Heavens, how long was I dreaming?"

"I've held you like this for nearly three days."

He'd held me.

For days.

"Adelaide." His lips pressed into a thin line for a moment as though my name had left cuts on his tongue. "I came into existence knowing my duty, my powers, and how to wield them. I know the world, its people, and all the languages they speak. Yet I do not know how to apologize in a single one." A deep exhale. "However, I shall try."

I lifted myself up a bit because I damn well deserved to hear it. "Go ahead."

He took a deep breath, twirling a strand of my hair around his finger like he'd used to before he tucked it behind my ear. "I have not protected you, letting you fall prey to chaos borne of my own mistakes. I have wronged you, accusing you of betrayal when your character has never given me cause to doubt your honesty. I have given you pain, such pain, emotionally abandoning you in your time of need. For all this, I apologize."

Seconds ticked into a silent minute, only for time to trap me in the echo of his words, touching my dead, cold core and breathing a warm spark of life into it.

I wasn't sure what I'd expected him to say.

But not this.

Not with such candor, where he exposed his failures without a single attempt at justifying them, causing a flutter in my heart that grew awash in the heat between our bodies.

I couldn't say how long I stared at him, but he eventually lifted a brow, adopting an almost sheepish look. "I did it wrong."

"No." He did it too well for a man, letting his cruelties of the last month fade too quickly into the darkest cranny of my stunned mind. "You practiced, didn't you?"

"For nearly three days." The corners of his mouth hiked and fell, as though uncertain if he should dare the hint of a smile. "I want us to start anew. Do you forgive me?"

Against the remnants of rage in my muscles, I allowed them to slacken, lowering my head onto his chest. I was only a mortal... a dead one. Neither resistant to this wash of heat Enosh provided after endless weeks of cold, nor immune to the rather poignant apology of a god.

"I'll consider it."

He scoffed, "Stubborn woman."

"Arrogant god, thinking that a handful of pretty sentences would make a woman forgive so easily."

"Nothing about you is easy, Ada, but you are worth all of my troubles ten times over," he rasped against my ear, providing me this sense of value only he could, in all its retched glory. "I realized my many mistakes when Yarin... confirmed it."

My chest heaved with an unexpected sob, but I swallowed it down, letting it rot among shattered dreams and broken wishes. *This is enough,* my mind chanted like a prayer. *This is as good as it gets.*

And yet the sob hiccupped straight back up, parting my lips as I said, "I wanted this child."

"As did I." Hushing me, Enosh wrapped his arms around me, likely expecting me to cry where I fought not to. "Among my many regrets, the way I failed you both weighs on me the heaviest. I do not know how to be a husband, understand even less about how to be a father. Yet I understand I have failed at both."

That flutter came to my core once more, drifting not on the words of a god, but a man humbled. Was this truly Enosh? Or was I still dreaming?

I pushed myself up once more, assessing the sway of his dark brows, the curvature of his lips, the straight nose. Still as annoyingly handsome, that bastard, yet something had changed.

What was it? His eyes?

Yes.

Not so much their gray color, but how the foreboding storm at the depth of his irises had somehow settled. What remained was a gaping cleft of emotions for me to stare at.

And he let me.

Enosh neither turned his head nor distracted from it with a twitch of his upper lip or the smug lift of a brow. I stared right into the face of my god husband, seeing the finest wrinkles at the corner of his eyes, the faintest blemishes of his complexion... and the pain of loss that so closely resembled mine.

He, too, had lost a child.

Twice.

At least in his heart.

Enosh reached his hand up, swiping a finger over my brow where it must have gone into disarray pressed against his chest. "What does my wife see?"

"You." Beautiful and terrifying, gentle and cruel. "I'm sorry you had to find out about Njala and the baby like this. I know you loved her."

"So I'd thought but..." His face scrunched up for a moment, and his gaze wandered into the room as though visiting old memories. "None of it compares to how I feel about you. Which makes me wonder if it was not so much her I loved, but the idea she resembled of children, family, life. In the end, this arrogant jerk could not inspire her love. Maybe gods ought not to be loved, but only hated, worshipped, and feared."

That brought a little tug to the corners of my mouth. "Or maybe you simply couldn't claim her heart because it had already belonged to another."

That returned his gaze to the here and now, which he set straight on me with uncoy intensity. "When you first arrived at my court, did your heart belong to another?"

"No."

"Good." He pushed himself up to sit and pulled me right along with him, leaning us against the wall of bone. "There's something I wish to show you, but we ought to dress you first to keep you warm."

"Dress." That word sent a shudder over me. "What happened to Orlaigh?"

"Not much... for now." He slipped out of bed and took my hand, pulling me to my feet as breeches formed around him. "I could either see to her punishment or watch after my wife, and I chose the latter."

"That must've cost you a great deal of self-control."

"Not at all," he said. "I wasted two centuries on hate and anger and will give the past my attention no longer beyond the necessary. Certain things ought to be taken care of… but after, I wish to live in peace."

"What will you do to her?"

That question gave him a moment's hesitation as he stared down at me. "What do you wish me to do?"

Braid her into your throne.

The words choked up onto my tongue out of nowhere, their taste bitter and unfamiliar, so I gulped them down. Did Orlaigh deserve to be punished? Yes. But she'd been betrayed by a loved one she'd tried to protect. How should that affect the severity?

"Punishment is your area, not mine. And now that we are speaking of corpses, Lord Tarnem was the one who helped shed light on all this in exchange for my promise."

"Promising what?"

"Um…" I thought for a second. "That I would shed light on this."

"And so you have, remaining as true to your vows as always."

"I guess that's one way of looking at it." My eyes fell to my belly and to the three lines where my wounds had been, each one now shaped into pale-puckered vines with flowers blooming beneath its foliage. "You gave me scars."

"I like your scars, your imperfections, written across your body like a story that tells me fragments of your mortal life. However…" Inhaling deeply, he took my hands in his, looking at me with solemn eyes. "One word from you, and I shall make them go away as though it never happened. The choice is yours."

My choice.

Such strange words.

My throat turned parched beyond its usual state. Did I want them gone? The wounds had caused me so much grief, yes, but the scars may serve as a sobering reminder of the world out there… the unfairness, the depravity.

"But it did happen." And if I stepped outside right now? It would surely happen again. "No, I want them to remind me."

No sooner had I spoken, did Enosh let a dress of brown pelts shape around me, heavy and lined on the inside. A black jacket was still forming around him as he took my hand in his, guiding me toward a set of stairs that hadn't been there before.

I followed beside him up the alabaster steps, letting my other hand trail over the smoothed bone of the banister toward a set of looming doors. "Where are we going?"

"I took the liberty of making you this while you rested." At his next step, the doors opened for him to lead me through. "A wedding gift I very much hope you will accept, for the last one ended in torture and death."

"A wedding—"

My words caught in my throat.

Devil be damned, my husband had been busy.

CHAPTER 16
ADA

Rendered speechless, I gaped at the atrium stretched out before me. Four slender columns formed the corners of the square, each adorned with grooved shafts. Flowers decorated the top of each, shaping outward like heavy leaves after rain.

At the center sat another pavilion, right beside what resembled a willow. Its bony-white branches wept down, carrying elongated foliage in shades of brown ranging from fawn, over to copper, to ebony. But it wasn't what took my breath away.

No, it was the birds.

My eyes lifted to the red-cheeked robins that flapped their wings, soaring toward the blue ceiling before they dove downward. Their *cuck-cuck-cucks* drifted on the gentle current as the birds settled on the branches of the willow or the translucent pavilion roof.

I crossed a patch of pale grass—its blades shaped from the sheerest skin—while what had to be beetle hulls formed colorful flowers here and there. "You brought the outside to the Pale Court."

"So you may see your birds and trees—as you requested all that time ago—no matter how death shackles your bone to my kingdom." He stepped up behind me, letting his palms brush along my arm before he pointed up, bringing my attention to the ceiling once more. "Behold, your sky. The children painted it for you before they shaped the leaves of the willow. Do you like it?"

"It's the most beautiful thing I've ever seen." I ran my finger over the criss-crossed ridges of the tree's white bark beside us. "You truly want that forgiveness, don't you?"

"Among other things... he rasped against the back of my ear, letting his warm hand settle on my throat, pulling me back slightly against his whisper. "You shall answer me this question, little one. Have you ever found any inklings of affection for me? Before I wrecked it all?"

I tilted my head back and let it settle against his shoulder, relishing the controlled possessiveness of how his thumb stroked the side of my throat. He'd once told me that love knew no precaution, turning us into fools for liars and monsters.

I was no liar.

Was Enosh a monster?

At his worst, he could be. And perhaps falling for such a man was wicked and corrupted—but so were the mortals out there. I'd suffered their cruelties, their judgment, their violence. The world was full of monsters.

But this one was mine.

"Yes, I was growing feelings for you." For this god whose love hurt as much as it healed. "Of all the bastards, devils, and monsters in this world, you are the one I chose."

An exhale stuttered over his quivering lips as the leaves on the willow trembled and wept toward us. “My goal to gain your heart remains unchanged, Ada.”

When his lips brushed along my cheek, my mouth turned toward them. “Kiss me. Don’t you dare turn away.”

His hand slipped from throat to chin, holding it in his ungiving grip as he slanted his mouth over mine. Our lips collided into a ferocious kiss, letting our breaths mingle and our moans meld.

Ash and snow flooded my senses. My tongue curled into the familiar taste of my husband’s mouth. My palm reached into the soft strands of his raven hair I had tousled a thousand times.

Breathless, Enosh pulled back, staring down at me from wide eyes. “The scent of ash might be burnt into my skin, but you are forever branded into my heart. Precious and forever treasured, this I vow. I love you. I want nothing more than for you to love me back. That, and...” his hand slipped over my collarbone, down between my breasts, and settled against my belly, “this child.”

Confused, I shook my head. “I don’t understand.”

“You once asked me how far I would go to see you returned.” The lap of his tongue at the nape of my neck sent an unexpected quiver into my thighs. “Little one, I will set the world ablaze and stand smiling at the center of its flames.” His other finger drew lazy circles around the side of my neck, numbing my mind with its warm caress. “I will kill, burn, and cut everyone who dared to bring heartache to my wife. I will do all this and worse to avenge what mortals did to you and me. And I will not stop until the lands are safe once more, and Eilam gifts you the breath of life, giving our child the mother it needs to grow.”

His threats against the world faded under the rapid flutter in my core, as though I sensed the robins’ wingbeats between my ribs. They swirled up a surge of deep longing until my breath fled, leaving enough room in my chest to fill with an overpowering wash of hope.

Was it truly possible...?

Dropping my hands to my belly, I placed them atop Enosh's. "My baby."

"Yes, Ada. Our baby." Pressed against my back like this, his heat seeped into my muscles as his fingers stroked along my bodice, letting it part and expose my breasts to the air. "What a wonderful mother you will be, growing it beneath the beautiful cadence of your kind heart."

I wasn't sure if I cared much about the kindness it held, as long as it would beat in my chest once more—a lullaby for my son or daughter. "Your brother was very eager to take my life. He won't give it back so easily, will he?"

His hand slid beneath my hair, gathering it up before he lifted it to rest over my shoulder while he kissed the other. "Not without some... pressure."

Which was probably where the burning and cutting came in. "Pressure?"

"Your life comes at the cost of others and has to be paid swiftly and with no mercy," he murmured between kisses behind my ear, letting my body grow heavy and slack. "There must be bloodshed, Ada... not only to restore your life and save our child, but to reestablish my divine rule across all lands."

That... made sense. So why did it ache my belly? My mind trailed to the lands beyond the Soltren Gate, empty and abandoned.

With or without my life, Enosh would kill those responsible for his torture and my death, anyway—something I'd known for a while and couldn't possibly hold against him. He needed to destroy the temples, the priests who worshipped there, and the soldiers who protected them.

That, or we would never have peace.

That, or I would not have my baby.

I gave a curt nod. “I understand.”

“Good girl,” he breathed into a kiss against my temple, letting my chest bloom at this praise he’d denied me for weeks. “You are so good, Ada. So honest and true, beautiful and kind. Annoyingly stubborn, driving me insane with her hardheadedness. I promised you a child, did I not?”

“You did.”

“And am I true to my promises?”

“Yes.”

“As I shall be true to this one.” His finger slid beneath the fur, drawing circles around my nipple. “You will have this child, Ada, and I shall hold the both of you in my arms very soon.”

Oh, all my body tingled.

I looked back at his handsome face, his gray eyes full of longing, a mirror of the hope I carried in my chest. Enosh was so easy to hate, but in moments like this, he was even easier to love.

Maybe I did?

A love born as a flutter in one’s chest, lying dormant in the cold clasp of death, only to sprout in this flood of truth, guilt, and hope between us. So all-consuming it left cuts and bruises and, once unleashed, would whirl into a storm that left nothing behind but justice.

I closed my eyes and tilted my head, allowing him to suckle the sensitive skin along my neck. Warm hands brushed over my shoulders, fingertips stroked the dips above my collarbone. Then, with one languid move, Enosh brushed my dress down, letting the pelt pool by my feet.

“Turn around for me,” he whispered as his fingers tugged

my waist. "Spread your legs. Do not make me repeat myself, for I shall not allow you to leave me wanting again."

When I did, I found him kneeling between blades of pale grass. His lips trailed along the vines of scars on my belly, kissing away the pain, the sorrow, the grief.

"Once your belly grows big with my child, I shall place a hundred kisses on it each day anew." His hand slipped between my legs, caressing my lower lips, massaging as he kissed along my hip. "Would you like that?"

I dug my fingers into his raven strands, loving their softness, yet how they refused to part easily. "A thousand."

"Two thousand kisses." With one quick move, he unbalanced me, only to catch me in his arms and lower me onto the soft carpet of silken grass. "Things will be different between us from here forward. Allow me to love you like only a god can. The rest will fall into place."

My back arched when he slanted his mouth over my cunt. He dragged the flat of his tongue over my entrance, suckled my folds into his mouth, letting his guttural noises vibrate against my clit.

Something tingled my arms.

And my legs, feet, waist.

Everything.

I lifted my head, watching how Enosh made a meal of my cunt as the silken grass stretched and moved. It caressed my entire body, like thousands of worshipping feather strokes, leaving not an inch of my skin ignored.

My mind descended into utter bliss, overwhelmed by this flood of sensation. Mercy god, the sky spun as I gave into the heat between my legs, the throbbing in my veins, and the ache in my belly only the King of Flesh and Bone could sate.

"I love you," Enosh said between suckles on my lower lips. "Missed you so terribly."

A shudder raked over my skin, hardening my nipples, sending sparks of heat into my belly. I spread my legs wide, inviting his wicked mouth to bring me back to life as I writhed and moaned.

"I missed you, too."

Had missed his attention, his total devotion, the way he touched me like no other ever had. How could one not love such a man who was so devout to me and our child?

His mouth stunned my mind as his tongue lured my clit from its little hood, sucking, circling, pinching it gently beneath the clasp of his lips. When his fingers entered me, thrusting knuckles into my center, they tossed me into the throes of scalding pleasure. Dipping and curling, torrential waves of heat flared around my cunt, pushing me into a harrowing release that robbed me of my voice.

I all but whimpered through it, drowning beneath the liquid wash of heat coursing through my veins. My hips bucked against his chuckle, my senses so heightened, each lazy lap of his tongue that followed scorched me down to the satisfied hum in my chest.

Enosh kissed his way over the curls between my legs, along every single rib, then positioned his hips between my thighs as his clothes faded into dust. "I daresay you are warm now."

I palmed his cheek, letting my thumb run over the scrape of his stubble along his chin. "Feverish."

"This is the most alive I can make you feel..." He set the throbbing tip of his cock at my slick entrance. "Letting your nerve-endings tingle as I push inside you..." Rhythmic pulsations let me stretch around his sizable girth, each inch of progress accompanied by a sensuous kiss to my mouth. "Sharing my heat with you, skin against skin..." He framed my head with his arms, staying closer to me than he ever had as he thrust deeper, rolled his hips up and back, then thrust again. "Making your cunt weep around my cock. And this..."

Ba-boom-boom.

Ba-boom-boom.

Ba-boom-boom.

The beat of my heart shuddered in my ears, a sound that startled me as it sent tingles through my limbs and into my core. "That feels nice."

"It takes me a great deal of focus to sustain it." His forehead lowered against mine as we stared at each other, letting our moans resonate the sliver of quivering air between us each time he drove into me. "Each beat of your heart is nothing but me thinking of you. Never again shall you go without it."

Enosh rocked in and out of me at a sensual pace, heating my inner walls with measured strokes. His hands closed around my wrist, slowly bringing them upward where the white grass slung around my arms, gently restraining me.

"Do you feel me? I am a thousand caresses upon your skin." More spread into my hair, sending one blissful shiver after another from my scalp down across my body. "Never again will I deny you my touch. I am all yours, Ada. Forever."

He fed me his kisses, assurances of his love, and each masculine groan that tumbled from his lips.

And I feasted on it, clasping his back, sensing the familiar shift of his muscles against my palms. My legs clasped around his waist as the grass lengthened with my motion, allowing me to pull him deeper into me. Back arching, I met him beat for beat, aching for completion with unrestrained need.

"I love you." His hand fisted in my hair, angling my head until the side of my neck lay exposed where he licked and kissed, only to growl his pleasure against my earlobe. "The ground shall tremble beneath my army of corpses, letting the depravity of mortals crumble by my queen's feet. However many wicked lives it takes, I shall sacrifice them all to have yours restored. I shall destroy this world wrought with corruption, building a better one for you and our baby."

Our baby.

My nails clawed at his back as my insides convulsed with an intensity that set my core aflame. The beat of my heart quickened, drumming so loudly inside my head that it overwhelmed all thoughts of caution, all lessons of morality, and even my scream as I peaked.

Enosh's throaty groans mixed into it. He gave a final thrust, pinning me between the weight of his body and the tickle of grass along my blessedly warm skin. Shudders wracked his body, but he remained otherwise still, his cock twitching and throbbing inside me.

When our breathing calmed, he nuzzled my temple. "We shall stay like this for a few days while I tend to you. Then, we shall provoke my brother to come into his form, and demand he gives you the breath of life."

I reached up, stroking black strands from his face. "Do you think he might agree, then?"

"If I can convince him of my determination and resolve, he might." Whatever he saw on my face had him hushing me as he cupped my face. "Let me deal with my brother. All I need of you is to trust me and to be hopeful. Can you be hopeful for me, hmm?"

"I can be anything you need me to be."

If only it would return my baby.

CHAPTER 17
ENOSH

I was a man of my word.

A god out for revenge.

And yet, here I lay, on a bed swaying a foot above the ground from the willow in my wife's garden, letting time pass us by.

For days, I'd put my grudge aside for the sake of enjoying my woman's touch. How she drew letters beneath my shoulder blade. Tugged on the ends of my hair. Traced the sway of my ribs.

When her movements slowed, I let a groan muffle into the furs. "Do not stop."

I sensed her cheeks bunch where her face rested inches from mine. "I thought you were asleep."

"Had I been sleeping, your heart would have stopped." Instead, I had found bliss in days of conversation and nearness, while eventually drifting into comfortable silence and quiet rest. "Your touch is... hypnotizing."

Ada increased the pressure, letting her nails gently scratch down each side of my spine until the fine hairs on the small of my back lifted. "Not cold?"

"Cold is all I have ever known, my love." I slowly blinked my eyes open, stretching my legs and inhaling deeply before I cupped her cheek. "You will be warm again soon. Until then, I shall be the beat of your heart, the throb of your pulse, the rush of your blood, and the salt in your tears."

A gentle smile curved her lips, pink again from the constant supply of warmed blood borrowed from others I sent through her veins. "When will we leave?"

"As soon as we have made ourselves look presentable." I rubbed my other hand over my cheek, smooth shaven since we'd bathed together the night before. "Black mink, white fox, or brown sable. Choose."

"Black mink."

"Excellent choice. But first..."

When I rolled her onto her back and climbed between her legs, she gave a pitiful shove at my shoulders. "You just had me."

"Mmm, yes, in the most curious way."

Oh, my brother called me a bore, but had he ever loved a woman at the bottom of a spring, encapsulated in heat while he happily drowned? How strangely wonderful it had felt, filling Ada with my seed as my lungs filled with water, unable to die but succumbing to the panic of its premise, nonetheless.

"Are you denying me?" Clasping her wrists, I brought them over her head, letting the ropes of hair that suspended our bed gently bind her. "Tell me, little one, what happens if you do not allow me to touch you, hmm?"

Ornery thing she was, she pressed her foot against my chest and wiggled her toes. "I'm sore, almost as though you refuse to ease it."

"Because this is how I prefer you, feeling me between your

legs long after we coupled." Shoving her leg aside, I lowered my head to kiss our child, as I had promised I would. "You are counting, yes?"

My kisses over her belly ripped the most adorable little giggles from her as she writhed beneath me. "I can't count that high."

"I shall teach you, but for now, it serves us well since the sun has long risen beyond that gate."

And yet I kissed her scars a dozen times more, letting my senses reach into her belly. I could not feel my child, so I touched it the only way I could. Focused on the tiny void, I caressed around it, letting it know I was there, never again to fail as its father.

Lips benumbed, I rose, then reached out and lifted Ada from the bed just as I removed the bonds and dressed my wife for the occasion. "Keeping you warm will pose a challenge, for the lands are sleeping beyond a layer of snow and the winds are biting."

"Which explains the sheer weight of this."

She glanced down at the dress forming around her, with long trumpet sleeves, a high collar with bone buttons in the shape of small robins, and a heavy cape that rested on her shoulders. Fur-lined gloves of black leather formed around her hands, and matching boots completed my creation.

I let a black leather outfit form around me, with inlets of the same mink, the inside lined. "Is it to your liking?"

She slipped off my arm and spun, letting the train fan out until the fine hairs of the pelts bristled. "Beautiful, like everything you create."

"It is still unfinished."

She startled when I let her strands weave themselves into a nest of golden braids, bringing a look of sheer wonder to her face. Oh, how little she'd seen of the powers bestowed upon me. Raven feathers fanned out at the back of her head, giving her a black halo for a crown.

Reaching her gloved fingers up, she let them tap it as realization widened her eyes. “Feathers.”

“Behold, the Queen of Rot and Pain.” I let black beetle shells compress into a crown upon my head—almost shaped like thick antlers—along with swirls which I imagined coming together by my forehead. “What say you?”

“Behold, the King of Flesh and Bone.” She rose onto her toes, running her assessing stare over my crown as she brushed strands of my hair back over my shoulder. “Out to break hearts.”

Among other organs. “Now we are ready to ask the world to bend its knee.”

A tug on my senses.

Had she just flinched?

Unable to find any traces of it in her muscles, I disregarded it as no more but an odd tremor and opened the gates of my kingdom. The ground shook, letting the beads of bone and nail above our heads *clank* together.

Ada reached for my arm. “What was that?”

I intertwined my leather-clad fingers with hers and guided her toward the stairs for the throne room. “Allow me to show you.”

I led her downstairs, into the familiar reek of death and decay barely dulled, for I had not bothered to do so.

Orlaigh slouched on the dais—as she had for days—her face puckered and grayish-green, painting her as the traitor she was. Her betrayal should not have come as such a surprise. She was mortal, after all, wicked and dishonest.

“Orlaigh.” I stared down at my gloves, tugging on one finger where they refused to sit right. “I have wasted two centuries trapped in the past, and I shall give it my mind no longer. Let us keep this brief. Will you climb into my throne, or shall I make you?"

The old woman slowly shook her head in acceptance of my judgment and struggled herself onto her legs. "Nay, Master. Ye dinnae have to make me. Aye, I'll go."

And yet she gave my wife an apologetic look, preying on my little one's goodness.

With success.

A small cluster of tension around Ada's shoulders. A set of muscles that contracted along her arms. A toe that curled slightly in her boot. My little one's flesh and bone betrayed the kind of unease that sharpened the edge I thought I had already crossed...

... only to find myself still balancing.

Ah, my love had told me she could be anything I needed her to be. I needed her to be cold, detached, and out for revenge—needed her to be all those things she'd accused me of. If only for a little while...

What if she could never be that?

A shadow fell over my chest.

Here I stood, a god shaped to perfection, powerful in so many ways, yet it bought me no reprieve from gravity and how it made me sway on this line with a deep crater to each side. One held the loss of my wife's warmth and child. The other, the loss of my cold wife's love.

Where would I rather fall?

The answer came easily.

I would rather embrace the cold body of the woman who loved me than desperately clasp to the warm body of the woman who grew our child in a core of chilling hate.

But alas, I was a god.

Gods ought to be above choices.

There was always my brother and his whispers—a last

resort should I fail at making my little one embrace the sad truth about mortals' corruption.

Until then, I would balance.

"I sense the tension in your muscles, unaware of how deep Orlaigh's betrayal might have reached." I cupped the back of Ada's head, pulled her in for a kiss, then placed my lips by her ear. "Have you ever asked yourself why we've been overwhelmed by such a large force in the forest? Curious, do you not agree? As though they had only waited for us to emerge that day?"

Her stomach clenched as her gaze dropped to my chest, and she ran a finger over the soft pelt of her sleeve. Thinking. Judging. Trying to find excuses for mortal's wickedness.

Her blue eyes sought out mine. "Pa told me how High Priest Dekalon had every town and village form a militia. You might be mistaken."

Yes, I might be, but that made Orlaigh no less a traitor. At least now, the old woman could serve a greater role in restoring my wife, helping me to stand by my word for I had promised Ada a child.

A traitor would make me no oathbreaker.

"Has she not left the Pale Court many times?" I asked, letting my fingers stroke over Ada's belly. "Knew her way around the markets and taverns?"

A rush of blood warmed Ada's veins—courtesy of my command—then her gaze shot to Orlaigh. "You informed people of our plan to ride out? And cost me my baby?"

Orlaigh shook her head so rapidly, it matched the tremble in her voice as she whimpered, "Nay, lass. Never."

"Perhaps you have... perhaps you have not." I rested my hand on the small of Ada's back, where I tugged her into motion before her anger could ebb away. "Such is the plight of the liar, never to be believed again. Go ahead. Feed your body to my throne."

Ada braced against my urging. "No."

No?

A muscle twitched in my jaw, and my lips parted as though eager to call upon the God of Whispers. If my little one could not watch the woman who betrayed her get her due punishment, then how could she possibly sit back and watch the slaughter of—

"I want to see how the throne swallows her." Ada's words cut through my thoughts and worries alike. "She knew I had signs of pregnancy. Oh, I'll never forget that look she gave me that day."

My heart stumbled over one beat, then another, only to quicken into a faster pace that set my arteries awash with relief. Perhaps this blade I balanced was still there, yes, but welded thicker than first assumed.

"And has Orlaigh not asked me to remove the rot from her before we left?" I circled her belly, reminding her of what this woman may or may not have cost us. "As though she knew we might not return for a while."

"Yes." The word fell from Ada's lips, a mere mumble before her voice took on the gust of an encroaching storm. "Three times she betrayed me. *Threatened* me with the throne. Now, I want to see her in it."

"And what my wife wants, my wife shall get." I whispered a kiss against Ada's temple before I said, "Orlaigh, you heard my queen…"

Trembling like leaves in the autumn breeze, the old woman stepped around the throne. She poked her head through the opening I shaped in the backrest, right between Lord Tarnem and Commander Mertok. It *was* getting rather crowded.

The bone closed but a second later, swelling around

Orlaigh's neck like white quicksand as she gasped. "Aaah... Ghrrr—"

The bone strangled her scream into a choking gargle while my throne reshaped. It swallowed her limbs beneath waves of thickening bonedust, weaving them into the backrest to the symphony of cracking femurs and joints that dislodged with several *pop-pop-pops.*

Ah, how satisfying.

The gruesome sight robbed Ada of breath, filling her empty ribcage with... something. Something I couldn't quite name, but it had her spine straighten and her shoulders square.

"Do you wish me to stretch her limbs, hmm?" I dove my face into the crook of Ada's neck, taking in the scent of salt and minerals from how I'd washed her hair in the spring last night. "Shall we needle her organs with bone, letting it spread through her like those roots of mortal's corruption? All you have to do is say it."

A swallow visibly ran down her throat, but she shook her head. "No, this is... this is punishment enough."

Perhaps another time.

I led her along the hallway toward the Æfen bridge as Orlaigh's whimpers faded behind us. "It is time for us to confront my brother. After that, we will ride for the village where I found you. From there, to the high temple."

When the hallway opened to the bridge, her legs froze. "Where did they come from?"

With a slow wave of my hand, I beckoned her gaze to pass over the corpses that lined the bridge, each armed with swords, pikes, and daggers of bone. "From the piles beyond the gates, sworn to defend us."

"I thought no mortal other than the children would ever enter your court again."

So much surprise in her voice over something she'd begged

of me for an entire month, as though she'd all but forgotten her former goals.

Perhaps she had.

"Even gods make mistakes." Why hold on to a vow given over the death of a woman who had betrayed me three times over, and deprive my wife and our child of the protection they deserved? "From what I sense, the Æfen Gate is blocked by a significant force of soldiers. How kind of High Priest Dekalon to supply me with an army and deliver it to my doorstep. Still, never again will I allow harm to come to you."

She turned to lift a brow at me. "Enosh, I can't die."

"But you can suffer, and you had enough of that." I let a dapple-gray horse shape in front of us, lifted her onto its back like I had done a dozen times before, then swung up behind her. "Suffering the pain of flesh is my duty; protecting you from it is my vow."

I willed our horse into a walk toward the gate, calling upon the dead to follow. Groans and stomps resonated in the Pale Court, and the bridge shook beneath the thunder of two hundred fleshbare heels marching toward the Æfen Gate.

"Do your master's bidding!" My shout joined the beat of hooves in my requiem of ruin, carrying it up the incline before it scattered into the wintery winds. "Seven men you shall bring me, alive and bound. Kill the others. Kill them all!"

CHAPTER 18
ADA

Kill them all.

Those three words spun inside my skull as my mind scrambled to comprehend what was happening right before my eyes.

A swell of corpses flooded the encampment outside the Æfen Gate, drowning soldiers beneath bone-shivering moans and the stomps of their feet. Whichever mortals survived the wave of death fought to its surface with their mouths agape, their faces distorted in pain, their screams tainted with panic.

To my left, a young man struggled up a sword. He severed the head off a dead woman. It was of no use.

The headless corpse gripped his face between the clasp of her fingers, letting bony digits dive into his eye sockets. A soft flurry of snow scattered around them, some flakes tainting red from the splatters of his eyes even before they landed on the battlefield.

No, not battlefield.

This was no battle.

It was a slaughter.

When a gag pushed past my esophagus without consent, Enosh placed his hand over my eyes. He shielded me from the viciousness of his vengeance as though the heart-rending screams and pitiful pleas didn't paint bloody pictures in the blackness before my eyes.

God confound me, my diaphragm convulsed as though I could still be bothered by such a sight after living through my own death. As though something inside me wanted to take pity on these men.

No, I wouldn't.

They *deserved* it.

This needed to be done.

"It's already over, little one," Enosh whispered into my ear as he lifted his hand from my face no more than five breaths later, sending black and white floaters through my vision.

Impossible. "What?"

"They can no longer harm us."

Because they were all dead.

An unwelcome quiver raked through my stomach. In five breaths, Enosh had decimated the entire encampment, butchering everyone.

Aside from a few soldiers who screamed here and there.

One stumbled over his dead comrades while frantically shoving his guts back into a hole in his stomach before he sunk to the ground. Another hung from a bone pike where it had gone through his shoulder, pinning him against a naked oak. He screamed the loudest as he tried to struggle himself free.

"You took what was not yours to take..." Enosh said too calmly for comfort, letting our horse climb over the carpet of slain under blood-curdling screams from those not quite dead yet. "Oh, brother... show yourself."

And there, beside a pile of twitching corpses, appeared his brother.

The wrong one.

Enosh groaned. “When I call upon him, he won’t come. When I ask him to stay away, he sticks like shit on a rock.”

Yarin hopped over a half-dead priest and strolled toward us, his forest-green frock lined with red fox pelt that matched his boots. Of course, the God of Whispers wouldn’t be far from such… madness.

Madness that made sense.

“And here I feared it would be another dull day,” Yarin said, weaving around a corpse with chewed off arms. “There I lay at my court, in a tangle of limbs, nearly—” Frowning, Yarin glanced over his shoulder at the soldier pinned to the tree who wailed in agony. “You know how loud noises ache my head.”

At Enosh’s dismissive wave, a bone spike drove through the man’s throat, finally relieving him of pain and suffering. “The same cannot be said about the constant noise coming from your mouth.”

“Wonderful, how you’re trying yourself at humor. Married life seems to have loosened you up. Anyway, I was nodding off when a barrage of the most atrocious thoughts reached me. *Oh no! The King of Flesh and Bone! He will kill us all!*” He glanced around, tapping a finger against his smooth-shaven cheek before he shrugged. “And so you have, brother.”

“Not all.” Enosh jutted his chin toward seven men with their arms bound behind their backs—three soldiers, two priests, and two squires—led to us by corpses. “Why are you here?”

“Believe it or not, I realized I have a personal interest in your success.”

Enosh dismounted, letting someone’s skull shatter beneath the impact of his boot before he pulled me down. “In case you are here for more holes to fuck, just know I require the bone and muscle of every soldier.”

"You're making me sound debauched, Enosh. No, my interest is inspired by this new title I shall acquire in... let's say nine months, plus however long Eilam remains stubborn."

"And whatever might this title be?"

"It is really quite simple." Yarin straightened his spine, letting a lopsided grin form a dimple beneath his cheek. "Am I not to be Uncle Yarin? Ada, is this not what you mortals call it?"

Enosh and I sighed before I said, "Yes. Uncle."

"I shall watch the little god or goddess while you two... kill priests or... otherwise enjoy yourselves in town every now and then," he mused. "Uncle Yarin. I quite like the sound of that."

Well, I did not, but it couldn't be helped now, could it? "With a madman for an uncle, what could possibly go wrong?"

"Precisely. Now that we are speaking on madness... Oh, how fine you look, Ada, with your hair decorated with feathers instead of loam." Yarin took my hand, guiding me around the dead soldier toward an area not littered by death, and let his lips hover over my knuckles in an almost-kiss. "Mmm, undeniably my brother's wife. But black...? Truly, there's no life in that color. If you were my woman, I would dress you in the finest brocade, embroidered with the richest threads of gold."

Enosh slapped his brother's hand away and pulled me against him. "If she were your woman, which she is *not*, she would be dead at her *own* hand."

"Yes, yes, yes, but much better dressed on her funeral." Yarin flung himself toward a pile of still twitching corpses, only to land on a tufted daybed that had appeared out of nowhere atop them, shifting in their final struggles as the legs sunk into their flesh. "Between us, Enosh, I shall never bed a warm woman again. No, I have sworn them all off. Since this renders Eilam's threat to kill all whores before I even touch them quite irrelevant—well, I might as well partake in this, um... divine vengeance, crusade, soiree... whatever you wish to call it."

Enosh clenched his jaw. "If you insist, *brother*. But at the very least, make yourself useful and watch my wife while I call upon the third." He lifted me over the carpet of corpses, put me on the daybed beside his brother, then leaned in for a menacing growl. "Watch. Not touch."

"I would *never*. If only because your possessiveness over her might be potent enough to get an immortal killed." The moment Enosh turned away with a sigh, Yarin let a golden platter of fruits shape in his palm and reached it to me. "Hungry? Oh, I forgot." He tossed it away, letting apples *thud* against skulls and grapes scatter across limp bodies. "Dead. No good with food. My apologies."

Enosh walked over to the bound men. "Kneel."

At the command, the seven fell to their knees in front of the corpses, lining up before us less than ten steps from the daybed. Fear flitted across their features, eyes wide and chins trembling. One of them—a squire who probably hadn't seen his fifteenth summer yet—soaked his breeches, letting them darken around his crotch.

"Still so young." The sight of his rosy cheeks, red pimples, and patchy blond facial hair brought an unwelcome hollowness to my guts that I couldn't afford. "What will Enosh do with him?"

"Something that will vex Eilam like nothing else," Yarin said with a devious grin lining his lips. "Never got along, those two. See, Ada, Eilam gets rather flustered when we cut a mortal life short before its due time, since it affects him in a way we cannot quite grasp. And there truly is only one thing that upsets him even more..."

My throat tightened. What could possibly anger the god of life more than such a slaughter, where hundreds died in seconds?

My husband slowly walked along the men lined up for

death, letting the snow crunch beneath his boots before he squatted before the youngest one—the one who'd pissed himself.

"Mortal, you have a choice to make." A bone knife formed in my husband's palm, of which he brought the sharp end to the squire's eye. "Deny what I ask of you, and I shall carve your eyeballs out with this, *slowly*. They will dangle on a string of cartilage as I hang you upside down from a tree."

No sooner had Enosh spoken that last word, did the earth tremble. Corpses tossed on the ground about half a furlong ahead of us as a flare of wind whirled up snow, blowing it toward them.

My breathing stumbled to a halt.

No, not snow.

Bonedust wafted from the copse of trees lining this valley, the old piles of corpses around the Æfen Gate, and the open meadows behind us. It came together in an avalanche, burying slain soldiers beneath a dusting of it as it roared toward us. The dead scrambled, crawling away from...

From what?

"As it so happens, my wife is fond of trees," Enosh said, letting his dark voice loom over the squire's whimpers like a foreboding shadow. "So I shall grow a magnificent tree right in front of our home for the world to behold, decorated with the twitching, wailing bodies of those who betrayed their god. Starting with you, mortal."

Raw, numbing shock looped around my organs as the waves of bone collided, sending a puff into the dreary sky. The impact alone shook the world hard enough that nearby twigs snapped and a few horses broke loose to take off in a flight, their hoofbeats a terrified substitute for my heart.

A massive tree shaped right in front of my eyes, big enough one would be able to see its crown from Hemdale and beyond.

Thick branches sprouted from it, gnarled and grotesque, like the gout-ridden fingers of an old witch, left naked without a single leaf of skin.

Instead, strings of something, hair perhaps, braided themselves downward like the swamp vines on the sunken trees in the western wetlands. From there, they formed offshoots that slithered across the ground. Some of them came toward us, only to wrap around the men's boots.

With a start, the squire glanced over his shoulder at the tree—as did the others—his mouth falling open wider the higher his gaze wandered—up toward the treetop scraping at the winter-gray clouds.

"From this tree, you shall eternally hang." Enosh pressed the bone blade against the squire's cheek, returning his gaze to meet the god's with a bloody cut. "And the crows shall peck at the two holes in your face. Greedy as they are, they will peel the skin off and dig their beaks through your skull before you manage to die. Or…" He tossed the blade in the air, gripped it by its blade until blood dripped from his knuckles, then reached the handle over. "Each one of you shall take a blade and, one after another, open the veins along your arms."

My survival instinct leapt in my chest, shoving a gasp past my lips. A whiff of iron and sweetness crept into my mouth, quickly tainting my gums with the stench of urine and guts, letting my stomach spin for reasons I didn't want to explore.

Had Enosh not warned me of his plan to bathe the lands in blood? Had it not made sense, terrible as it may be, for mortals had brought this day of reckoning onto themselves? If we wanted revenge on those who'd wronged us—to destroy all under the Sun of Helfa and gain life for me and our child—then these men needed to die.

But the squire was no man.

He was a boy.

Innocent.

Barely old enough to grow a damn beard, let alone lift a sword. Devil be damned, he'd probably spent all week watering the horses, filling cups of ale, and pouring the commander's pisspots into the latrines.

"P-please, Your Highness," the boy stammered, letting my gloved fingers curl into the mink of my dress no matter how I didn't want them to. "I... I have a younger sister at home who... She's carrying my babe."

Well... maybe not innocent.

But not terribly guilty, either.

Yarin chuckled. "*Tsk, tsk, tsk...* not even I am depraved enough to rut my own sister."

"If only because we do not have one," Enosh clipped over his shoulder, then turned his attention back to the man. "Are you suggesting that you wish to feed the crows?"

"No!" the boy blurted, eyes nervously flitting from Enosh to the blade as he hesitantly nodded. "Unbind me, and I... I will do it."

His arms fell forward right then.

I breathed.

Breathed again.

It was all I could do to keep down this desperation, this inkling that these lands I called home might soon resemble those beyond the Soltren Gate.

And if we found a young alemaid in some tavern, would she have to cut her wrists, too? What of the stable boys? What of the motherless babes screaming inside the temples? When Enosh had said bloodshed, whose blood had he been talking about, exactly?

Watching this boy pick up the blade... it shook me beyond comprehension.

As it shook him, for he dropped the blade into the snow

with how his hand quivered. Nausea bit at my throat when he lifted it from the white powder. He shoved back the leather covering his arm, brought the blade to the pale skin, and—

“Stop,” someone said.

Me.

I’d said that.

CHAPTER 19
ADA

My chest caved in.

Why had I interfered?

Enosh turned while gesturing the boy to halt, then walked up to me. He sunk his knees into the corpses, letting his concerned stare flit across my features as though checking me for bruises.

"I sensed the mounting tension in your muscles." Kneeling at eye-height, he clasped my chin, then leaned in to nuzzle my temple before he placed a kiss on my lips. "Is it the cold? Do you wish me to fashion you a blanket?"

I was terribly cold, shivering at the white mercy of winter and pity alike. "It's not that."

"The carnage?"

"Your wife has an onslaught of morals and compassion," Yarin said, followed by a sigh. "I get those sometimes. Once a century, or so. At least every other."

"It's just... I've never seen so many dead people." In a world where they didn't rot, that meant something. "This has to be at least a hundred, maybe more."

Enosh frowned at me. “These are three hundred and two soldiers joining our forces.”

Three hundred and two.

In five breaths.

My guts shifted at such high a number that escaped my counting and imagination alike. “Enosh this… this squire, he… he’s an innocent boy. He probably doesn’t even know why he’s here.”

Enosh’s gaze drifted to Yarin. The brothers exchanged a silent stare, though it seemed to say a great many things for Enosh shook his head as though in answer.

My husband glanced over his shoulder at the boy, then turned his attention back to me. “Are these not the kind of mortals who have attacked us, standing under the banners of houses that support the high priest? Who have… tortured me and brought about your death?”

My throat turned parched with thirst—a sensation I hadn’t felt for nearly two months. “Yes, but—”

I swallowed.

But what? Had we not discussed this? After all, they’d waited for us out here, armed with swords and ill intentions. Had I stepped a foot out here, I would be the one cowering before these men.

Maybe even before a squire.

Three hundred and two.

In five breaths.

I expected Enosh to lift a brow at me, asking if he was not merciful. Cutting one’s veins was worse than a quick death, sure, but still preferable over hanging upside down from a giant tree as a crows feast.

Instead, he rose, sat beside me on the daybed, and pulled me onto his lap. He palmed my cheek, stroked along my earlobe, and took his time to dote on me as the lined-up men cowered in fear. The boy started sobbing, of all things.

Three hundred and two.

In five breaths.

Enosh placed his hand on my stomach. “Are these not the kind of mortals responsible for the loss of our child?”

My chest curled toward my belly in a protective reflex, all while Enosh circled my stomach like I had done a dozen times. “Yes.”

“Yes,” he echoed, clenching his eyes shut as he rubbed the tip of his nose over my forehead, inhaling me. “My throne shall have the high priest’s head in it before the snow grows by another foot, this I have vowed.” When he opened his eyes again, he let them lock with mine. “This, you shall not hold against me, Ada.”

“I won’t.” Understood his urge for revenge, our need for corpses, and the urgency to destroy those who meant us harm, but... “I’m just not sure if my vision of this matches yours anymore. What of the people between here and Elderfalls? Here and the high temple? *Innocent* people? The farmers along the road, the women finding kindle, the... the children playing in the snow? You will spare them, right?”

“Innocent people...” There was a moment’s hesitation. “Tell me this, little one, who chased you?”

“The priests.”

“Who gave the command?”

I swallowed. “High Priest Dekalon?”

“Yes,” he said. “Tell me, who killed you? Who drove in the blade? A priest? A soldier?”

I shook my head, sensing my stomach hollowing as the point of his questions dawned on me. “People.”

“People...” he echoed once more, thumbing my cheek as though rewarding me for a terrible lesson finally learned.

"Innocent one moment, wicked the next. Men, women... even the sick, old, weak, and boys mounting their sisters. Mortals are wayward creatures."

So he would spare none.

A strange ringing came to my ears as my mind spun, letting innocence and guilt blur into one obscure tangle. "But if I stand by this, idly watching how corpses bite the face off an old man limping down the street half-blind, am I not wicked, too?"

"How can you be?" He took my face between his hands as though to keep my thoughts from spiraling out of control. "Have you not fought me for a month to get me to rest the wicked? Ada, have you not *tried* to save them all?"

"Yes."

And paid for it with my life.

My baby.

The one I'd promised to protect.

The one I'd failed so miserably.

"You, too, have a choice to make, little one. Tell me, my love, who gets to live? The mortals, or you? The mortals, or our baby?" A second's pause, and then, "For you cannot have both."

My lungs collapsed.

I cannot have both.

All that made so much sense again, in all its terrifying truth, because we needed Eilam to save this baby trapped alive in my belly. "Are you even certain your brother will come like this? Three hundred dead... in five breaths. I don't see him anywhere."

"Little one, he is already here, drifting on every final breath expelled. I know my brother and what aggravates him. Mortals ending their own lives...? Oh, it provokes Eilam like nothing else, no matter its... *inspiration*."

"Oh, what a fuss he made at the brothel, all because of the one I had... *inspired* to slit her throat at Airensty," Yarin added. "And what a bore that one turned out to be. Always crying. Boo-hoo, my poor dead boy. Boo-hoo."

Amid the expectant silence, time moved slower, one second for each caressing circle of my cold palm around my belly.

Cold because of people.

"Then why stop at all?" I asked Enosh. "You don't need my permission."

With a deep exhale, Enosh let his forehead drift against mine. "You know why."

Because he wanted my love.

The lack of one might threaten the other.

Dread slid down my spine, wanting to curve with the knowledge that there wasn't even a choice to be had. Nothing would give me what I wanted while sparing me the weight of what might become many gruesome deaths—innocent deaths—on what was left of my tattering conscience.

Not truly.

Because while Enosh seemingly needed my sincere love like air, the same was not true for my blessing. All it took was one of Yarin's whispers, and I might merrily giggle at the sight of a bone blade hacking into a wrist. Why else had they exchanged that look?

One deep breath to clear my mind.

Enosh had forced a great many things on me—and had robbed me of twice as much with neither blessing nor permission. That he now tried for my understanding instead of simply stripping me of this hindering compassion running riot in my chest...?

It meant a lot to me.

And if I sat back and watched it all unfold, would that truly make me culpable? Evil? What mother wouldn't do *everything* in her power to see her child returned? Why not at the cost of those who took it?

Besides, what if those seven men were all we required to convince Eilam? We could be at the high temple in two days, maybe three, kill those who defend the high priest, then kill him, then go back home.

Alive. Pregnant.

It would all be over.

I took a deep breath, letting my chest expand so wide there was no room left for pity. "Alright."

"I love you so," Enosh rasped. "Mmm, Ada, I know a great many things but not how to raise a child. You shall teach me, yes?"

"Yes," I said with a weak smile, amused by the thought of a god changing soiled clouts. Enosh barely ever ate; no doubt he had little experience with shit, if any. "Are you certain Eilam will appear like this?"

Another kiss to my temple, then his silver eyes found mine. "Oh, he will show himself. And then, we will demand your life breath back, hmm?"

That roused another flutter behind my ribs. "Yes."

Enosh slipped me off his lap and returned to the line of men kneeling in the snow, who shivered from frost and fear, letting a new bone blade shape when he reached the squire.

Gulping, the boy took it, and brought it to his wrist.

"*Tsk, tsk, tsk.*" Enosh gripped his hand and guided the blade a smidge more to one side. "Right here, mortal, along this very vein, blueand oh-so swollen with dread. Cut."

From ten feet away, it looked like no more than a nick, but I knew how sharp a bone blade was. It sunk into the vein easily, immediately staining red before rivulets of blood collected in the man's palm. From there, crimson *drip-drip-dripped* into the white snow.

"Return what you stole from my wife," Enosh mumbled as the boy's head slowly drooped, chin sinking toward chest. "Or else I shall unbalance this world until it turns upside down. Show yourself!"

Enosh's shout echoed across the silent field, letting a flock of birds take flight from a nearby tree. All the while, the young man's arms slouched, pulling heavily on his shoulders until he tipped forward, slumping against the god.

Nothing.

No Eilam.

A tremor shook me, caused by equal parts of cold drifts from the north and despair. How many more needed to bleed out before that bastard finally showed up? I just wanted my baby.

When Enosh rose, letting the squire's face fall into the snow, I averted my gaze. "This is upsetting..."

"Agreed," Yarin said on a sigh. "Upsettingly *boring*."

Enosh handed the blade to the next man in line, a priest. "How many priests with their soul still about?"

"Five," Yarin said. "Seven with the two in this line."

"Bind the dead ones. I shall trade you one for one."

Offshoots of hair spread across the field of demise, slithering toward the sudden echoes of scattered wails and prayers. When they retreated toward the trunk, they pulled the corpses of priests with them.

Soulbound.

One after another, they rose toward the branches. They tossed and writhed until their robes slipped over their heads, letting the shit-stained underpants of some air out. They screamed and cried, praying to a god who would not help them.

"Wonderful," Yarin said with a grin and an excited clap. "Oh, Enosh, I do love it when you lose your mind every couple of centuries. Such skill. Such creativity."

The soldier who kneeled in front of my husband shot his hand forward, taking the bone blade from Enosh's palm. With a slow cut, he opened his veins to the chill of winter and death.

"Good man," Enosh whispered as the soldier slowly slumped into himself as he crawled toward death. "I can do this for the rest of my life. Tell me, brother, how long might that be?"

When Enosh picked up the blade where it had dropped in the snow, a sudden sense of despair settled onto me like thick tar poured over my very soul. It slithered into my chest, robbing me of air, leeching the little warmth I had left from me like *he* had done the day I'd died.

"Eilam," I rasped, making Yarin scoot away from me and Enosh to rise to his full height.

'Ada.' My name whispered from an aura to my left, almost like the caress of light one felt when the sun poked through the windows in the morning. Not a sight; a sensation. *'Still so much life in you, refusing my command. An atrocity.'*

Eilam slowly came into his form beside me, his windswept hair as white as snow, his black eyes seemingly fixed on me, though it was hard to tell. Oh, and he was naked.

Yarin rolled his eyes. "I would have gladly waited another moment if only you would have found a rag to cover that white fur of yours."

"By Helfa..." the other priest mumbled, rocking on his knees and swaying back and forth as he stared at Eilam. "Give me the blade so I can depart this unholy place of dark magic."

Enosh let the man's arms fall forward and handed him a fresh blade, but his eyes remained locked on Eilam. "As you wish."

The daybed shook.

My gaze snapped to Eilam, who trembled beside me as he watched the priest slit his wrists. It truly upset him, didn't it?

A flutter of hope.

Would he give in?

We had four more left...

"You knew she carried my child." Enosh stepped up to us and, with a flick of his hand, let a leather shape on Eilam's crotch. "Give her your breath."

"I did not know what it was when she died, not that it would have mattered." Eilam leaned into me, bringing his eerie eyes so close to mine, I stopped breathing, if only to remind myself that I no longer needed air. I was dead. He could take no more from me. "Her life was twice forfeited. Once stolen."

I lifted my chin no matter how it trembled. "I just want my baby."

Perhaps I imagined it, but his eyes appeared to slip to those lips he'd once kissed, letting the hairs rise along my arms.

"Enosh, did you know that our brother kissed your wife?" Yarin blurted, letting my husband's jaws clench with such force his ears twitched. "Ada, how bad was it?"

I looked straight into Eilam's pitch-black eyes. "Clearly so terrible, I died from it."

Yarin laughed.

Enosh did not.

"Strange creatures," Eilam said, seemingly unfazed by it all. "Women. So different from us."

Yarin leaned back into the daybed. "At long last, you took notice."

"Give her... your... breath." At Enosh's growl, all those soldiers who'd lost their lives stood and turned toward us, stares abandoned, sending a shudder across my chilled skin.

"Or on my word, I shall kill every soul I come across until you restore her."

"I do not think you will, Enosh."

"You are not powerful enough to stop me."

"From the moment you have claimed your first death of the day, I have been watching, listening." A strand of Eilam's hair fell forward, scenting the air between us with crisp breeze and lavender. "No, I am not powerful enough... but your wife is. And stopping you, she will. Already she has... doubts."

"So certain, brother?" Yarin asked. "All it takes is one whisper."

"As I recall, our brother has no want for your illusions. No, he longs for... unadulterated love grown from her uncolored inclination. Tell me, Enosh, how much will she love you once the first house collapses onto a child under the weight of corpses? How many whispers will it take to dull her hate once a wave of bonedust suffocates a girl in hiding? Come to think, have you ever told her how many children died in the Soltren lands?"

When my gaze flicked to Enosh, my husband sunk his head —if in regret or to escape my judgment, I couldn't say.

"Children. So innocent. For a while." Eilam cast his judging stare over me, lifting a smug brow. "All this ordeal over a mortal woman, little more than an insignificant speck on our memory. Here one day, gone the next."

Insignificant.

A rush of hot blood itched beneath my skin, tossing me into the biting throes of rage and utter despair. He would not do it. Would leave me behind cold. All because he... expected me to protect the innocent?

And what of my trapped baby?

Was it not innocent?

It was, and I refused to fail it again.

"You think I'll do you the favor and stop Enosh?" I leaned into Eilam, then a bit more when he shifted back, as though uneasy about my closeness. "Think again, Eilam, because right now, I'm very tempted to help."

Why did Yarin sink his face into his palm? Why did Enosh hiss? What did I do? Wasn't this what he'd wanted of me? To stand behind this?

"Will you truly help?" Eilam opened his palm, letting a wooden stake form there. "Show me how mistaken I am in my assumption, mortal. Of course, my brothers shall not interfere, guiding neither hand nor mind."

"What?" Gaping in shock, I looked at Enosh, who's eyes narrowed with concern, then back down at the stake. "If I… if I do this, you'll give me my life back?"

"A mortal's breath in exchange for yours sounds fair to me."

Without a moment's hesitation, I reached for the stake, letting my fingertips stutter over Eilam's palm before I closed it around the smooth wood. He thought I would give up on my child? That I gave a rat's ass about one measly soldier?

I rose and hurried toward the line of men. Positioning myself behind a gray-bearded soldier, I brought the stake to the man's throat, scratching it bloody with how my entire arm tossed under the strain.

Yarin grinned.

Eilam narrowed his eyes.

Enosh, however… oh, he looked as though he was only waiting for me to stab the man's throat so he could fuck me in the puddle of blood. Maybe I'd let him right after I did this. And I would; I could. For my baby, I could.

I gripped the man's hair.

I pulled back on it.

I pressed the stake against his throat.

The man screamed.

Thud.

The stake suddenly lay in the snow, clean and innocent and unused, all while my empty hand shook uncontrollably. Tremors wandered up my arm from where they invaded my core, making me twitch so hard, the world around me distorted.

Eilam vanished where he sat, the only remnant left behind was the sound of his words. "Point proven."

CHAPTER 20
ADA

Limbs, lifeless and heavy, tossed about where I sat on the horse in front of Enosh, scolding myself for my damn weakness.

If only I'd stabbed that man's throat...

After hours of self-imposed silence, I blew out a breath, watching it billow into a night colder than death itself. "You c-can say if you're ups-set with me."

Enosh wrapped what had to be our third fur tighter around me, but not even the King of Flesh and Bone could keep my teeth from chattering anymore. "How could I be upset about something that made me fall in love with you in the first place?"

His sweet words weren't helping my goal to rack up some of that wickedness he claimed I had little of. "Had I k-killed the man, I might be alive now instead of f-fr-freezing my arse off. We could ride to the high temple, kill all the p-priests, then fa-finally go home. I only ever killed damn fish, and they don't s-scream."

"Not to mention that injured bird you accidentally stepped

on as a child," he mused. "The one you once told me about... and had you in tears for two days."

"It made an awful popping sound." I rubbed the cold tip of my nose on the cape, pulling frigid air into my lungs in an inhale of courage. "Can I ask you something?"

"The answer is *many*," he said while stiffening behind me, clearly aware I'd wanted to know about the children beyond the Soltren Gate. "Caught in the outreaches of my anger and grief. A number you cannot possibly imagine."

But I was gaining an idea with every stray soldier or night-guard we met on our way to Elderfalls, for Enosh killed them all in passing. "Do you ever regret it?"

"Not for the reasons you would wish, Ada. To me, mortals are nothing but flesh and bone, sweat and scars. Being born only to die, so I may strengthen the bridges of the silent grave-yard that is my empty, empty home." A heavy sigh followed by what had to be the hundredth kiss of our journey right atop my head. "I know it is not what you wanted to hear."

No, but it was exactly what I *needed* to hear to gain clarity. "Are you still spreading rot for the children?"

"Ever since we left the Pale Court."

I twisted on the horse's back and stared into the blackness from which we'd emerged. Hundreds of corpses trudged behind us, gathered from one town, seven villages, and a tavern we'd come across by chance—where Yarin had chosen to spend the night.

Over a hundred self-murders.

Not a single glimpse of Eilam.

Enosh spared women and children wherever we went, focusing on soldiers, priests, and the occasional idiot who came at us with a pitchfork or shovel. Perhaps it was his way of showing me he truly wanted to be the man I'd asked him to be—for as long as he could.

The problem was, I wasn't sure if that was good or bad anymore. Bad, probably, for it chipped away that determination Enosh wanted to prove to his brother, and in turn, strengthening Eilam's belief that Enosh would be forced to stop.

Because of me.

I settled my hand on Enosh's where he held me by the waist. "Did you ever ask your brother to twist my thoughts?"

"On the contrary. I asked him many a time to leave them alone."

Because Enosh longed to be *truly* loved, just like Eilam had said. "Would you ever do it?"

"Not to gain your love."

He wouldn't have to.

Somewhere between the forest, death, and drowning, I'd fallen in love with this man against principle, peccancy, and precaution. Could no longer disguise lust for loathing, pleasure for pain, or even love for lunacy.

Enosh was complicated and cruel, yes, but he was not without his merits. Regardless of his twisted morality, he'd showed me more love, attention, and care ever since I'd crawled out of that grave than others had in my entire life. Killings aside, he tried hard to behave himself.

"To strip me of compassion, then?" I asked. "I saw how you looked at each other."

"I contemplated the necessity to have Yarin... flare your hatred for these mortals so it would not fall to me once more." Several hoofbeats shattered the drawn-out silence, until he finally added, "Of course, that was before Eilam tested your resolve. Easing you into a content bystander would have been easy enough, for a while."

I glanced behind me, finding his stare unusually dull. "A while?"

"Even the God of Whispers has limitations."

"Enosh, the woman at Airensty slit her own throat."

"She grieved her fallen husband and, from what I understand, had also recently lost a son. Has he not whispered into your mind in an attempt to rouse tender feelings for me, back when you still wore that pretty necklace—"

"It was a collar."

"So *pretty*. A shame it went missing. I might fashion you a new necklace, though less tight around your beautiful neck." His voice carried a hint of jest, letting me hear his grin even in the darkness. "Once his whispers faded, did you love me?"

"I hated you before and loathed you after."

"Precisely, and oh-so painfully honest." There was a hint of a laugh. "Eilam is now convinced of your wavering, counting that Yarin will reach his limitations before I reach the kind of devastation required to end this."

"You should have done it the moment Yarin showed up. Strip me of that damn compassion. Maybe then I would have killed the man."

"Two hundred years of lies, deceit, and illusions. I did not want to bring this between us unless necessary. Perhaps it was, but it is of no consequence anymore. At this point, all we have left is the hope that my perseverance will bring about his surrender before it brings about your renewed hate."

My throat narrowed.

We needed a better plan.

Because the longer I sat on this horse as a silent observer, the more people would die. At the same time, watching how Enosh turned the lands beyond yet another gate into a boneyard would only drive a new wedge between us. The worst part...?

It might *not* return our child.

That much, Enosh had made clear.

If I wanted my baby and to stop this killing, to finally gain some peace now that Enosh and I had grown closer, I had to convince Eilam that I would not stop my husband's vengeance. The fastest, most reliable way of going about that...?

Becoming the vengeance.

"We will find a solution," Enosh said, for he had probably sensed my unease, although we both knew that I'd turned this into an impossible situation when I'd threatened Eilam that I might just help, unprepared to follow through. "Until then, I shall gladly do the killing for you."

As though no dreamier words had ever been spoken, I curled deeper into his chest. "You are awfully romantic tonight."

But his ease around sending a bone spike through a stranger without even looking at him would make no difference—it didn't need to. I knew now what I had to do.

I had to become the Queen of Rot and Pain.

Beautiful and terrifying.

Gentle and cruel.

Starting with those who'd killed me.

My husband steered our mount toward the row of crooked fisher huts, which slept quietly beneath the new moon. Its light reflected on the snow crystals which crunched beneath each hoofbeat, having frozen into a thin sheet of ice atop.

The cold tip of Enosh's nose nudged my temple. "Show me where the man who did this to my wife lives."

"Two men. One's Rose's b-brother, Henry. I know his house, but not where the other one lives or who he is." To our right stood my old home, the door wide open and barely hanging on to its bottom hinge, with a dusting of snow scattered into the hut. "It's abandoned, and Pa is nowhere in sight."

As expected.

I'd never been a fountain of abundant positivity, but anyone with half a brain would know that Pa was likely dead. If not killed by villagers or priests, then by whatever had eaten up his lungs from the inside.

I pointed at the second house to the left of the brick well, the bit of smoke coming from the chimney proof enough that the bastard Henry was inside. "I don't want Pa to wander."

"We might find him yet," Enosh said and slowed his horse when the corpses scurried into the shadows surrounding Elderfalls. "The latest death count, Ada."

An odd wave of pride flooded my core, having counted every single one with Enosh's help. "Six hundred and twenty-eight."

He dismounted and helped me down, my legs stiff from the cold and hours on horseback. "Did he touch you, this... *Henry*?"

"Not that I remember." I followed behind him to the oaken door, many homes of Elderfalls abandoned or quietly asleep, aside from a hound that barked somewhere. "The other was the one who d-drove in the knife. But Henry c-came after me just the same, and threatened to deliver me to the priests dead if I wouldn't fo-follow him."

"I hate how you're shivering..."

Enosh kicked the door, letting its bolt break with a loud *chink*. The hound barked louder, adding howls to the song.

Groans and incoherent mumbling joined from the inside of the home, along with the familiar scent of salted fish. In the dim light coming from the poor excuse of a fire in the hearth, a figure struggled from a mattress of straw.

My molars pressed together. "Hello, Henry."

"What's this about?" Swaying from drink or sleep, or both,

he gripped the rough-hewn beam that supported some sort of hay mow sitting above. "Who are—" His eyes locked on me and he sidestepped, stumbling over his feet before he slinked behind a rocking chair, bringing wooden spindles between him and us. "You! You should be dead. I saw it. Saw you bleed out from your belly. No, no, no... you're dead!"

"I am." The same fate would await him. At *my* hand. A choice I had quickly made peace with on our way here. "F-freezing my tits off because of you."

I watched how the hollows beneath his cheekbones filled with shadows, making him look sickly and weak—not at all like the man with the felt hat who'd cornered me.

Now *I* cornered him, sidestepping, driving him toward his reckoning that was my deadly husband. Until Henry's gaze flicked toward the hay mow. And again.

"Someone's up there," I said.

"I know, my love," Enosh said. "*Boom-boom-boom* goes his heart, pumping liquid terror into his veins."

"Let me k-kill this one." The conviction in my tone died at another biting chatter of my teeth, extending itself into my arms as a tremble.

Enosh's eyes wandered to my quivering hands, then met mine as he shook his head as though to say, *"You will fail, further strengthening Eilam's resolve."*

No, I would not fail.

The thought of taking a life terrified me, but I had to keep my wits together. If I couldn't even kill those who'd brought about my death, then this would not end well. Would never give me my baby.

Now was the time.

"Give me a blade," I said to Enosh, and his brow arched. "What your wife wants, your wife shall get, remember? Your wife wants a bone knife."

Once again, that hungry glint flickered in his eyes as he opened his palm where the blade shaped, the handle carved with the same vines on my belly, offering a solid grip for my fingers.

"No! I… I… It wasn't me who—" A gag hiccupped from Henry's throat, eyes frantically darting between Enosh and the door. "Arne did it! My cousin drove the knife into you; I swear on my mother's grave. It was him! He's the one you want. He's up there!"

My heart gave a jolt in my chest. Head tipping back, I stepped away from him for a better angle, stomach going queasy.

Then I saw it.

Nothing but the red glint of embers reflecting from the edge of a rust-speckled knife. Its pointy end rested on a wooden slat, and a finger tapped the handle while the rest of Arne remained hidden in shadows.

Devil be damned, there was no way I couldn't kill *that* one. "That's the man who drove the knife in."

One quick step forward, and Enosh gripped Henry's face. He slammed the man's spine against the beam until the mow shook, letting threads of skin bind Henry to the wood as Arne scooted back into the shadows.

"Where is my father?" I walked up to Henry, pointing the blade at him. "What happened to him?"

"I swear, I did him no harm! Oh god. Oh, Helfa, help me!" Henry pleaded. "Rose! She brought the priests to him for coin, then up and left."

So that bitch wasn't even in Elderfalls anymore. "Where to?"

"Hogsbottom. Three day's walk, upstream."

"And the priests did what with my father?"

"Rose might know, but I swear, I know no more!"

Of no use to me anymore, then.

A thick swallow went down my throat. Heavens, I should have paid more attention to my husband's killing. Just how did one kill another? I brought the pointy end of the blade right beneath his navel.

Like this?

"Very painful, as you might remember." Enosh stepped up behind me, placing his arm around my belly and his whisper against my ear. "Death might not come for a day or two as he bleeds out, depending on the organs injured, poisoning himself from the inside with his own excrements."

"Painful sounds good." Yet, when the blade turned unnaturally heavy in my hand, I glanced over my shoulder at Enosh. "I don't know how to kill."

"Shh... Say no more." He stepped closer to steady me while his fingers reached for my hand that held the blade. "Like this, my love."

With his fingers closed around my wrist, he brought my hand to Henry's throat, pointy end aimed straight at the bobbing lump there. My focus scrambled, however, when Enosh lapped at my earlobe and pressed himself against me.

He was *hard.*

His cock rested against my lower back as he kissed the sensitive skin behind my ear. Quickening breaths tugged on the fine baby hairs at the nape of my neck, sending a wonderful shudder over my pebbled skin.

An indecent moan escaped me as though I wasn't about to stab someone. "You are depraved."

"Says the woman who raped me on my throne."

Now I had to grin a little. "I was cold..."

"Place your other hand on the butt of the handle, right here." He released his arm from my waist, took my other hand, and placed my palm onto the wide, smooth end of the handle.

"One hand holds it steady; the other hits the handle, driving it through his throat. Fast. Simple."

"I don't want fast."

Wanted him to suffer.

"So impatient, so deliciously stubborn." Enosh gave a teasing thrust against me, letting me feel the hardness and size of his hunger. "Fast leaves little room for doubt."

He had a point there. "Well, I guess one has to start somewhere."

I pulled back my hand.

My fingers stiffened.

"Don't help me," I blurted. "I have to do this on my own, so don't be the one making me hit it."

"I have not moved an inch."

A deep breath.

I am the Queen of Rot and Pain.

Beautiful and gentle.

Terrifying and cold.

My palm hit the handle.

The blade drove into Henry's throat.

Blood, deep crimson and warm, shot from the wound in quick intervals, some speckling my face. More of it bubbled from his mouth, only to drown his groan and drip down his chin while he slowly bled to death.

There. I was a killer.

I braced for shame, guilt.

None came.

Instead, my next breath expanded my lungs wider than ever before, sending a strange thrill through my body. Who would have thought killing was so easy? Making me feel so... alive?

Enosh clasped my chin, turning my lips to meet his in a

fiery kiss as a sudden breeze came in through the door. “Look at you, good girl, punishing the wicked for their crimes.”

I groaned into his mouth, mind spinning from all those tingles racing up and down my body, tasting Henry’s blood between the mating of our tongues. “It was too fast. Not at all what he deserved.”

“Ah, but my brother is rather troubled at the sight, nonetheless. Not bothering yet to come into his form, but too furious to contain how he moves the air.” His hips rolled against my backside, and not even the mink could hide how much harder he had gotten. “He is the mortal’s last expel of breath, the chill coming upon the room, and the gust shifting the atmosphere. Do you feel him?”

“I take your word for it.” I reached behind me, letting my gloved fingers follow the curved outline of Enosh’s length against all sense of decency. “What should we do?”

Enosh lapped at my ear. “Give death something to watch.”

CHAPTER 21
ADA

Enosh grabbed my shoulders, spun me toward the table, and brought my hands to its edge, commanding me with a squeeze to hold on.

My calves tensed as the mink hiked along the backside of my legs, its heavy weight settling onto my hips. "There's still one left."

"The mortal will wait his turn." He kicked my legs apart before the weight of his chest came down on me and, at my impulse to look back at the mow, his teeth clamped down on the side of my neck before he whispered, "Trust me."

Trapped beneath the hot weight of Enosh's body, I could only dig my nails into the rough planks of the table as he spit into his hand. A hand he brought between us a moment later, lubricating my cunt.

"Stay a while, brother. Watch how I fuck my wife in the blood of the man who did her wrong. The one she *killed*. Oh, how well she's done it, without even a gasp. Would you not agree?" One shift of his hips, and Enosh pushed inside me. "Lift for me, little one. Take me deep and fast."

Lost between the searing pain of heat against my stretching entrance and the rush of gooseflesh pebbling my skin, I barely noticed how he pressed down on my back. My chest hit the table and my arse lifted, letting the scalding pleasure of his next thrust prickle deep into my womb.

"Enosh," I moaned on an exhale, pushing back to take him deeper.

The table jumped beneath me with every rapid snap of his hips, every sharp sting as his thick cock rubbed along my cold inner walls. God or not, Enosh had no other choice but to fuck me so violently, chairs tipped and hit the ground with loud cracks.

And I wouldn't have wanted it any other way. Braced as well as I could, I ignored the pain for one guttural moan tumbling from his lips, two, three. At the fourth, a prickling sensation emanated from between my legs, throbbing and tingling as cold flesh did when held against a flame.

"Oh my god," I moaned, melting beneath this glorious heat. "I'm so cold. Faster!"

"A mortal's breath in exchange for hers." Enosh drove into me faster with staggering strength, letting his ungiving thrusts pin me between the feverish heat of his body and the tremble of the table as its legs moaned across the floor. "Is it not what you offered? Are you not true to your word?"

A wave of warmth lapped around my clit, bringing with it the foreboding sparks of heat that made my insides convulse. Enosh felt it, because his hips rolled against me in that way of his, letting his cock stroke and steer me toward my orgasm.

"Mmm, more," I moaned, needing him to set me ablaze, and I didn't care if a dead man hung his head tied to a fucking beam beside us. "More. More!"

"More." The word came out a dark growl as Enosh's grip

likely bruised my hip through the mink. "What my wife wants..."

He fucked into me harder.

Oh god, I was so close.

Only a couple of thrusts more, and—

"You helped."

At the sound of Eilam's voice, every vertebra along my spine stiffened and Enosh stalled, letting a mewl whimper from my lips that would have put a cat in heat to shame. "Now he has to show up? Now?"

With a chuckle, Enosh slung his arm around my belly and lifted me, letting me dangle with his cock up my cunt. Like that, he turned us around—toward where Eilam leaned against the wall—and lowered himself to the ground with me still sitting on his length.

"My wife does not appreciate your timing." Angling my legs and lifting my feet to each side of his bare thighs, Enosh spread me in the most indecent way, though a shred of mink dangled from my knees and offered cover. "As for helping... I steered neither tendon nor muscle as she hit the handle. Oh no." Rolling and shifting his pelvis beneath me, Enosh grabbed my hip and pushed me down. "My sweet Adelaide did that all by herself, determined to take back what you stole."

Eilam frowned at us where he stood bare, apparently with neither fondness for clothing nor care for the cold, his arms crossing in front of his chest. "You guided the knife to the mortal's throat. Positioned her palm on the handle. She would not have done it otherwise."

"Ah, so you have been watching us for longer than I thought, and still, you are mistaken. Mmm, let me consult with my wife."

Hand climbing to my throat, thumb pressing against my jawline to keep me looking straight at his brother, Enosh leaned back. When he straightened, he brought his other hand toward my face, dripping crimson from its fingertips. Henry's blood?

"Adelaide, would you have spared him and given up on our child?" Dark red fingers painted along my jawline, my cheek, and up toward the corner of my lips, the blood still wonderfully warm. "Or would you have driven the blade into the mortal's throat to let him bleed out like the retched soul he was?"

Eilam's black stare followed his brother's hand and how it slipped from my throat down, lower and lower, until it gathered the pelt of my train, each tug like a flush of energy spinning at my core. Surely Enosh wouldn't—

I gasped as Enosh pulled the mink up, exposing me so lewdly to his brother and how he set his finger at the top of my throbbing clit. "He can see."

"Shh..." He pressed down on the little bud, making me squirm and moan as he slid his other damp finger across my bottom lip as though teasing me to open and have a taste. "Tell me, brother, did she sound like this when you dared to put your lips to hers? Once this is over, you and I shall have a talk about the liberties you took when you touched my wife."

Eilam tilted his head, staring at how Enosh rubbed my clit, but his other body parts seemed rather disinterested in this erotic display. "Your arrogance is worse than Yarin's perversion. This will not end the way you hope, no matter your provocations."

"Not true to your word then, after all," Enosh said, taking his time to guide my pelvis into a circle while simultaneously pushing me down on his swollen length. "Little one, I asked you a question, and my wife always speaks true. Would you have pierced the mortal's throat?"

A sobering chill dripped down my spine, reminding me of

the fact that this was more than a fuck—it was a ploy and a terrible taunt. A mortal's breath in exchange for mine. That had been Eilam's offer, and I would damn well collect what I was due.

Against all remnants of modesty, I steered on Enosh's cock, relishing the thrill of this obscene moment with shocking intensity. I'd told myself I could be anything I needed to be for our baby.

I only needed to be one thing.

The Queen of Rot and Pain.

"No, I wouldn't have pierced his throat." I rolled my hips faster, because queens took whatever they wanted, and I wanted Eilam to see that I could be as terrible as my husband. "I would have stabbed him in the belly. Make a damn mess of it, probably, leaving him to squeal like a sow."

Eilam pushed himself off the wall and slowly padded over on his naked soles, squatting inches from my foot with his impressive but rather limp cock dangling from a thatch of snow-white curls.

The moment his torso shifted forward, bonedust rushed from all directions, forming dozens of spikes that levitated before Eilam's face.

"If your toe as much as stubs her ankle, we shall have to delay this disagreement, for I will make you believe you are dying a million gruesome deaths, over and over again, for the next decade." Enosh breathed so heavily behind me, I heard the air suck through his nostrils. "Now, stand by your word. A breath for another. Do it!"

Eilam raised his gaze and shifted his weight onto one leg, taking a long look at Henry. Then his black eyes returned to me, so void of any color, but it was the lack of conviction on his face, the blatant indifference, that made me shiver in his presence once more.

Whatever he saw, it was neither killer nor queen. Beautiful and kind, perhaps, but not nearly as cruel and terrible as one needed to be to survive among monsters. Certainly not among gods.

But I lifted my chin, refusing to flinch under his persistent stare. Perhaps I was no queen.

Yet.

But over the course of two months, I had been held captive, stripped of all decency, made a deal with the devil, died, and had my soul shackled so I could grieve the loss of my child.

I was no longer the woman I'd been.

Neither worthless nor insignificant...

... but a queen in the making.

I placed my hand onto Enosh's, guiding the size of the circles his fingers drew around my clit, the speed at which he teased the little bud, and the pressure he applied.

Enosh groaned, letting the masculine sound rumble against my shoulder where he kissed, sucked, and nibbled. He thrust upward, lifting me ever so slightly as I rocked back, driving him deeper into me, then forward toward his dusky sac.

"Second to none," Enosh whispered into my ear, fighting hard to keep his rhythm as he neared completion. "Made for me."

This much in control over our movements, I bucked against his fingers, letting them drum the sparks in my lower belly into roaring flames. Once again, they scorched across my entire body in one terrifying wave of heat and pleasure as his brother watched.

Instead of allowing myself to succumb to it or the way Enosh's hips first stalled then twitched, I leaned back against my husband's chest. Bracing against it, I reached behind me, letting cold fingertips climb the floor.

Wood.

Wood.

Blood.

Wet and thick, it had created a puddle beside us. I swirled my fingers through it, then leaned forward toward Eilam as Enosh sent spurt after hot spurt of seed into me. With a quick swat of my hand, I sent speckles of crimson across the god's face and into the white of his hair.

"A mortal's breath in exchange for mine." I brought my bloody fingers to my lips and stroked them into my mouth, letting the blood of the man who'd aided in my murder spread slightly salty across my gums. "You still think I will stop my husband? Dear brother-in-law, you need to start worrying about who will stop *me*."

Eilam neither blinked nor said a word.

Only faded away.

My bloody hand dropped to my belly, shaking from a rush of rage and vigor alike. "He doesn't believe me."

"Doesn't believe you?" Enosh chuckled behind me as his fingers tugged on my braids, opening them up. "Eilam hates coming into his form with such intensity—decades pass between the occasions. Twice, he has come into his form today. You know what he hates even more...? Not having the last word. Little one, you made him *furious*."

"I did?" My chest lifted with an inhale of renewed determination. Enosh knew his brother a great deal better than I did, so I had to take his word for it. "You can't help me next time." Strange how the mention of my next murder brought not even a quiver to my fingers as I glanced back at Enosh, gulping down Henry's blood. "The next time, I want to look like a queen."

Enosh rose and slipped me off him, gingerly brushing the

mink of my dress down. "No, Ada, you shall look like a goddess, with a crown upon your head like none before."

No, not a crown.

Not until this was over.

"Make it a tiara." I spun around and pointed up at the mow. "Using his jawbone."

"That can be arranged." Enosh shaped breeches around him as he stared at the mow, where strings of braided skin writhed and slithered, lowering a bound Arne down from it. "Between us, mortal, I have fantasized about many a punishment. Oh, so torn was I between all the possibilities of how to make you pay for what you have done to my wife."

I watched how the grayish-brown vines of skin stood Arne up, the veins on the white of his eyes bright red and visible even in the dim light. "Let me do it."

"No, Ada." Bone knife already shaped in his hand, Enosh cut Arne's nightshirt, laying the trembling man's torso open to the cold. Enosh set the pointy end of the blade against Henry's stomach, an inch above his navel. "I swore to avenge you. And little one, *this* mortal is mine to punish."

Instead of driving the knife into the bastard's belly with a turn as he deserved, Enosh gingerly cut along his skin with the precision of a bricklayer. One long line from navel to the hem of the cotton trousers.

It didn't bleed. Barely.

Arne trembled, throwing himself forward, only to bounce back at the mercy of hair strings tied to the wattle in the walls to bind him in place. "Please... it wasn't me. Rose killed her!"

"Liar," I scoffed. "But don't worry. She'll be next."

And if all worked out, the last.

"Shh... stop moving, mortal, or I might damage an artery." Enosh pushed one finger into the cut, then another, letting it rip open into an oozing gap as Arne stared down at himself, too shocked to even scream. "Death shall be your friend, mortal. But only until my brother shackles your soul, for you shall serve a higher purpose. An honor, truly."

Enosh pulled back, his fingers hooked around... something. Intestines? Yes. Oh, that was even better than stabbing.

Pale pink and streaked with blood, Arne's guts emerged from the hole in his stomach. The rippled organ lowered to the ground in sheer never-ending length—one foot, two, three... oh, goodness. It eventually changed shape and turned a grayish-brown, covered in a layer of mucus.

Enosh gave a little tug.

That was when Arne screamed.

"See, mortal, you shall remain alive like this for a while, watching your sustenance turn to shit." Enosh stepped back from the tangle of guts on the ground and haphazardly wiped his bloody hands on a nearby rag. "Terribly painful, dying of a wound from the belly. Even more so if something tugs on the organs."

"Disembowelment. How lovely." Yarin leaned in the doorframe, and I only now noticed the commotion outside as corpses chased people from their homes, filling the night with their screams. "You wife's thoughts told me you are in need of me?"

"Only after a few hours of suffering, so he may reflect on what happens to those who dare touch my wife."

I nearly moaned at the violent possessiveness. "What will you do to him?"

A smile came to Enosh's lips, not as rare as they used to be but all the more stunning to behold set into my husband's perfect face. "He shall warm my wife as we ride for Hogsbottom. But first..."

A shaggy, mange-infested dog stepped into the house, its body covered in festering wounds, its eyes milky white. The dead beast immediately bit into Arne's guts, tugging without ripping, letting the man jolt from his state of shock and scream.

Oh, how he screamed, and squealed, and shrieked, but the ear-stabbing sound soon muffled behind a gag of skin that wrapped around his face—a sight that brought another rotten smile to my face, just as my title commanded.

"The sun is nearly coming up. We shall spend the day here so you may warm yourself by the fire." Enosh rubbed his palms up and down my arm. "Traveling by day will only get us seen and cause surrounding villages to flee. This woman who knows of your father might get away, so we shall ride there tomorrow night and find her in the morning."

Yes, we would find her.

Then, I would kill her.

CHAPTER 22
ADA

"The one with the fish cages stacked beside the door." Sitting astride our horse upon a hill, I pointed at the house in the valley before us near the forge, the wattle and daub freshly whitewashed, the roof neatly thatched. Pretty. "She should be in there."

As requested, Enosh had once again dressed me for the occasion. This time, my husband had outdone himself with a dress of feathers, the bodice swan-white, then turning grayer and grayer down along the train, only to end in black plumes and a fringe of soot-covered fingers.

Courtesy of Henry and Arne.

The house we'd stayed at had been low on wood, and my husband proved quite incapable of finding more in the forest. His solution? Let their parched bodies climb into the hearth, feeding the flames as he continuously restored their bodies.

Enosh cast his gray eyes over the powdery-white village, his cape of crow feathers matching the train of my dress. "Unless the farmer lied."

"You'd be surprised how merrily people turn against

strangers." As Rose had done with me, and as I would do with her. "What if I want her in your throne like the others? Will you do that for me?"

"I will not."

My gaze shot over my shoulder at him, finding a lopsided grin that tugged on the corner of his mouth, playful in a way I'd never witnessed before. Was he... trying himself at humor?

I stretched my arm out, warming my black-gloved fingers on the seven-foot flame a soulbound and gagged Arne so kindly provided beside us with his remaining body parts as I tried to decipher my husband. Enosh looked younger like this, carefree, lending him an air of mortality.

I arched a brow, twisting further in the saddle to ensure he saw it. "How was that? Your goal to gain my heart remains unchanged?"

A single, breathy laugh burst from his throat. "Negotiating with a god once more, that mortal woman who has neither patience nor a shred of obedience?"

"You prefer me that way." My cheeks bunched at the playfulness between us, the familiarity we'd grown around each other. "Rose in your throne in exchange for an inkling of love."

"As though your chest is not full of it already, fluttering so nicely between the beats of your heart for me to sense and revel in." For a moment, he lifted his chin by a haughty inch the way he'd used to, but I saw the twitch on his cheek, the teasing twinkle in his eyes. "My throne is rather crowded at the moment, but are you not my Queen of Rot and Pain?" He stroked a strand of my hair back, twirling it around a joint on my jawbone tiara, letting the veil of teeth strung on threads of skin at the back *clank* at the motion. "Once we return home, I shall fashion you a throne beside mine... right after I have made a cradle. Decorate it as you please."

"Her head in my throne, and her legs, drumsticks for my child to play with."

He dipped down, letting his lips warm mine in a gentle kiss, followed by a quick nuzzle of my nose. "What my wife wants, my wife shall get."

Willing our horse into an unhurried walk, he followed a narrow trample path that led into Hogsbottom. Smoke lingered between the quiet homes, mingling with the wet fog of the early morning. How strangely narrow all this seemed, walls creeping toward me as though I no longer fit into such a place.

Somewhere, a creek prattled underneath a thin sheet of ice, coming together with the *ca-lops* of hooves hitting the cobblestone cleared of snow. Until we came to a halt by the fish cages.

An old man leaned against a stable with a pipe hanging from his mouth, puffing into the air as he squinted at us. If he were smart, he would stay just like that.

Enosh dismounted, glancing around and assessing our surroundings as he helped me down. "You are still determined?"

My gaze went from the snow gently rolling from the roof, to the breeze tugging on the naked twigs of a shrub, to the gentle flutter of the feathers on my dress. Was Eilam watching?

"More than ever before."

Arne might have driven the blade into my belly, but who had taken my help only to betray me? Who had chased her brother and cousin after me like hounds? Who had sold out Pa? Who had set this entire mess into motion?

Rose.

Beneath the unholy hate quivering in my core and the determination to end this once and for all, I had neither capacity for doubt nor pity. I wanted her dead with an urgency, and I might just kill her like I'd done with Henry.

Fast. Simple.

Get on with my life.

Literally.

At my gesture, Enosh kicked the door in, letting out a swath of heat that lured me toward the crackle of flames and the screeching of chair legs over wood.

With unbending resolve, I stepped inside the home, only for shock to paralyze every single muscle in my body. My joints locked. My mouth gaped open. My temples throbbed with the echo of my foolishness.

There she stood, peachy-cheeked Rose, scrambling back like the rat she was until her back hit the wall so hard the baby gave a warning cry.

The one in her arms.

I swallowed air, my eyes so fixed on the bundled-up babe that I barely registered how her husband lifted a chair before his chest as though it would offer protection. Curse me, I'd forgotten all about the fact that she'd been pregnant back in Elderfalls.

No, not exactly forgotten.

I'd simply worried so much about my own child and it hadn't occurred to me once that I might find her with a baby in her arms, its dimpled cheeks red from the generous heat in the hearth.

Should that deter me?

Enosh must have worried so, because he kicked the door shut, then placed his heavy hand on my shoulder, giving a sobering squeeze. "Is this the mortal woman responsible for your death?"

Lips trembling, tears streamed down her cheeks as Rose's eyes flicked to her useless, cowering husband, who mumbled prayers, then back to Enosh. "I… It was my brother's idea, my cousin who held the knife. I swear, I—"

"Mortals swear a great many things, though few of them prove true." Enosh gave the onsets of trembles on my fingers a concerned side glance, then straightened and jutted his chin toward Rose's husband. "Give him the child, for I shall remain true to my vow and punish those who have brought misery to my wife."

"No, please!" Rose clutched the baby to her chest, letting it startle and flex its chubby arms from the woolen blanket with another warning cry. "Please, I... ask of me whatever you wish but... please, my baby needs me."

Enosh smacked his lips. "Yet another conundrum, for my baby, too, needs its mother. I shall not place yours above mine."

When Enosh extended his arms to take the child and shifted forward, I stepped in front of him. "No, I need to be the one."

I had to do this.

On my own.

"Very well." Enosh let the same blade I had used to kill Henry shape there in his open palm, my husband's forehead wrinkling with a dozen justified doubts. "The wind picked up when we arrived."

"I know," I said when I took the knife, the handle somehow going slick and damp in my grip as I looked at Rose. "Give your baby to your husband."

"No..." Rose whimpered, holding it tighter as she sniffled and cried until snot drooled onto her upper lip. "Oh my god, Helfa, I just wanted a better life for me and my baby instead of fish stew every damn day."

My stupid stomach clenched as though recognizing the hunger pains any fisherman's wife or daughter experienced whenever the damn beasts wouldn't bite. But only until I looked around the house.

Fragrant, golden straw poked from the linen on the mattress, a fire that burned away throwing barely any smoke into the room, and a fat cured ham hanging from a rafter. Oh, she'd made herself a nice little home, indeed.

With the coin from the priests.

I took a strong step toward her, gripping the handle of the blade tighter. "You sold out my father. Where is he? What happened to him?"

At my questioning, Rose's feet slowly slipped out from underneath her, and she sunk along the wall until she pooled into a puddle of cries on the floor. "They t-took him. Said he'd be useful to the high priest, paid me a handful of c-coins, then put him on a mule. Elisa... Adelaide, please... look at my baby." Before I managed to focus my gaze elsewhere, she turned the little thing, showing me its stubby nose and flakes of white on its chin from when it must have spit some milk. "Look at my... my baby."

I did look.

God help me, I stared down at the baby, its eyes hazel-brown. A handsome thing, with chubby cheeks, full lips that rooted for a nipple, and a thatch of brown hair poking out from the blanket draped over its head.

A heavy weight came over my chest, so overwhelming I squatted before them. If I killed Rose now, this child would never know its mother—just like I had never known mine.

That ached me.

For a moment, I might have contemplated to spare her. There were plenty of other wicked souls out there I could kill to show Eilam that I had meant what I'd said. Maybe.

Until the god took shape right beside Rose, ripping a startled yelp from her but leaving her no direction to flee. Trapped between walls on two sides, the bare god to her left, and me in front of her, she simply folded her arms over her baby.

'*Ada*. His voice filtered not into my head like his brothers, but rather, into my very core. *Will you truly rob a babe of its mother? Condemn it to grow up without ever knowing her embrace when it scraped a knee, or the sound of her voice when she sings it to sleep?*'

"Shut up," I mumbled, probably sounding like a madwoman, rambling to myself like this, and perhaps I was because the weight of the knife tripled as though I truly wanted to spare that bitch. "You think this will hold me back?"

It couldn't.

Not with how Eilam sat there with that smug smile all the brothers seemed to have inherited from whatever hellhole birthed them. All this killing would continue if I succumbed to doubt now. All those corpses out there...? They would have died for *nothing*.

Was this not better?

To kill one, yes, but spare the rest?

Did that not make me a hero?

Besides, what if I failed now, and Eilam would go back on his offer? What if he didn't? I couldn't bring myself to kill someone less deserving of punishment than this woman. What if Enosh would wipe these lands like he'd done before? What if—

'*Ada.*' Eilam's voice had my nostrils flare and my molars grind together. '*Think of the baby. The innocent boy—*'

"Quiet!"

Rose startled so hard at my shout that the baby shook in her arms. One warning wail, and another, then the boy started to cry with vigor. Tiny red veins popped up all over his wrinkled face, chunky fingers clenching and unclenching.

"Shh..." On instinct, I reached my hand forward, hushing him, wanting to pick up this boy and hold him against me.

Rose pulled him away from me.

Did what I had wanted to do instead.

She lifted the boy's head to rest in the crook of her neck, rocking him, swaying him, comforting him, hushing him. All the things I wanted to do with my baby, she did right before my eyes... The woman who had cost me the opportunity to do so.

For eternity.

Hot and biting, anger carved itself into my beating but dead heart, letting my fingers tighten around the blade. Why did she deserve to hold her baby and I did not? What had I ever done to anybody to be denied hushing my child? Why would I deny myself, when all this could end with a single stab?

I'd done it before.

I could do it again.

Just one more time.

For my baby.

For the *world.*

Eilam cocked his head, brows furrowing. '*Have you no heart, murdering—*'

"I told you to shut up." With a swipe of my hand, I lashed out at him. The blade cut across his collarbone before tearing open his neck, letting rivulets of blood run down his bare chest no matter how he pressed a hand to the wound, staring at me in shock. "Take the baby!"

I'd only shouted it into the room, but Enosh immediately stepped up beside me. He leaned over with hushing sounds, plucking the screaming boy from Rose's arms.

Perhaps she would have gone after Enosh, if it wasn't for the ropes of skin wrapping around her, disabling all fight. Still, she tossed on her arse and screeched frantically, her face a mess of tears and auburn strands clinging to damp cheeks.

I leaned closer to Eilam while readjusting my grip on the

blade. "I might rob the boy of its mother, but I'll also make sure that many other boys will get to keep their fathers."

Or at least, that was what I told myself when I brought the blade to Rose's throat with one hand and let the palm of the other touch down on the butt of the handle.

Fast. Simple.

My eyes flicked to her belly.

Throat. Belly.

Throat again.

The next time my gaze dropped to her upper belly, a bone knife protruded from it, close to her lungs, its handle resting in the fist of my hand. How it had slipped so low, I couldn't say. Maybe the weight, maybe not.

I watched my hand turn, driving it in deeper until a wet cough called my attention back to Rose. Red-cheeked Rose, whose lips parted like that of a fish out of water, unable to take a breath under the flow of blood that gargled from her mouth.

"I am the Queen of Rot and Pain, beautiful and kind, terrible and cruel," I murmured to myself and Rose, then stared down at Eilam, who still held his hand pressed to a wound already closed. "Now give me my baby."

CHAPTER 23
ENOSH

I was ruined.

For eternity.

There she stood—my woman, my wife, my queen—with a wicked mortal bleeding out by her left foot and a stunned god sitting by her right. Yes, my little one had ruined me, for there could never be a woman beside me ever again but my Ada.

That made the premise of her resurrection as frightening as the thought of her renewed mortality.

"Her breath for mine." Leaning over, she brought the blade close to Eilam once more, then let the bone *clank* to the floor. "Or I swear I'll not just be a speck on your memory, but a lesson on what those strange creatures called women are capable of once they have nothing left to lose."

I rocked the crying boy in my arms like I had witnessed mortals do, loving the monotony of the motion, but I must have been doing it wrong for he kept screaming. "If you want her soul bound, we ought to call upon the God of Whispers."

"I changed my mind." Ada turned toward me while

forming a cradle with her arms, her features warm as she blinked down at the baby, yet a stoic, almost resigned strain came to her jawline. "Let me see if I can calm him. Shh..."

Tugging on the woolen blanket, I covered the child and lowered him into her arms, watching how she hushed him. How she gingerly stroked from his forehead down along the bridge of his nose, again and again, until... yes, it calmed him.

I committed the sight to memory.

So much to learn about babies...

Once his cries faded, Ada carried him over to a nearby cradle, like she would soon do with our child... if my brother proved true to his word.

The trembling, uttering mortal who swore he had no involvement posed no threat, so I strolled over to my brother. Oh, he looked positively shaken, unaccustomed to the pains of the flesh and taken by surprise by who had inflicted it.

Eilam rose, still bare, snarling down at his bloody hand. "Your wife dared to cut me."

"And if you refuse her once more, she *will* cut you again in places far more painful." I let breeches form around him, along with a plain leather jacket. "It is over. Stand by your word and give her your breath, or on my vow, I shall turn these lands into a boneyard and dance with my wife upon a carpet of skulls."

His lips twitched with renewed anger, so unlike his usual apathy. "At what cost?"

My stomach tightened.

I glanced at Ada where she stood by the cradle, rocking it with her knee while her bloodied hand rubbed over her dress. *Desperate to wipe it off.* But it were the abrupt movements that caught my attention. Was she resolved? Shaken? Were her muscles twitching from unbridled energy? I could not determine one or the other.

If the latter and my brother still refused, how would she

continue? What if my little one had fulfilled my brother's demand out of desperation? How much more death could Ada witness before she would distance herself from me once more?

I bit the inside of my cheek if only to keep myself from slamming Eilam against the wall for forcing me to yield some. "What else is it you want?"

A pout played around his lips. "Will you not guess?"

His damn balance. "Very good. Villages, towns, peasants... I shall spare it all until High Priest Dekalon is dead, the temples are destroyed, and the priests strung to Ada's tree. After that, we shall return home and be peaceful."

"I do not think so, Enosh." Eilam straightened, making him stand taller than me, if only by half a hand. "I demand you open your gates and return to your duty of spreading rot, cleansing the earth of all that once lived."

A small concession, considering that I had given this promise to my wife already and would see it fulfilled as agreed upon. "You shall have my promise."

"Not only that, but you will end your crusade against the temples and priests now, and your quarrels with them shall not cost another mortal life."

"Impossible!" Daub rilled from the walls, and the wooden planks beneath my boots creaked with how old bone in the ground writhed with my anger. "Each time I step foot into these lands praying to a false god, I will be hunted, captured, and burned, returning home to my wife and child eventually, yes, but charred to nothing more than cartilage and bone."

"Had you done your duty, it would not have come to this," he said in all his glorious ignorance, so oblivious to the hardships of being the *only* god bound to his form. "Time shall restore their beliefs and—"

"I vowed to have the high priest's head in my throne, and you will not take that from me. Brother, you will not. I have suffered pains you cannot possibly imagine, and I will have my vengeance on this mortal."

In no hurry, he stepped toward a wicker basket that stood on a stool, and pulled an onion from it, which he examined with utter fascination. "Choose, Enosh. Your revenge or your wife. Now, before you question the value of my word once more, hear this." Onion tossed back into the basket, he turned to face me. "She shall have her breath regardless of your choice... but for how long can she keep it this time? Mortality is nothing but a sickness. She suffers it like all her kind, making this nothing more than one quarrel between brothers... of many more to come."

Bone shivered across the lands, ready to shape into a spiked rod to shove up his prick sideways. And while nothing would delight me more than to see him bleed out from his genitals, I willed it all to settle in the ground once more.

Oh, I hated him so.

Righteous, dull, celibate Eilam.

Unfortunately, his words made sense.

Decades, centuries, eons... As old as time, I had witnessed a great many crossroads, yet none had felt as significant as this one. I ought to think on this for a moment.

My Ada called me ill-tempered, and she was correct, for I was tempted to turn around, take my wife, and keep on killing. Eilam would be forced to return her breath eventually. Oh yes, he would restore my wife's life... after I'd either killed her feelings for me or eradicated the part of her I loved dearly.

And if we demanded her breath now while I refused to bow to his demands...? He would chase after her breath for eternity, and then I would chase after him to return it. Armies of corpses, beheadings, bloodshed, gods at each other's throats...

There would be no peace.

Only hatred and revenge, both of which I had sworn off for

it had cost me my wife and child once before. I could not let it affect my family a second time.

"Give her the breath of life and, on my word, I shall do as you ask. I will revoke my vow of vengeance to the high priest." For my wife and child, I would do this, so they would be alive and well within our home. "However... you will promise not to take her breath again should anything ever happen to her."

Eilam shrugged. "It leaves her soul fragile just the same."

"Her soul shall be of no concern to you, so as long as you leave her breath alone," I said. "Do you promise me this?"

His eerie black eyes took me in for another moment before he gave a curt nod. "We are agreed."

I turned away and walked over to my little one, stepping up behind her with a kiss on her shoulder. "My love, are you ready to receive the breath of life?"

She stared at the sleeping boy for a moment longer, then turned just as her lips struggled up a weak smile with the oddest answer. "We need to ensure he's taken care of."

"Gold coins take care of mortals, I have learned." I clasped her chin, bringing those bright blue eyes up to meet mine. "Are you well?"

"No," she said in all her painful honesty, yet a nod followed. "But I will be. Once this is finally over. I need this to be over, Enosh."

"Then come."

With my hand on the small of her back, I guided her toward my brother. At the same time, I extended my mind, commanding the dead to spread out and secure a path to the Pale Court. I had to protect her better from now on.

"Ada..." Eilam walked up to us, assessed my little one for another moment, then took a deep breath. "Cure her of any rot and decay, or she will come back to life ridden with foul sickness, and I refuse to take the blame."

Removing even the tiniest specks of corrosion from her form, I stroked her cheek, willing her muscles to ease and give where her shoulders wanted to stiffen. "Shh... it is almost over now. Take two deep breaths. One for you. One for our baby."

"Our baby," she said, then inhaled.

Inhaled again.

Nodded.

"Wait," I said when Eilam stepped closer, letting my arm clasp around Ada's waist while I cupped her face. "Any moment now, you will leave the prison of your death. I will be neither guard nor master, neither punishment nor absolution. Only your husband who loves you very much. The question is, what will you be? I need to hear it."

Say that you love me.

For a couple of breaths, Ada only stared at me, but understanding soon dawned on her as she mirrored my gesture and cupped my face. "And if I don't answer, will you keep me trapped in death?"

I forced a smile. "Facing the premise of losing you this very moment, I just might."

Ada smiled back and patted my cheek, thumbing the emerging stubble on my chin the way she did often and seemed to enjoy. "If that is true, then you don't deserve the answer until after."

That made me grin with its painful truth. No, I had botched our relationship once by wearing it down with old distrust, and I would not risk it again. Would trust she had found some love for me. That my little one would return to me. Always and forever return to me.

If not... well...

...I could always collar her again.

I gave her a nod. "Stubborn, obstinate, beautiful woman."

"Arrogant, cruel, annoyingly handsome god."

I placed a kiss to her lips, trying to taste the remnants of the vows she had given, the devotion with which she had once spoken them. "I shall ask you again once your heart beats on its own."

Eilam leaned slightly forward, bringing his lips close enough to hers that my jaws clenched, leaving but a sliver of air between them. Air which turned frigid, letting even my little one's breath billow. Eilam's eyes blackened further, seemingly turning into liquid tar.

I watched with sheer wonder, having never witnessed my brother's power of giving and taking life.

But only until all strength was sucked from Ada's form, as though she was nothing but a puppet with its strings cut unexpectedly, and I could not keep her upright.

Heart hammering in my chest, I caught her in my arms and pulled her against me. "Ada! Ada, what is it?" No reaction. Not even a blink. "What have you done to her?"

"This has never been attempted before, Enosh." Eilam frowned at my wife, observing her, and I could find no malice on his face so unaccustomed to hiding its emotions. "I presume she requires more life than I usually give, its force so strong that her form cannot endure as it enters her. You ought to... do it for her somehow."

"If it is strong enough to threaten her form, the same might be true for her soul, and we ought to call upon the God of Whispers," I said, then spoke into the room for Ada and the other mortal to hear. "Yarin, brother, you are needed."

Nothing.

No Yarin.

I mumbled a dozen curses before I tried again with more vigor. "Uncle Yarin, you are needed."

"Anything for my little niece or nephew. Ada, is that not what you mortals—" He stiffened while he still came into his form beside us, wearing nothing but breeches and one boot. "My, my, my... it seems as though I have missed all the fun. Whyever is your wife's soul spinning?"

"You ought to ensure that its chains remain intact while Eilam gifts his breath. It was strong enough that even I failed to keep her standing." When my little one shifted in my arms, I cupped her cheek. "Nothing but a fainting spell of some sort. We will try again now, yes?"

A heavy gulp tugged on her throat, but she nodded. "I'm ready."

Yarin stepped closer, bringing his palm to her sternum as his eyes narrowed with focus. "Let's get this on with. There is something I need to... finish."

When the air turned frigid and Eilam's eyes blackened once more, I braced against the violent force of his breath. It swirled around us, cold and biting, leeching all strength from my muscles, unleashing havoc on my focus as it tousled through my hair. Until, with a beat of entire stillness, as though time suspended itself for one breath, we all froze.

Ada sucked in a deep breath and stared at us as color flushed into her face, eyes frantically bouncing from Eilam to Yarin and from there to me. "Have you done it?"

I swallowed, extending my mind toward her as shock paralyzed my extremities. "I cannot say."

We had certainly done *something*.

Because I no longer sensed her bone.

No longer felt her flesh.

CHAPTER 24
ADA

Three gods stared at me as though they'd witnessed lightning for the first time, all while a rush of energy drove the coldness from my bones. It tingled in my fingertips, the roots of my hair, beneath my toenails. What was happening?

'Mistress.'

A jolt went through me at a woman's whisper, her voice utterly unfamiliar. "Who said that?"

Enosh lifted a brow at me. "Who said what?"

'Mistress, my mistress,' came in a cacophony of different voices from all around me, as though hundreds of people whispered in unison. *'Mistress. Let me come to you, my mistress.'*

'Mistress.' A man.

'Mistress.' A girl.

'Mistress. Mistress. Mistress.'

"Oh my god." I swallowed a gulp of saliva that had pooled beneath my tongue and wiggled off Enosh's arms, all while sweat pearled on my forehead. "Something's... something's not right—"

A billion thoughts flitted through my mind. Pictures of strange lands, the resonance of words I'd never heard before but understood nonetheless, how the sun and moon danced in a pattern through night and day... It all came to me, pouring into my head until my temples throbbed.

Worse was the pounding panic.

The one that didn't belong to me.

At least... I didn't think so, for it came not from within me, but right over there. From the mortal man. The rush of blood in his veins trembled the space between us, every change in his body like a language I understood.

The hot blood pumping through his arteries, that one clogged vein in his left leg that tore with hairline cracks, how the hairs at the nape of his neck lifted, growing, stretching, changing. I felt it all, and my brain tumbled inside my skull at the potential explanation for this madness.

I stared from one god to another.

They stared right back.

Eilam slowly tilted his head. "What... is... she?"

Exactly! What *was* I?

Alive, yes, with a heartbeat that quickened with every passing second and breasts that suddenly ached like they had in Elderfalls. A realization that brought a spark of joy to my core, but the confusion of this lingered.

In a movement too quick for me to dodge, Enosh gripped my waist, fell to his knees, and pressed his ear against my chest. There, he listened to the beat of my heart, presumably, only to stare up at me from wide eyes two beats later.

"A heart shaped to perfection, not a single out-of-tune beat." A tremble hushed over his bottom lip before he added, "I believe she is... like us."

Like them.

I swallowed more saliva as though I'd forgotten in death to

do that regularly. And did that not explain how I sensed the strong beat of the boy's heart, how his inhales scraped on the snot in his nostrils, and how his eyes still felt puffy from all the crying?

'Mistress.'

I flinched.

Yes, and that.

Eilam let out a hissing snarl. "Another atrocity."

"Do you truly believe we have created an immortal? A goddess in her own right?" Yarin eyed me up and down, a slow stroll of green eyes from tip to toe. "Presume there is only one way to find out."

His left hand gripped my hair at the back of my head until my scalp burned. The right one suddenly held a golden, tooled knife, which glistened in the light of the hearth's flame as it came toward my face.

"No!" Enosh shouted, reaching for the blade.

He needn't have to.

On reflex, I shoved Yarin's chest.

The God of Whispers flew across the room, hit the wall with a groan, then collapsed to the ground. Pieces of daub cracked from the wall, only to shatter into a puff of white dust until Yarin fanned a hand before his face and... giggled?

"I believe you are right, brother," he said and struggled himself up, brushing the dust off his breeches, but it was a lost cause. "Oh, I commiserate with you already. Good luck putting this one in chains."

Enosh frowned.

No doubt he might have considered it for a moment when I'd refused him my answer, but I might as well be above those things now and opened my hand.

"I need a knife." It shaped right there in my palm, plain and a bit... crooked. "Thank you?"

"My love," Enosh all but exhaled the words, "I did not put that there."

Oh my god.

Oh my god.

Oh my god.

Cautious excitement pooled in my belly. Taking a steadying breath, I clasped the knife and brought it to my other hand. One cut across my palm, the blade so sharp it didn't so much hurt as it burned. Blood percolated in the narrow wound, but not a single drop rose to the surface.

Because it closed too quickly.

Oh. My. God.

I was like them.

Terrible and cruel.

Beautiful and kind.

Perfect.

Exhilaration, fear, and confounded shock rushed through me. Until the ground shook, and a water jug stuttered off a wooden stand before it shattered on the ground with a splash. Only fear remained then, and I scurried into Enosh's arms.

Had I done that?

Beside me, Yarin staggered over the shaking floor as if on sea-legs, laughing more heartily each time he banged his head on a beam or cupboard. "Enosh, get your hysterics under control."

"It is not me, but her," my husband snarled, then he wrapped me in the calming embrace of his arms. "Little one, you ought to calm your nerves before you accidentally bury us beneath a wave of bone dust."

Everything shook harder.

I startled.

No, not me.

The boy did. With a cry.

That didn't calm my nerves in the slightest, driving my pulse until wood moaned somewhere. "Get me away from here!"

Enosh lifted me into his arms and hurried out the door, passing an Arne charred to bones before the house, then lifted me onto the horse before he mounted behind me and clutched me to him. "Shh... calm, little one, or bone will rip the ground open and pull the world into darkness."

"INTERESTING." Yarin paced before us in the snow, right underneath some dormant maples near the village where he had shaped us daybeds. "What about the mortals' thoughts near us? *How much longer until that lazy bastard shows up with the wood? She'll be a good girl and not tell anyone of what I've done with her. What if I'm the only one touching myself like this?* Do you hear them?"

"God's bones, no!" And if Yarin did, then no wonder he was the maddest of the lot of them. "Only the dead calling me mistress, but it's never-ending."

"Only Enosh's powers are yours to yield, then. Good. A goddess yielding the power of all three would be disturbing indeed."

"In time, their voices will be nothing to you but the constant patter of rain on a roof," Enosh said where he slouched beside me with a smile on his face, one leg draped over my legs and one arm behind his head for support. "Nonetheless, this is... I am still quite stunned, truly."

"Indeed. A woman undying for us to have for eternity." Yarin opened his palm, letting sand form there that moved like the waves in the ocean as a tiny wooden boat drifted on the rolling motion as though it calmed him. "I have a strong inclination to go looking for a bride to kill and resurrect. So many problems solved at once. If only it did not require... Eilam." Who had disappeared once more, leaving nothing behind but the echo of a growl. "Oh, this must vex him like nothing before. Where to now, brother? The temple?"

Enosh sighed. "I have given Eilam my word to abandon my vow for revenge and not let it take another life. In exchange, he agreed to never take her breath again."

"A fool's deal."

"Quite so, but I had not anticipated my wife to turn immortal." Enosh tossed himself up, plucked me from where I sat, and lowered himself back down with me draped over him. "None of us have. Our brother wants me... peaceful."

Yarin let the sand drift from his hand, but it never reached the snow and simply vanished instead along with the boat. "A shame. I would have loved to witness whatever you had planned for the high priest."

My shoulders slouched.

Why?

This was good, was it not?

I took Enosh's hand and placed it onto my belly. Resurrected into a goddess capable of growing our child, what else was there to want? And with Enosh forced to abandon his goal for revenge...? Nothing.

Except...

I tilted my head back and looked up at him. "What of my father?"

"I shall try to find him while I ride about the lands once more." Yet his long exhale let my head sink lower, right along with my hope of ever seeing Pa again. "Eilam also demanded that I open the Pale Court to all mortals again and ride the lands to spread rot."

That lured a snort from me. "As if that is for him to

demand. You promised me that a long time ago. And we still need that cradle!"

"Is that so?" A smug grin came to his lips, fingers clasping my chin to keep my gaze on his. "I daresay, wife, my promise came with certain... contingencies. Come to think, do you not owe me an answer?"

"I do."

I lifted my head, letting my lips search for his. They came together in an unhurried kiss as we pressed against each other in this moment of complete peace, where the world finally left us alone. Until the ground shook once more, nothing but a tremble at first, but branches moaned louder as our kiss turned heated with need.

"That is disgusting!"

Enosh and I broke the kiss, looked over at his brother, and found the god wrinkling his nose at a near-skeletal arm that pulled itself through the snow with the tips of its fingers.

"The dead must think you at great risk, little one," Enosh scoffed, but his hopeful stare betrayed the tension in him, the waiting for words I'd once refused. "Tell me, little goddess, what had you shake the ground just now, hmm?"

I brushed my lips over his, not in a kiss but a mingling of our breaths as I stroked my fingers through those heavy black strands of his. "And if I still won't tell you? You can no longer make me."

"Once again, you have not been listening, Ada, for I have *never* wanted to make you."

A moment of silent understanding passed between us, nothing but quiet and invisible flutters amongst two people who had fallen in love unbidden.

I nodded, letting my thumb stroke over his bottom lip only to feel its tremble. "I love you."

Snow fell from the branches of the maple as the tree trembled down into its roots, giving a moan that must have shaken the entire world for just one second.

"And I love you," Enosh said. "Will love you until time ceases to exist. I shall search for your father as I ride the lands, and I will find a way to bring him home."

How?

I'd only ever been to the high temple once as a young girl, but its high walls had left a lasting impression. It would be difficult for Enosh to gain access to the temple *peacefully*, and impossible to get Pa out alive.

And that was not the only problem.

"They will hunt you down, Enosh." Call upon every house sworn to protect the faith, quickly overwhelming my husband by sheer numbers. "Trap and torture you for who knows how long until you manage to free yourself. As long as the temples stand and the priests live, you won't be safe."

We wouldn't be safe.

His lips pressed into a thin line, hard and ungiving against my own as he kissed me. "There is always the God of Whispers to aid me."

"Have you not listened, brother?" Yarin asked. "I will look for a woman to wed and kill. Oh, our love will eclipse even the sun. As such, I ought not to tempt Eilam's wrath by aiding you, for I shall need him for my woman's resurrection."

"You will also need me."

"A conundrum indeed." Yarin sunk his face into his palm. "I would have preferred sisters. Less eager to quarrel for dominance. Prettier to look at, too, to be certain."

Which meant Enosh would be on his own against two hundred years of hatred. "What if I ride the lands with you? I could..." *do the killing,* "...help you."

"I would never allow it," he said as though he could keep

me from doing it anyway. "These lands are dangerous, and immortality offers no protection from pain. On the contrary."

Focusing on the age-old bone scattered across the lands, I let it drift together. Then, with one sudden blast, I let it clash against the maple, felling the tree with enough skill that the trunk split, groaning until it hit the ground and shook the daybeds.

"I can protect myself now." Just like Enosh had told me that he'd been created knowing his duty and how to yield his powers, I knew it as well. Felt it deep inside me. "That rabbit hopping through the snow earlier...? I made that."

I *made* that.

That word brought a smile to my face.

"Adorable." A kiss to my head. "But the answer is still no. The high priests have gone through much trouble to prepare for a confrontation with me. I shall secure the lands so you may enjoy them... eventually. Until I can guarantee your safety, you will remain at the Pale Court or move about safer lands, if that is what you take issue with."

The issue was that this still hadn't ended.

It would go on, and on, and on.

And I was tired of all this suffering.

His. Mine. Everyone's.

So tired.

I turned onto my side so I may look into my husband's calm gray eyes and stroked the rough whiskers along his jawline. "Do you think it's truly growing? Our baby?"

"I have no doubt, but only time will tell," he said and, when I sensed the corners of my mouth droop, he smiled and let his forehead drift down against mine, his next word a familiar whisper. "Patience."

Something eternity would surely teach me at some point. "As long as people pray to Helfa, our child might as well grow several inches each time they trap you somewhere. I don't want them to hurt you, Enosh."

He pressed a kiss to my forehead, then another, taking his time before he said, "Never lose faith that I will return to you. Always and forever, I'll return to my Ada, the midwife from Hemdale."

His Ada.

My heart fluttered.

"You sacrificed yourself for me once before. I won't allow it a second time." Would not let this world rip us apart ever again. "Let's ride for the high temple. *Together.* You will spread rot and open the Pale Court like Eilam wants in any case. And if that isn't enough for your brother, what can he do to me now? You might have promised him to abandon your revenge, but I made no such promise."

"Ada's crusade," he mused, and a smug grin tugged on the side of his mouth for just a second before he shook his head. "I presume my brother ought to have placed more care into his words, but the answer is no. I will not let you."

"I asked neither question nor permission."

"Headstrong, obstinate little goddess." He made a disgruntled sound at the back of his throat and pinched the bridge of his nose as though he'd just realized that no bone chain would ever *not* dissolve at my command. "Ah, Adelaide, my love for you might yet make me a liar."

"My love for you might yet make me a monster."

"We are all monsters in someone's story, little one," he said, then finally gave his nod of approval, "except in our own."

CHAPTER 25
ADA

I rode my dead horse toward the stone archway of the small temple we'd found in the forest, my beast's hide a patchy mix between chestnut and brown, and its rump in dire need of a tail. Alas, I hadn't inherited my husband's creativity.

"No! Helfa, oh please!" The young priest scooted his arse over the ground, letting his threadbare black robes rip as he frantically made the sign of Helfa. "Please, I beg of you, please spare—"

With a flick of my hand, I drove a bone dagger into his belly. He gasped at first but screamed shortly after when I commanded the blade to cut upwards into his lungs. His scream lodged in time with the severing of an artery. Warm and thick, his blood speckled the back of my hand.

A hand Enosh took into his as he rode up beside me. He lowered his lips to my hand, frowned, then wiped the blood off with the sleeve of his raven jacket.

"How finely tooled your dagger was." His lips pressed an ardent kiss to the back of my hand, then Enosh sat straight, letting our fingers intertwine. "Still, a spike through the neck is less messy."

"Enosh, I'm a midwife." I had worse bodily expulsions on me. "A spike through the neck is too fast, too painless. Did I ever say a word? No. You have your way, and I have mine."

"Quite so." Just then, he sent a volley of bone spikes into the necks of three other priests who'd tried to make a run for it, turning the temple grounds silent at once. "If memory serves, then the high temple should come into view at the end of this forest."

For two days, we'd cantered across the lands without stopping, killing every soldier and priest on sight. Temples, we'd torn down together, sending blasts of bone dust into the structures from two sides at once.

With the rising sun flickering through the pines and the last rays of the moon disappearing behind a chain of hills ahead, we willed our mounts toward the edge of the forest. And there it was, the high temple. It had grown over the years, spanning several stone buildings clustered into nothing but a fortress.

Enosh stopped his horse and pointed at the bailey rigged with what looked like massive crossbows mounted on iron blocks. Bolts sat in the grooves, large enough to kill a bear. Several fires crackled on torches along the battlements, where archers overlooked the valley below. Walls of wooden spikes, arranged in several rows to the left and right, lined the pathway heading for the massive gate.

"To catch corpses," Enosh said, looked behind him at our quiet army of the dead, then smacked his tongue. "It will take time to breech this and gain access to the interior of the temple."

"They sure built this to keep a god out." Yet one thing, they had not planned for. "But not a mere woman."

Dutiful and obedient.

Worthless and insignificant.

Enosh frowned at the plain dress I'd bartered from an herb witch in exchange for a mortar and pestle shaped of bone. Not a single embellishment on my woolen dress gave me away as more than a woman, and certainly, not more than Enosh's mortal wife.

In that lay my power.

The humor of it didn't escape me.

"You have anticipated this, have you not?"

"I've seen the temple as a child and knew that it wouldn't be easy for you to get in there. You'll be shot and set ablaze before you even reach the gate." I pressed a hand to my belly, circling a bodice reinforced with ribs of bone, the inside of the train that fanned out at the hips lined with bone chips. "Putting Pa at risk the moment you step out of this forest."

Enosh's hand curled tighter around mine, and his jawline hardened. He didn't want me to go in there, but what could he do to stop me?

Nothing.

"This is the fastest, easiest way for one of us to get inside," I said after a moment of brittle silence. "Perhaps I can negotiate my father's release. Or at least find out where they keep him. If anything, it'll draw their attention away from the gate. I'll fight them from the inside, and you'll fight from the outside."

His heavy sigh puffed into the frigid air until he brought my hand to his mouth for another kiss. "One scream. One billow of smoke. If I sense a single mortal in there draw a weapon, I shall let death overrun this place even while they set me ablaze."

"Sounds fair," I said, willing my horse back into a walk. "If I leave you anything to kill, that is."

Enosh's hand held mine until the growing distance ripped

our fingers apart. I rode toward the gate alone, a woman whose worth was determined only by the marriage she'd struck and the child she carried in her belly.

The two soldiers standing guard exchanged a look, then one of them approached with wariness in each of his slow steps. "Turn around, wretch. The high temple is closed for pilgrims until the King of Flesh and Bone has been recaptured. High Priest Dekalon's order."

When the other soldier tilted his head this way and that, taking too much interest in my dead horse, I dismounted and commanded it to turn and trot off. "From what I've heard, High Priest Dekalon asked for me. Is he here at the temple?"

"Aye, he is," the first soldier said, my pulse quickening with excitement. "What would he want with you?"

"Bring me to him." Of course, they chuckled at my words, the audacity of a woman making such a demand. But only until I said, "I am Adelaide, wife of the King of Flesh and Bone."

Both choked on their amusement, stared at me wide-eyed, then lowered their short pikes. One soldier glanced behind me, likely searching the horizon for signs of Enosh before he looked up at the battlement that had fallen into commotion.

"You see anything up there?" he shouted.

A metal helmet reflected the first rays of the sun from where it poked out from the barbican to the left of the gate. "Empty and quiet. Not a sign of him."

"I came alone." I took a taunting step backward. "Of course, if you don't want to admit me, I might as well turn around and—"

"Open the gate!" the first soldier shouted as he quickly rounded me, bringing the metal point of his pike close to my spine. "You'll walk straight up that corridor without making a fuss."

A corridor that opened up to the squeak of heavy oaken

doors on damp hinges, letting out an unexpected whiff of pine, so intense it scraped my throat. White marble lined the inside all around, woven with specks of gray and polished to a shine.

I breathed in too deeply, sensing my ribcage expand until the pike's point scraped at my dress, letting me shift forward into my first step. Dimness swallowed me whole, the corridor nothing but one poorly-lit straight line, with only a handful of golden fire basins lining it with great distance between them.

Strange.

Behind me, the door creaked shut, sending a shudder across my entire body. Only nerves. In five minutes, I had done what might have taken Enosh hours—accessing the temple so I may bring death to the heart of Helfa.

Ignoring the soldier's spiteful remarks, I walked along the corridor, counting the furrows in the marble across the floor and even the walls. Amber in color, they reminded me of honey, yet appeared as solid and polished as the surrounding stone. Precious glass, perhaps.

I extended my mind, letting it brush along the flesh and bone of nearby mortals. At least a hundred with considerable weight strapped to their aching muscles and calluses on their hands. Soldiers.

However, I couldn't sense Pa.

Nothing that would single him out, anyway.

Where was he?

"This way. Turn!" When the corridor parted, the soldier shoved me to the right, where it all slowly opened into some sort of round chamber. "Stand on the Sun of Helfa while you wait for the high priest, you bitch, and don't dare make a single move."

I positioned myself on the golden emblem set into the stone at the center of this high-vaulted chamber, right across from the wide dais with a golden chair sitting atop. The same amber-colored lines veined along the wall, pouring down to the ground where they came together at the gilded edge of the Sun of Helfa.

A glance over my shoulder confirmed that the other soldier had not followed. Unfortunate, considering how the bone beneath my dress quivered with the urge to shape into a dagger just for—

Someone was coming.

I didn't so much hear the footsteps as I sensed the motion in the man's knees, the strain along the muscles on the left and right of his spine as he approached.

He stepped out from behind a gilded metal screen of some sort that crowned the dais, rounded the golden chair, then stood at the edge of the first step. The way he stared down at me over his hook nose let the fire in the basin beside him reflect off his bald head, the man dressed in the white robes of the high priest.

"What a curious scenario..." He eyed me for another moment, then sunk into the red velvet of his chair. "Weeks of searching for the midwife from Hemdale called Adelaide, only for her to knock on my door? Light of hair, blue eyes..." His gaze trailed down my legs, then found mine again. "How do I know it is indeed you? Certainly, Enosh would not have allowed his wife to step before me, considering how eagerly he protected her."

"Obedience was never my virtue," I said. "Where is my father?"

His lips pursed, noisily sucking little gulps of air as his throat narrowed to the width of a grass halm, undoubtedly believing me now. "Why have you come?"

The vibrations of many soles pounding the ground drummed along my senses. He'd called in soldiers. Good.

Would've been a shame if there was nothing to kill in this chamber but an old man and the soldier behind me.

I widened my stance so my dress would better hide how the bone chips shaped into small daggers beneath it. "Like I said, I came for my father."

"And wherever might your husband be? The lords of the realm have their soldiers observe each path toward the high temple with cages full of doves in their tents. That none of them reached here with a message would mean you have truly come alone, leaving your husband and his army of corpses behind."

It also meant that I had to make this quick and hurry to find Pa. They hadn't spotted us in the forest, but the temple was likely sending doves out this very moment, commanding said soldiers to come here. A force we may be able to take on, but only together.

"Or it might mean that they're already dead." I grinned as I prepared a dagger just for him, the handle maybe or maybe not tooled with vines, but I sure tried my best. "I came to negotiate —something my husband has little interest in. Therefore, I came alone, but I will leave here with my father."

The echoes of boots slapping the marble resonated in the corridor. Sure enough, a wave of soldiers marched into the vast chamber. I counted around sixty. Dressed in mail armor and white tabards embroidered with the Sun of Helfa, they surrounded me with their hands on the pommels of their swords.

High Priest Dekalon leaned back in his chair and let his hands steeple before his chest. "Or perhaps you won't leave at all."

One after another, I gingerly shifted the daggers where they levitated above the ground, aiming them upward in the direction of sixty-one necks and one stomach. "Bring me my father. Let me leave here with him unharmed, and I will convince my husband to spare your soul."

"Would you listen to this woman?" His chuckle held more arrogance that Enosh's ever had. "You have a great many demands."

"My husband said the same."

A moment of stiff silence passed between us, then his pout took on the gut-roiling sway of a smile. "I am afraid I cannot agree to this. See, dear Adelaide, your father never stepped a foot into this temple, and instead, suffocated on his own blood on his way here. It is my understanding that the priests left him by the wayside. Unfortunate."

Suffocated on his own blood.

Left him by the wayside.

My heart shattered.

A sob built at the back of my throat, pressing painfully against my esophagus the harder I tried to contain it. An old man who'd never done anybody any wrong, and they'd just... left him without even a burial, wicked wayward mortals.

Beneath my dress, sixty-two bone daggers shook and trembled out of aim at the rage in my core, the utter disgust I held for these... monsters so sickening that—

No. I had to remain calm before the ground trembled, giving away what I was.

Except... everything remained still aside from the bone I carried on me, and that realization caused cold sweat to break out along my spine. My gaze flicked around the chamber, everything in here encased in polished marble.

Not a single speck of bone.

I took a deep breath, no matter how the sharp bite of pine irritated my airway. All the more reason to find my bearings and end this once and for all. No matter how meticulously they might have kept the bone out, I was about to make more available, anyway.

"My husband was right." Sixty-one daggers waited patiently for my command. The last one I slowly reshaped in the grip of my closed palm. "You're a terribly dreadful kind, full of wickedness and depravity."

The high priest grinned. "Capture her, and chain her to—"

Bone daggers cut through the wool of my dress, whistled through the air, then embedded themselves into the throats of soldiers. A cacophony of *thuds* and *clanks* resonated the chamber as they collapsed onto the marble.

I climbed the dais, gripped the high priest by his robe, and pulled him from his chair. "I won't ever wear a chain again, be it shaped of bone, iron, or the scrutiny of mortals."

His lips parted and clenched shut several times before he managed another word. "Adelaide, let me—"

"You do not get to call me that, mortal, for I am the Queen of Rot and Pain." One stab, and I drove my dagger between two ribs and into his lungs, so he may suffocate on his own blood like Pa had. "Kind enough to allow you a quick death, right before I tear down your damn temple and bury your bones beneath the rubble with the rest of you traitors."

Ransacked by trembles, he stared down at his blood-drenched robes, then lifted his stuttering hand onto the metal ring of the fire basin beside him until his flesh sizzled. "May H-Helfa save... save y-your soul."

He pulled on the metal.

The basin tipped.

Clank.

Coals rolled from it and skipped down the dais. They scattered across the chamber, over the amber glass—

Whoosh!

A massive flame shot toward the ceiling, so potent I let go

of High Priest Dekalon. He rolled down the dais, his body coming to a stop near the emblem as fire broke out all around him. It followed the amber lines, spread out in all directions from there, climbed the walls—

No, no, no...

I stumbled back as panic gripped my heart and squeezed the battering organ. That wasn't glass; it was pine pitch, dried into the furrows of the marble to set the entire temple aflame.

And me with it.

CHAPTER 26
ADA

My nostrils burned with the smoke quickly filling the chamber as flames came together into nothing short of an inferno. Worse was how the corpses littering the ground caught fire, skin melting to their faces like wrinkled leather—something they hadn't done for two-hundred years.

Enosh must have lifted his curse, but I commanded them to rise, regardless. If they tossed themselves onto the flames blazing along the furrows, I might be able to escape, but where to? The corridor I'd come from had been full of pine pitch and was likely already roaring.

Eyes burning, I glanced back at the metal screen, trying to blink it into focus against the violent heat that brought tears to my eyes. If I ran that way, what were the chances they hadn't poured the amber resin into the stone there as well? Small.

With a single thought, I commanded the corpses to throw themselves onto the flames back toward the corridor. At least there, I knew where I was going.

Obeying their mistress' command, they collapsed onto the

flames two and three at once. I sprinted down the dais and crossed pile upon pile of soldiers like bridges.

Bridges doused in oil and set ablaze, for the flames engulfed them too quickly. They blackened the train of my dress, singed my hair until its bitter reek crept into my nostrils, scalded along my arms until it blistered.

Pain prickled my skin like a thousand needles driven into my flesh at once, ripping several whimpers from me until the first scream wedged from my throat. A cough doused it, doing my lungs no favors as I heaved and pulled boiling air into my chest.

Was I going the right way?

Orange flames depleted the air as they frantically danced all around me, suffocating me, making my mind go blank. Floor, walls, ceiling... everything burned.

W-where is the temple?

Where...? Oh my god, which way lay the gate?

A sudden roar ripped through my focus as my dress finally caught fire. Dissolving one of the corpses into nothing but bone dust, I let it sprinkle onto me, extinguishing the flames. Another end of my train caught fire instead.

My chest heaved in tight convulsions as my legs gave underneath me. I collapsed to the ground, screaming in silent agony as the fire burned me alive, causing such havoc on my focus that I couldn't sense a single speck of bone. This was it. I would crawl out of here charred to—

Gravity shifted around me.

No, *I* shifted as someone picked me up, pressing me against the ungiving hardness of a familiar chest.

Enosh!

He said something, his voice nothing but deep vibrations against the roar of flames as I tossed in his arms. Darkness devoured me as he let something form around me, leather perhaps, shielding me from the worst of the flames while they certainly devoured him.

I jostled about, screaming against his chest as the heat continued to bite at my body. The pain was agonizing, but it had nothing, *nothing* on the shock of gnawing cold that suddenly drove its sharp fangs into my flesh. Were we... outside?

Enosh shook the leather off me, hushing me from lips black with soot, set into a face almost as disfigured as the day I'd died. He looked like the monster people made him out to be. But this one was mine, my god husband, who had gone through fire to save me.

"Soldiers are coming," he ground through his teeth, visibly in pain as he spoke. "The valley is too narrow to escape them easily."

Mind reeling, I only reached up, watching my fingers, charred to the first knuckle, cup his blistered cheek. "You saved me from the fire."

"I have told you I would stand at the center of flames for you and our child, have I—" Enosh stumbled, and everything spun once more before he sunk to his knees with a hiss. "Listen to me, little one. Gather bone with me as fast as you can from wherever you mind reaches and pile it around us, yes?"

It wasn't so much his words that instilled blood-curdling fear in me, but the tension in his voice. When I looked around the distorted landscape, I understood the urgency.

A frigid breeze numbed my face, amplified by the sight of mounted soldiers galloping toward us. Hundreds of them, maybe even a thousand. Their hoofbeats drowned beneath the roar of flames coming from the open gate of the temple, and smoke rose in raven-black billows from the stone buildings.

Chaos surrounded us, trapping us between a large army storming ahead, archers running to the wide arrow slits in the battlement behind us and chains of hills to our left and right. How could we possibly escape this without—

"Ada!" Enosh shouted, startling me out of my daze. "Bone. We need bone!"

Bone. Yes.

Against the panic in my chest and the pain of my burn wounds, I focused on whatever bone was in reach. Skeletal remains of rodents trapped between boulders, beetle shells hard enough to break through the frozen ground, the corpses inside the temple... I gathered it all, letting it drift toward us like a snowstorm.

Arrows whistled.

One embedded itself into Enosh's upper arm, ripping a grunt from him. More followed, thudding into the snow all around us as the hoofbeats of too many horses shook the ground on which we kneeled.

"Enosh," I whimpered, fearing immortality more than I had ever feared death. "They're closing—"

He threw himself atop me, ripping me to the ground with a hiss. Another arrow must have struck him somewhere with the way he flinched, and again, curling himself around me.

"When I say now, you blow the bone in all directions at once with as much force as you can!" His command was harsh because it needed to be, yet I sensed how his fingers stroked along the back of my head, offering comfort as he pushed me into the snow. "Wait."

Pressed against the ground like this, I couldn't see much. But I didn't need to. I heard the sharp *thuds* of arrows puncturing the ground, sensed each flinch when one struck my husband, and felt how the beat of hooves bore all the way into my heart.

When the bone around us trembled, barely distinguishable

from the snow, Enosh stroked my head with more fervor. "Patience, Ada. Patience."

He jerked once more.

Another moan.

"Wait," he mumbled as though he'd sensed the panicked rage build in my core, the brutal urge to kill all those out to hurt us. "Wait. Wait. Now!"

It emerged as a cry toward the gray clouds, the energy that thrust the bone we'd gathered into all directions like a deadly tidal wave, rippling on the surges of my rage and grief.

Trembles ransacked my entire body, stiffening my spine to such a degree, not even Enosh could hold me down as the surge of bone ripped through the line of soldiers.

Like a powerful gust, it threw everyone and everything back, lifting horses off the ground only to let the beasts collapse several feet away. Some of the spiked walls blew across the field, lancing soldiers and horses alike, leaving them to wiggle and squeal.

My chest nearly burst with glee.

The army was... gone.

Whatever was left screamed and wailed, but a loud rumble soon overshadowed it as parts of the bailey broke off with a deafening boom. The crumbling stone ripped the archers down, burying them and their pestering arrows beneath it.

A smile ached my cheeks.

The temple was gone, too.

Nothing remained around us but severed limbs, chaos, and a few soldiers who walked about the field of slaughter disoriented. But not much longer.

I struggled myself onto my wobbly legs and lifted my arms, my voice a mere whisper but the dead heard it just the same. "Rise."

Soldiers pushed themselves up to stand, screaming in

panic and confusion as their limbs moved at my will, their souls mere onlookers that would depart soon enough.

"Kill them," I said. "Kill them all."

They spread out like a mischief of rats, cleansing this place of its remaining depravity.

I kneeled back down where his upper body swayed, where he sat with at least five arrows protruding from his back. "Enosh."

"Cannot die," he murmured as he strained to lift his head, his face still badly burned, his lips black with soot and crimson red from the blood he coughed up.

"I'm so sorry." For how I, one after another, pulled the arrows from his flesh, sending jolts and grunts of pain through him. "You'll heal faster like this."

"You have done so well..." Enosh wrapped his blistered arms around me and pulled me against him. "We will... rest here for only a moment, little one. Only... only a moment. Then we will go home."

Home.

To our Pale Court.

Nodding, I allowed myself to go slack against him, only now noticing my badly burned legs, not a shred of wool left around them. No, he was right. We needed to heal before we would return home.

So there we sat for an hour or two or forever, a god and a goddess mending in each other's embrace. Perhaps he was the liar. Perhaps I was the monster. I didn't care.

Neither did love.

CHAPTER 27
ENOSH

A few months later...

"You are counting, yes?" Kiss after kiss, I pressed my lips to Ada's swollen belly where she lay sprawled out naked in the grass of her garden.

Until something pressed back.

I jerked upright, barely able to contain the nervous excitement in my veins as I watched for more movement. Ada had told me how our child had begun to stretch in her womb, sometimes showing a hand, other times a heel. Always when I was out to spread rot.

Ada lifted herself onto her elbows and grinned. "Did you see it? Because I felt it."

"Sensed it against my lips," I said, my eyes fixed on her belly with rapt attention. "I am starting to wonder if I will ever—"

There!

What had to be a foot so small pressed against her belly from the inside, lifting the skin before it sunk back down. My child poked a limb up from the other side instead, letting Ada's stomach ripple and shift with the movement, filling me with wonder.

Here I sat, a god undying, who sensed all the dead, all the living. An immortal who had witnessed the rise of civilizations and their downfalls. Had seen the world turn to ice and fire steam into oceans.

Decades. Centuries. Eons.

But never had I seen anything so precious.

There it was, my godly child, turning its father speechless, rendering him mute with astonishment. How small a limb it was, showing me that he or she was alive and well, growing beneath the beat of Ada's heart.

"It is... beyond words." I gently lowered my hand onto the protrusion, laughing at the way our baby did not yield, but rather, pressed into my palm. "As stubborn as its mother, to be certain."

Ada turned onto her side with a smile and a groan, allowing me to behold the beauty of her condition and how it was changing her form. Her breasts had become fuller, her hips a bit wider, and a few pinkish lines of torn tissue appeared below her belly now and then.

I lowered myself down behind her, pressing my bare body against her backside. "Where is the pain?"

"Everywhere." A sigh accompanied her hand as it motioned toward her lower back. "But especially there with all the kicking your child does."

I brought my hand to her waist, gently kneading toward her spine and up along the muscle from there. Ah, gone were the times where a second's thought had cured her ailments. No, the King of Flesh and Bone now rubbed his wife's strained muscles until his thumbs ached.

Like a mere man.

My chest lightened at the thought, and how this woman had given me the responsibilities of a husband. Soon, those of a father would follow, turning eternity into a precious promise indeed.

How our child would place itself in this world remained to be discovered. Perhaps it would one day ride the lands with us, as I allowed Ada from time to time whenever her pleas became too pestering.

Or whenever she just left without my permission...

As much as death had emboldened her, immortality had turned her into a force to be reckoned with. She, too, had the power to spread rot. But mostly, she spread death, which angered Eilam greatly. Together, we had returned order to the lands beyond the Æfen Gate.

Across most parts.

Others would follow.

One ought not to expect mortals to worship their true deities after two centuries of absence. Not until we would tear down every temple and string every priest onto Ada's tree. No, such transitions took time, understanding, and patience.

I placed a kiss onto the nape of Ada's neck, her hair somehow darker than it had been, though she accounted it to the pregnancy. "Better?"

"No," she said, running her fingers over the silken grass. "Perhaps because you're pushing more fervently against the wrong part of my body. My pains are along my *spine*, not between my legs."

"Yesterday, you claimed the opposite."

I pushed my hard length against her thighs, and the way she braced to feel all of me didn't go unnoticed. My little one had become rather insatiable as of late, demanding much of me. I gave her all the attention I could. The world could wait. My little one remained impatient.

"Spread yourself for me." I took her hand and brought it to her buttocks, giving it a hard squeeze. "Open yourself wide and invite me in. Show me how much my little one wants my cock."

She didn't.

Of course, my woman didn't, and instead, she reached behind herself to grip me, placing my crown at an entrance slicker with need than I had first assumed. "Is this invitation enough?"

"Quite sufficient."

I pushed into my little one's needy cunt, groaning at the way it gripped me so tightly, beckoning me deeper with how wet she was. "Dripping with lust, taking all of me so eagerly, my good little goddess."

How sweetly she moaned, her back arched to allow deep thrusts while my hand cupped her belly. How strangely arousing this was, sensing the movement of my child against my palm while I drove into my wife.

And yet, Ada soon pressed a hand to her forehead, her hips stilling. "Not again."

Another spell of dizziness. It happened often lately when she rested on one side too long, likely because the weight of the child narrowed the blood flow of an artery, but who could say? Her flesh and bone evaded my powers, but a good husband ought to work around that.

I slung my arm around her, helping her up as the leaves of the willow above us rustled. "Up with you."

Skin braided itself down from the bony white branches of the tree, weaving together into a harness beneath her buttocks. Two thicker ropes formed beside her arms so she may hold on to it, creating a kind of swing that lifted her off the ground.

Stroking her thighs apart, I stepped up between them. I brought Ada's hands to the ropes, then once more pushed inside her. Suspended like this, she gently shifted back at each thrust, only to fall onto my length with more energy.

"More," she said as her knuckles stiffened beneath my hands.

I let my hands fall to her hips, holding her steady in the contraption of the swing as I fucked her harder. I observed the angle at which she shifted her pelvis, listened to the sound of her moans, and paid close attention to the rise of her nipples.

However much of a god I was, my divine wife left me stripped bare to the skills of a man. And when we reached our pleasure together, only to fall into each other's arms after, neither of us could disguise what we had as anything but love.

Achingly true love.

For eternity.

CHAPTER 28
ADA

One year later...

I stepped into the tavern, the air thick with the scent of sausages, herbs, and sizzling lard. It had brought many a patron to the rough-hewn tables that stood about, most decked with foam-capped tankards and wicker baskets that held slices of bread.

Men and women turned their heads, then bowed as they ought to as they mumbled, "My queen." Amidst the occasional screech of bench legs over wooden planks, none dared to leave. That might have earned them my suspicion—something best avoided.

Because worse than a god in love...

... was a goddess out for revenge.

I walked over to the keeper, an old woman whose wimple hung as crooked as her back, and handed her a coin of good-will. "How many?"

"Your Grace," she said with a bow that lacked more grace than my own ever had, and jutted her chin toward the stairs.

"First room to the right. Three priests and two men with swords."

A sigh escaped me.

Five men?

How dreadfully boring.

But alas, such was our plight these days, chasing those last followers of Helfa from the small taverns, musty cellars, and secret hideouts in damp caverns.

I lifted the train of my dress, its fabric the sheerest skin, with petals of black beetle shells shaped like a thousand spring roses. Around each, white feathers shifted with each of my steps in lieu of leaves. A crown of fingers that had once pointed at me came together into a crown upon my head, scraping along the low-hanging ceiling as I ascended the stairs.

Traitorous mumbles soon resonated the corridor, hushed whispers and lies that came muffled from behind the door. A door I kicked open but a moment later, letting a priest tumble from a bench while the rest of the lot scurried into the corners.

"The Queen of Rot and Pain. *My* queen!" One of the priests, who hid a metal pendant in the shape of a sun behind his cotton tunic, raised his arms. "This is but a small gathering of friends, I swear it."

The hairs bristled along my arms.

Oaths. Promises. Vows.

Nothing but lies.

Proven at my first step toward them, when one of the men unsheathed his sword in all his foolish courage. "We meant nobody any harm."

Except for me and my husband with how they'd preyed upon us last month, when we wanted nothing but a peaceful walk with our daughter about the meadows.

My eyes fell to the pommel of the man's sword, engraved with the spread wings of a falcon. "Ah, the crest of House

Tertiel. Remind me, mortal, how long has it been since your lord bent his knee, vowing us his loyalty? Three months? Four?"

He slipped his hand from hilt to pommel, covering the symbol as though it could be made unseen. "I came of my own account."

"I shall put your statement to the test once I come for the bones of your lord's ailing wife." What a fine new archway she would span by the Æfen Gate, along with these five dissidents. "For now, I am convicting you for planning an upheaval against your deities. Up, up, into the branches you go."

"No! Please, Your Grace," one of them shouted as chains of bone shaped around his wrists. "Please, have mercy!"

"Oh, but I do." After all, in the generosity of my kindness, their souls would be allowed to depart to the Court Between Thoughts. "You are lucky my husband—"

One of the armed men stormed at me, sword raised high above his head and ready to strike. "I won't let you slaughter me like—"

I sent a bone dagger at him, letting it *clank* against his sword and rip the blade from his palm. Metal hit wood. I gripped his throat. A foolish mistake, because something bit me in the belly.

I stared down at the knife protruding there, close to my waist, where he'd driven it in with his other hand. Nothing too severe. Bleeding, yes, but I was more upset about the damn hole in my dress. Fashioning myself such an ensemble was no easy feat.

"Fool." I pulled the knife from my body, turned the blade around, and rammed it into his belly. "Such a mess on my dress for nothing. You want to cause me pain? Make me suffer? Well, mortal, then you ought to stab like so." One pull, and I cut upward into his ribcage before I stepped back and let him slump to the ground. "How wasteful of my time."

There I stood, counting the minutes to eternity while the man bled to death. The others waited neatly bound and attached to a bone chain, whimpering, and begging, and regretting their—

Ah, finally dead.

"Now rise." I watched how the man stood, how he stared down at himself in shock, as they always did. Next, he would scream, so I gagged him with a patch of skin. "Take the chain and lead your friends outside. Hurry now. Against what rumors may say, I do not, in fact, have all the time in the world."

I turned around and went back down, the tavern as silent as the grave aside from how the five men shuffled behind me, bone chain *clanking* across the ground.

"Follow me," I said as I crossed the empty market, and left the little village through a slender copse of trees that opened into a spring meadow dotted with orange tulips. "No need to litter this quaint little place with your intestines. That is far enough. Now kneel before your queen."

Against the dead man's grunts of protest, he kicked his four friends into the back of their knees. At my silent command, he unsheathed a knife, bringing it to the priest's throat as tendrils of braided skin slithered about the calf-high grass. Hay season. My favorite.

"I'm growing tired of the likes of you." Most of all, I was growing tired of how the priests prayed to Helfa. Still. "You know, if you prayed to me instead, the kind part of me might yet be swayed. Ask my husband. Too caring, he calls—"

"Ada! Come and see!" Enosh's voice came from downhill, strained with unbridled excitement. "Ada!"

"What now?" I mumbled as I turned away, leaving the men behind to piss themselves some more.

I walked down the sway of the hill, palms outstretched so I may feel the gentle scrape of the cat grass along my knuckles. Not far down, Enosh sat on a blanket of braided hair, his hair tousled from the spring breeze, carrying a blueish tint with how generous the sun shone down this day.

And there, in front of him, was Amelia.

A chain of red clover blossoms her father must have tied together sat among her black wisps, bringing out the rich blue of her eyes. She gingerly rocked back and forth on her hands and knees. Would she do it this time?

I stopped several feet away from them with an excited tingle in my chest, watching our sweet daughter with rapt attention. How she carefully lifted one hand and reached forward, chunky legs going wobbly. With a high-pitched squeal, she shifted her balance forward. So close.

Until her other arm gave out underneath her. She quickly jerked herself back into a sitting position, skipping the warning cries and going straight to screams and tears of disappointment. Dramatic, just like her father...

"Shh..." The sweetest hushing sounds resonated the meadow as Enosh picked her up, pressed her against his chest, and tenderly rocked her. "Patience, my love. Not much longer now, and you will crawl about court. Oh, how Orlaigh will groan as she chases behind you."

Something the old woman would do gladly, considering that it kept her out of Enosh's throne. It had taken little more but soiled clouts, a bout of colic, and teething pains to convince my husband that we needed a maid.

Raising a child is more exhausting than I had anticipated, Enosh said often, usually right before he went to bed. There, he lowered Amelia onto his chest, one arm wrapped around her as the two of them slept for a day or three.

My heart clenched at the memory, but it burst with ardor when Enosh pressed a kiss to Amelia's forehead, then shoved the tip of his nose into her hair, breathing her in. He was a good father, showering her with attention and love, often taking her on walks.

Enosh glanced over his shoulder back at me and smiled. "You missed it."

I walked over to them and sat on the blanket, and gave my little Amelia a kiss. "I've been watching you all along."

"My little princess is in need of a nap," he said as he gently stroked his thumb from her forehead down the bridge of her nose. "The mortals?"

"Waiting for death up the hill."

"Finish, so we may go home." He pressed his lips to mine in a loving kiss, but it was the way his other arm came around my middle that had me hiss in pain. "What's this?"

I looked from the blood on his fingertips up into the approaching storm in his eyes. "It is but a scratch, borne of a mortal's stupidity and my eagerness to get this over with."

Enosh was having none of it and rose, pressing Amelia tightly against him as he stormed up the hill. "Who was it?"

"Not now, Enosh. She's tired." I got up and hurried behind him. "Besides, the mortal is already dead."

"With his wicked soul still about," he growled down at the gagged corpse, who shuffled back a step. "You dared to touch my wife? Draw her blood while our daughter is learning to crawl only a handful of feet from her?"

Beside them, Yarin quickly came into his form with a wide grin lining his lips. "Amelia finally crawled?"

"No, she got scared, but it can't be much longer now,"

Enosh said, then lifted our heavy-lidded daughter into Yarin's arms. "Hold her."

"Sweet little thing, Uncle Yarin is here." He took her, drumming the tip of her nose in a way that never failed to lure a giggle from her. "Oh, how tired you look, but there is mischief to be had, Amelia."

Enosh swatted the chain from the corpse's hand, gripped the hair at the back of his head, and all but dangled him by it to a nearby boulder. "Another family memory stained by the likes of you."

He slammed the mortal's face against the rock. *Crack.* And again. *Crack.* And a third time. *Slosh.*

The corpse hadn't slumped to the ground yet when Enosh spun around, assessing the cut on my side even as he let out an annoyed grunt. "You promised to be careful."

"I was." Not truly. I'd been bored, letting down my guard at the dreadful premise of coming all this way for merely five men. "It is nothing, Enosh."

After he convinced himself of it, he nodded and took my face between his palms, letting his forehead sink against mine. "No more, Ada. Not until your bleeding comes, and certainly, none of this should you be with child again. Yes?"

"Yes," I whispered, finding a strange comfort in this hint of ash sprinkled over snow that we shared in. "Let me finish this real quick."

One after another, I shaped a bone dagger in my palm, ramming it into the bellies of three men.

The fourth one, one of the priests, stared up at me from tear-drowned eyes. "I cannot say, Adelaide, which one of you is worse. You or your husband."

"The answer to that is simple, mortal." I leaned over and stabbed into his belly, placing my lips by his ear. "We're equally terrible."

~SAVE THE WORLD, FUCK A VILLAIN~

Made in the USA
Columbia, SC
26 September 2024

defc0bc2-1f70-4bf3-ab7c-d760b536ba03R01